■ □ ■ □ ■

COMPULSORY HAPPINESS

■ □ ■ □ ■

WRITINGS FROM AN UNBOUND EUROPE

■ □ ■ □ ■

NORMAN MANEA

COMPULSORY HAPPINESS

Translated from the French by Linda Coverdale

NORTHWESTERN UNIVERSITY PRESS

EVANSTON, ILLINOIS

Northwestern University Press
Evanston, Illinois 60208-4210

Printed in the United States of America

ISBN 0-8101-1190-X

Library of Congress Cataloging-in-Publication Data

Manea, Norman.
    [Bonheur obligatoire. English]
    Compulsory Happiness / Norman Manea ; translated from the French
by Linda Coverdale.
       p.   cm. — (Writings from an unbound Europe)
    Four novellas originally written in Romanian, collected in French
under the title "Le bonheur obligatoire."
       Contents: The interrogation — A window on the working class —
The trenchcoat — Composite biography.
    ISBN 0-8101-1190-X (pbk. : alk. paper)
    1. Manea, Norman—Translations into English. I. Coverdale,
Linda. II. Title. III. Series.
PC840.23.A47A24   1994
859'.334—dc20   94-17021
                                                                                      CIP

Originally written in Romanian:
Biografia Robot (Composite Biography) © 1981 by Norman Manea; first published
    in Romanian in 1981 by Editura Dacia (Cluj)
Interogatoriul (The Interrogation) © 1988 by Norman Manea; first published in
    German in 1989 by Steidl Verlag
O Fereastră Către Clasa Muncitoare (A Window on the Working Class) © 1988 by
    Norman Manea; first published in German in 1989 by Steidl Verlag
Trenciul (The Trenchcoat) © 1989 by Norman Manea; first published in German
    in 1990 by Steidl Verlag

    These four novellas were first published together in French under the title
Le bonheur obligatoire in 1991 by Albin Michel. This edition was translated from
the French by Linda Coverdale with the approval and assistance of the author.

The paper used in this publication meets the minimum requirements of the
American National Standard for Information Sciences—Permanence of Paper for
Printed Library Materials, ANSI Z39.48-1984.

■ □ ■ □ ■

CONTENTS

THE INTERROGATION

A METHODICAL SCHEDULE, REPEATED DAILY, FROM FIVE in the morning until ten in the evening. Without any modification, the same ordeals, over and over, repeated indefinitely. To humiliate, intimidate, destroy. From morning to evening. Sometimes at night as well.

The same precision, the same cruelty, for several months now. And then, suddenly, a change.

One Tuesday morning, without any warning, an unbelievable change. They hadn't beaten her, and instead of beating her, they'd moved her to a bigger cell, on the first floor. She was allowed an extra hour of exercise, alone in the courtyard, before lights out. In the evening, a fat, grumpy guard replaced the toilet can with an enameled chamber pot.

The next morning, hot sugared tea; the meals were better than usual, too. In the afternoon, at the time formerly reserved for her harshest punishment, she was taken to the shower. When she returned, she found a sheet on her bed, and a clean blanket, and some clothing, neatly folded. The most astonishing thing of all: the small rectangular mirror and the slender tube of Nivea lotion found among the clothes.

Thursday morning, they took her through a maze of corridors, going left, right, down, up, left again.

A room with white walls, like a doctor's office. A woman was waiting there, smoking, sitting on a couch covered in brown oilcloth. She seemed like a former colleague, or a vaguely remembered acquaintance.

They were left alone together for almost an hour. The unknown woman sat with her legs crossed and wrote in a notebook propped up on her lap. Above her white knee, an elegant little fountain pen flew back and forth; every once in a while, the knee would twitch.

Then a doctor entered the room. Judging from the questions he asked, he had to be a psychiatrist. The unknown woman listened to all these routine tests with a bored or, rather, a blasé air. She must have been a person of high rank, because a simple gesture from her was enough to dismiss the doctor. Later she explained to the prisoner the reason for the unexpected changes of the last few days.

But only after making her stand completely naked for

an hour, during which time the woman did invite her to
sit down, true, and offered her cigarettes (which she herself
chain-smoked), but she would not allow her to go anywhere near her clothes.

"Leave them alone," she'd barked imperiously. "Later."

The woman had carefully studied the different parts of
her body. Without malice, with a cold, professional eye.
The inspection finished with a smile.

"Sorry about your hair—I can't make it grow back in
three days."

So it seemed she was the one who had thought of, or
at least supervised, the details of this new program.

"Too bad they shaved you. Did you have pretty hair?"

She didn't seem bothered by the lack of a reply. Her
questions were more in the line of amused hypotheses.

"As for everything else, you've taken fairly good care
of yourself. And you haven't even become too bitter. Actually, that's quite a triumph, I must admit."

She smiled again, as though giving a handout to a poor
relative.

"Today you won't have to follow any schedule. This
afternoon, a nice hot bath. It'll do you good, you'd be silly
to refuse. I've had some magazines and newspapers taken
to your cell. If you need or would like anything in particular, let me know, I'll take care of it. Here, I'll make a
note of it right now, if you want something."

She took a blank sheet of paper from the desk. She
waited, unruffled by the stubborn silence of the naked
woman sitting before her. She folded the piece of paper

several times and then slipped it into the breast pocket of her black satin crepe blouse, which had a pointed collar and long sleeves.

She stood up. A dainty brunette, almost tall, her waist tightly encircled by a wide leather belt. Hair worn loose about her fragile shoulders. Slender legs, arms too long, nervous hands. Bluish circles under her eyes. Very, very white skin, like the milky white of her short skirt, which didn't quite cover her thighs.

"We're getting you ready to see someone. An important meeting for you."

A tense, pinched smile.

"The gentleman would like you to look nice. In other words, normal, at least. He can't stand violence. He's a sensitive soul, you see."

Her eyes seemed to have changed color, grown even blacker, with a steely blue glint, and her voice was stern.

"As you'll find out, he's doing you a favor. A lucky break, you'll see."

She lit a cigarette, then turned her back, looked out the window, her thoughts elsewhere. Suddenly she whirled around, her hands clenched tightly together. Her face flushed, her expression pained. She slammed the door on her way out.

She didn't come back. The only indication that she might have remained in the vicinity came two hours later, when a somewhat panicky young man appeared, obviously instructed to be polite.

"Sorry, they forgot you were here."

Yes, the prisoner had put her clothes back on quite a while ago and was waiting, sitting rigidly on a chair.

"Please follow me."

She saw that her cell had been swept and aired. On the cement, a pile of newspapers and magazines.

At around three o'clock, her reading was interrupted. Two of them escorted her. She went downstairs, around corners, along lengthy corridors. This time, to a bathroom. Not the shower she'd already used. A gleaming white bathtub. Big, colorful, fluffy towels. A cake of perfumed soap. All sorts of little bottles. Slippers, nail polish. When she got back to her cell, a cup of hot tea was waiting for her.

And now, here it was, the fourth day. "Would five in the afternoon be convenient? Would it be convenient at five?" the woman had asked, as if speaking a line from an opera libretto, tired of the absurdity of what she'd been told to do and say.

So, the appointed day. That morning she was taken to another wing of the building. An elegant room. Thick carpets. Beautifully paneled walls. She was seated in an armchair, before a round, glass-topped table in a corner of the room. The table shook, the silver coffee service and china tea things tinkled. Croissants in a basket. Cherry preserves. Butter. Honey, apples, sugar cookies.

A large desk, running almost the entire length of the room. Not a single picture. Bare walls, except for a big round clock resembling a barometer, over the desk. Two windows, heavy drapes. Three chairs, including hers. Beneath one of the windows, a credenza with two shelves; on the lower one, a radio. A telephone and a lamp on the desk.

Lunch at two o'clock. Carp's eggs, green salad, deviled eggs, pork spareribs, slivovitz, tiny meatballs, spicy sausage, pickles, wine, mineral water, baklava pastries.

She fainted. Before passing out, she'd vomited until she was exhausted, and vomited again. She was taken to the bathroom, the one with the tub; she hadn't realized it was right next door. They cleaned the stains off her collar, they rubbed her temples and forehead with a damp washcloth. They stretched her out on an air mattress, to let her recuperate . . . They took her back to the same room, supporting her under the arms. Eggplant caviar. Meatballs. Deviled eggs. Carp's eggs. Slivovitz. Rum. Spareribs. Escalope Milanaise. Wine. Cake. Everything came up again. They caught her at the last moment, as she was falling. She sat down at the table once more. She picked up the knife, the fork. Then the bottle, the glasses, one after the other . . . When she awoke, the table was bare, cleared. There was only a slim black bottle, with a golden label marked *Eau de toilette*, and beside it, a tiny flask, hardly bigger than a thimble: *Perfume*. She looked at the clock. Four-thirty.

So she'd fallen asleep while eating, had slept with her head on the table. She pulled a handkerchief from the pocket of her dress. They'd given her handkerchiefs, and a dress. A kind of chemise, long and loose, of a thick material, like a new blanket. She moistened her face and hands with the toilet water. So she'd fallen asleep. She looked at the clock again. She'd have liked to go back to sleep. She felt groggy from the food and drink, and would have loved to rest some more.

What could the important person have to say? Why should he waste any of his precious time on her? Would he say the same things, ask her the same questions? Would the Plenipotentiary turn out to be more subtle than his subordinates, the gorillas who carried out his orders? Would he confine himself simply to doing his job? Send his report, in turn, to his bosses, and nothing more? Indicating that he has personally contacted, that he personally visited, that he made an effort, that he personally knows, etc., etc. Yes, yes, yes, he thinks there's nothing more to be done, he suggests immediate measures, no leniency, and so on.

But what about that strange, lovely go-between, who seemed like someone from her past, like a refined, sadistic former colleague? "Your hair—I can't make it grow back in three days." "Did you have pretty hair?" The question hadn't seemed malicious; it had been asked quite simply, in a vaguely pensive tone. Perhaps the most surprising thing that happened the whole time they were together.

Nine minutes to five. If this wasn't some new ordeal, intended to fray her nerves to shreds, if this important person really did exist, if he'd actually set up this appointment, and if, moreover, he arrived on time, then there were nine minutes left. What else could he propose or ask of her beyond what she'd already heard day after day? Threatening her family, her friends . . . Could the fate of the man she loved be made even worse? Would he ever forgive her if for one crazy moment she believed their lies, their promises? If she gave in, for a single instant, to her desire to know that he was free? They were planning something; she had to be ready for anything.

In only a few days they'd succeeded in bringing her back almost to normal. Ready to remember the rules of normal life. How to wear a dress, set the table, serve a meal. Yes, it was the food, the meals that had softened her up. Good food, and lots of it. Probably brought over from a fancy restaurant. Contrary to the usual practice, they hadn't starved her first; they'd revived her little by little, over the course of a few days. So that she'd then be able to sit down calmly in front of the food. Be able to choose. To eat her fill, not from hunger, but from greediness. To stuff herself at leisure, delighted to experience once again the refinements of good living. To bask contentedly in the warmth and benevolence of the world. To become docile.

She'd noticed that her stubborn determination had lost its edge, especially during the last few hours. The sweetish, fruity wine had made her tipsy. Ever since her fainting spell, she'd felt weak and lethargic. She would have liked to sleep for weeks in a big clean bed, in a quiet, spacious room. Only waking up occasionally to soak in a steaming tub, with perfumed bath oil, like the last time. And have brightly colored, refreshing drinks.

The door opened quietly, very quietly. But there were still two minutes left! Was he early? No, it was only some minor employee who hardly dared set foot into such an important room. Humble, hesitant, on tiptoes. Some timid functionary, sent to dust or air out the room, who knows?

He was carrying boxes of different sizes. He piled them carefully against the wall, in a corner, next to the door. He left and returned with a long, fat tube. A kind of cardboard tube, with a cover on one end. He moved silently, stooped over, without looking up, trying to be unobtrusive. He came in, disappeared, reappeared, gliding noiselessly. Clearly terrified by the importance of the person for whose arrival he was preparing. The cautious movements of this dogsbody—possibly one of the maintenance or clerical personnel—were enough in themselves to show that the expected personage was a very high-ranking official indeed.

The prisoner checked the clock. One minute past five. So he was late! They were making her wait on purpose, of course, they were hoping that she'd become upset and wonder what they were up to now. An old trick: they weren't showing much originality with that one. She'd learned how to protect herself.

Weary, no doubt, the silent employee sat down behind the desk! The poor man had some nerve! Snatching a moment's rest, sitting in the boss's chair! And what if he were to appear at that very moment? Just look at him: to cap it all off, he's smiling, shamefaced but proud, like an imbecile! He was looking at her, yes, he was staring at her and grinning. Pleased with himself, but lacking in confidence; his timorous and silly smile was a way of begging for encouragement.

"Be so good as to come closer. Bring your chair, bring your chair. Or rather, no, why don't you sit in one of these two here?"

She started in astonishment. The voice . . . There was nothing ordinary about that voice, which certainly didn't seem to belong to that puffing flunky, done in by the weight of too many boxes too heavy for him.

The prisoner didn't know what to think, what to do. She was unable to move. A cold sweat broke out on her forehead; her hands and back felt clammy. A bad joke, right before the arrival of the Plenipotentiary, because a few minutes are all he's got left, this, this . . . nobody . . . this . . . this janitor, stock clerk, cashier with too many mouths to feed, this post-office drone, doorman, storekeeper, salesman, plumber, whatever, with his voice, so . . . yes, yes, so . . .

"I was on time, you noticed. Come closer, please. I'm used only to small audiences, short distances."

He swallowed syllables, ran words together, telescoping them. He seemed to think only in leaps and bounds. A warm, tentative voice. And yet a commanding tone. Affected. A bizarre mixture: firmness and fear, gentleness, power, yes, and harshness, and, also . . .

"Well, would you please come over here now?"

As he watched her stand up and walk to the armchairs in front of the desk, he pulled a slim flask containing a reddish-brown liquid from one of his jacket pockets and gently set it down flat on the glass surface of the desk. Once she was seated, he studied her closely for a long time, allowing himself to be examined by her in return.

He wore a kind of knitted shirt of fine wool, mustard-colored, with buttons and an open collar. A jacket in a gray check. He had few teeth, and those were bad, stained by nicotine. Tiny red spider-veins on his nose. Pale, flabby face. Small ears, scrawny neck, frail hands. Short, thin fingers, twisted and yellowed. Nails bitten to the quick. A high forehead, extended by a bald pate. Large, dark eyes. Intelligent, yes, lively and black. A penetrating gaze, restless, glittering, searching, observing, evaluating. There was a wild, glassy sparkle in his eyes that suddenly became fixed, unblinking, dead. Extraordinary, the look in those eyes! This was definitely the man in question. Yes, it was, no doubt about it now.

He began waving his hands around, and pointed at the prisoner's head. It took her a while to understand what he wanted. Then she removed her cap and placed it on the right arm of the chair. But the man gestured again, not without a hint of irritation and disgust. Telling her to get rid of it, throw it away. He couldn't stand having to look at such a rag for one more instant. So she tossed the cap over her shoulder. It struck the window, plopping limply to the floor like a dead bird.

The man stopped staring at her. He looked down at the sheet of glass covering his desk, as though he wanted to avoid hurting her feelings, since the cap no longer concealed her shaved scalp.

He started to speak like that, keeping his head and eyes lowered. "I hope you're beginning to get used to me. We'll be able to have a chat. You see, I detest the picturesque. Anything distracting."

Then, what about the cap? Why had he made her take it off and exhibit her shorn skull, as smooth as a billiard ball? She looked at him, vexed at having been tempted for a moment to judge him by logical criteria, thus falling into the first and crudest trap.

"I demanded that everything be done to put you in a normal state. So that you would look normal. So that you'd react normally. So that you'd seem and even be, eventually, as far as possible, unobtrusive, colorless. Almost insipid. So that you wouldn't provoke any inordinate interest. I hate surprises, anything disruptive . . . I'd like you to get used to me. Don't be upset that I'm probably not the way you imagined I'd be. Try to do this. So that we can be on an equal footing. So that you can follow and understand me . . . This room we're in now, you were given time to get used to it as well, weren't you? I find distraction aggravating. As I told you, I don't like shocks, surprises, useless emotion."

Although the prisoner wasn't looking at him, she sensed that he'd raised his head to watch her.

"Let's go back over a few things now. You've been here for several months. Beaten, tortured. As much as could be borne by a woman of steadily weakening stamina. Between periods of unconsciousness, I mean. You were cursed and insulted, of course. You've probably never heard so much foul language, screamed with so much pleasure. They never stopped demanding from you the names of people you'd met. The hideouts, the clandestine activities of all your friends . . . Later on, they beat you a bit less. A few hours a day. A more varied schedule was introduced. You were made to stand in the courtyard, for three hours at a stretch, in all sorts of weather. Then, for several hours each day, you had to stand at attention within a chalk circle of about the same diameter as a basketball. Your feet swelled terribly. They were rather large to begin with, I'm told. The flesh started to puff up over the edges of your shoes, which you could no longer remove . . . Once or twice, at night, you found rats in your bed. If you can call it a bed. A narrow coffin, made for a shrunken corpse or a dying person who was to be constricted like a mummy. Didn't they turn on a siren, at night, out in the corridor? Didn't they bring in cats, so they could chase and beat them, right outside the cell doors? . . . Despite everything, perhaps they didn't rape you. Not because they didn't want to, naturally. Especially when they were beating you. When you were exhausted. Extreme weakness is very arousing, just as strength is, as you well know . . . Doesn't it count that they didn't rape you? You'd tell me they made up for it in other ways. And yet it counts for something, believe me, it counts."

She expected to see him smile smugly. But suiting his expressions to his words must have been the least of his worries.

"After shaving off your hair, they forced you to make it into a kind of feather duster. With which they made you wipe something besides dust . . . In fact, they'd forget to bring back the toilet can. Particularly on the days when you had intestinal trouble. Induced diarrhea? You must have suspected that. Kept standing, at night, targeted by the beams of four floodlights. Your head shoved into a barrel of soapy water? A crude idea, so primitive. Forty-eight hours locked in a closet? Forty-eight hours in total darkness. Without forgetting, of course, the usual third degree. Mocked, mistreated, starved. Not too funny, this recap, is it?"

Could he have noticed, even though his eyes were closed, that the prisoner was growing paler and paler?

"And why, after all? Always the same questions. Which you didn't answer. They knew beforehand. The answers didn't interest them. In any case, they wouldn't have stopped torturing you. And answers would have been an additional reason to punish you. To make you repeat what you'd already said, to tell you that your accomplices were claiming the contrary. To trick you into contradicting yourself: Yesterday you said that, and today, this."

He didn't anticipate any reply. Resting his elbows on the desk, he watched her without expecting her to react in any way.

"Nothing you can do about it. It's their job. Sometimes they get some results, though. Given their level of intelligence, it's difficult to show them that they're wasting their time. Besides, it's what they're used to, of course. And they enjoy it, let's admit that. You won't have to undergo any more harsh treatment, I promise you. It's not in their interest anymore to have you die or wind up an invalid. They'll make concessions, you'll see. Conditions will be . . . not excellent, but ordinary . . . So, you were arrested on a Wednesday afternoon. At seven-sixteen. In front of 7 Mandicevski Street. A few steps from the bus stop where you'd just gotten off. You were late. Annoyed and irritated. It bothered you. You were always very careful, however, and I'm sure you got ready early every time, so you wouldn't be late. You were very particular about being on time. But occasionally, at the last minute, you'd notice that your stocking had a run. That your coat was missing a button. That the zipper on your skirt was jammed. That your shoes weren't polished. You felt guilty that day, I suppose . . . The meetings of conspirators are in some ways—but not all—like lovers' rendezvous, aren't they? And the meeting that day was a little bit of both. Which made your lateness even more serious, of course. That Wednesday, your delay was caused by the bus. Not only, in fact, not only by the bus . . ."

From time to time, he would adroitly draw over to him, she now saw, the flat bottle lying on the desk. He'd unscrew the cap and fiddle with the flask, which he held under the table, down by his chair, without making any noise. You had to pay close attention to see what he was doing. You didn't hear him drinking—each swig went down quickly, almost while he was talking. He counted, probably rightly, on the curiosity aroused by his appearance and by what he had to say, which overshadowed all the rest, making it hard to focus on details.

"The bus's delay was not entirely accidental. We're the ones who made it late. Not by much, just enough for what we needed . . . I'm glad to see you're not rolling your eyes, that you're not easily impressed. I'd find that taxing. I'd become impatient, aggravated. Whereas this way I can begin to trust the person with whom I'm talking. I hope we're going to get on well together."

Abruptly, he drew his chair nearer. He looked vulnerable, unhappy. As though he was asking for help. Ready to let down his guard, to pour out his heart to a friend.

"You see, I can't bear to go up against an unworthy opponent. It unnerves me. I insisted, I told you, that you should be presented to me in a normal state. Otherwise, I'm at a loss . . . I can hardly function when I know that the person listening to me has been beaten, terrified, humiliated before being brought before me. Really, I can't . . . No, it makes me plain nauseated. And afraid, I must admit. Of myself. Of them. Of what might happen to me as well one day . . ."

He noticed that the prisoner suddenly seemed attentive, tense, as she confronted the face and voice of this aging, lonely child, helpless and complaining.

"And so you were late. Your comrades were arrested before you arrived. You know, sometimes our little game obliges us to play dirty . . . Before you panic, let me assure you that I know just about everything you could possibly confess. Besides, I'm also aware that you feel more or less incapable of judging the relative importance of what you know and so have prudently resolved to consider every fact of vital significance. So that you absolutely won't give anything away. I know the names of the regular visitors to the house in question. I've enjoyed reading the reports, and have requested further information on the subjects. I was given what amounted to in-depth biographical studies. Practically monographs, and not just on comrade Simona Strihan. Your friends call you Sia, don't they? So, Sia Strihan . . . I'm perfectly familiar—as though I'd known your friends for a long time—with Barbosa's liver ailment and still rather tidy fortune, plus the fact that young Patraulea, known as the Poet, has a definite penchant for the ladies. Which doesn't explain that other penchant of his, his passion for the arts, does it? And it can't be his rural background, either, since his parents were atrociously poor. Still less his very, very delicate constitution . . . The distinguished Mrs. Mărgărit is a fanatic. Although she looks like, and even is, an accomplished woman of the world. Acquainted with all the ordinary—and not so ordinary—pleasures of the eternal upper crust. Which she detests, naturally. Nothing but a fanatic, one would say. Unlike the engineer . . . Is that a draft I feel?"

He jumped up in distress, turning this way and that. On the alert, sniffing, nostrils flared, ears perked up, like a rabbit's. Ah, that was it! Yes, he did look somewhat rabbity, why hadn't she noticed this before? Or did he look more like a hare? And a little like a snake, perhaps? A slightly aquiline nose . . . They say the great men of history had aquiline noses . . . A high, broad forehead, like theirs? But the eyebrows, which reveal temperament, were not very thick. Rather sparse, actually. Beads of perspiration formed on his temples, then on his nose. His hair was thinning, but some still remained on the sides of his head. His face was pale, and he blinked constantly, as though nearsighted. A sign of timidity?

He gesticulated wildly, but stayed right where he was. His jacket had come unbuttoned, and one could see that his polo shirt had grown faded and baggy from too much wear, for it hung on him in a series of sloppy folds. The end of his worn belt had slipped out of the belt loops and dangled in front of his fly, looking silly.

Feeble tremors ran through his body. Hunched down

between his shoulders, his head jerked and twitched, as did his hollow chest. His bald spot, which grew larger toward the top of his skull, began to flush deeply . . . Taking a handkerchief from his pocket, he squeezed it in one fist, then in the other, lifted it to his nose . . . and sneezed.

The prisoner couldn't help smiling. Just then he looked her way and caught her at it. Despite his sneezing, which gave way to a coughing fit, he smiled, too, guiltily.

"I've got an allergy, you see," he mumbled. "The smallest, the slightest, the least little draft is a disaster for me."

He trotted over to the door and pushed on it, even though it was closed. He leaned—trembling, sighing, defeated, shaken by a series of salvos, bent double, as though stricken—on the doorknob. He went over to the window, making an attempt to stride forcefully. In passing, he placed his hand on the back of the prisoner's chair. He examined the window frame, the casement bolt: everything was shut tight, and yet . . . he was sneezing! A pathetic, helpless wreck. He sneezed, and sneezed, and you'd have thought he was doing it on purpose. His nose, which was already covered with little red veins, now became a dripping blob. He kept pocketing and fishing out again first one hanky, then another, in which he'd bury his face, hands clenched. Racked by convulsions, ashamed.

The prisoner watched as daylight waned outside the window, becoming grayer and grayer. Perhaps quite a while had gone by. She looked at the clock but couldn't make out a thing. The numbers had vanished, just like the hour and minute hands, from a clock face obscured by dust, as though lost in mist.

The fragile fellow was finally able to catch his breath, not without difficulty. But he seemed no longer willing or able to play out his multiple roles. The challenge didn't interest him anymore, and worse than that, he was just fed up. As though he'd had enough of wearing all the complicated masks of intelligence. As though the skeptics were right, for all is vanity and absurdity. He succumbed to laziness . . . Nothing mattered anymore, nothing could be more profound, more tempting, more certain, more prudent than laziness, he seemed to say. Why wear yourself out? And then, bam! A burst of energy.

The prisoner was still smiling. But her smile no longer expressed the compassion, even the sympathy, that she'd felt for a moment. Only disgust and contempt remained. A fixed smile, a rictus. One might have thought she'd fallen asleep, or, at the very least, that she was beginning to doze. Or that she'd fainted, died, with that horrible grimace on her face . . . Then he banged the metal top of the flask, violently, on the glass top of the desk.

A demented look gleamed in his eyes. The impact had been forceful, like the crashing blade of a guillotine.

But he was immediately sorry . . . He'd tried, moreover, to soften the blow at the last moment . . . to pretend he was simply looking for his flask. Which he then openly lifted to his fleshy lips, tipping his head way back to drain about a quarter of its contents. Then, reinvigorated but embittered, he collapsed into his chair.

"I hate boredom just as much as you do, little lady. You can tell, I suppose. I loathe boredom, I hope that's obvious. Along with work, perseverance, labor. Even logic. Sometimes truth as well. Frequently, frequently. I'm a . . ."

He'd pronounced the first words in a loud voice, which had then grown weaker. He was recovering his composure, his detachment, and wanted to make this clear.

"Yes, it's useless to tell you everything I know about Sia Strihan. Or Dinu Barbosa, Tina Mărgărit, the engineer Mateescu. Kahane, known as Agahane, or Patraulea the poet. Or that so very clever worker, Victor Vaduva. Or even our prize customer, the one you admire so much. It's not just admiration, I know, I know, I know all about, how shall I put it, how you love him 'body and soul,' as they say. I shouldn't annoy you by reciting everything I know about one and all, I shouldn't, I admit. I should tell you instead what I know about myself. To make you understand that I'm a decent sort. Tell you things about myself that are as important as the ones we've learned about Simona Strihan. So that you'd respect me? I had the impression I'd succeeded in awakening your interest . . . For me, there's no other form of esteem. You'll see that I know quite a lot about myself, too. Even though I'm . . . That's what I wanted to mention just now . . . Even though I'm a dilettante, a hopeless dilettante. That's what I am . . ."

Shoulders bent over the desk, over his liquor flask, he soliloquized in a low voice, head bowed, no longer looking at his audience.

"They tolerate my little foibles: my carelessness, my

idleness, my caprices, my weaknesses. They tolerate them. They've finally come around to considering me a necessary evil. Because I'm more than useful to them, I'm indispensable. They're convinced of that. Even though they don't understand my actions, my tactics, my deductions. Even though they despise me . . . They'd be so happy to stuff me into a cell. To take revenge, using the methods that you know, for everything they can't understand. And, better yet, they'd probably love to toss me into a coffin. Months go by without them calling me in. They leave me alone, the hell with me. But when they finally summon me, they don't haggle. They accept my conditions, in other words, my fee and complete freedom to do things my way. They've given up imposing their program on me, their rigid schedules, all that foolishness they think so much of. The bottom line is, they go along with me without any understanding of how I work. Or of what I'm saying when I go into my big speech . . . Every once in a while, you see, I wax eloquent. I explain to them why they should expect 'special' cases to crop up on a periodic basis. Exceptions! Spin-offs from life, which are nevertheless vital to it. Against which their disciplined hatred and stupidity have no effect. Different worlds, different species that will never understand each other. They ought to know in the first place what life is, so that they'd comprehend what I'm saying to them. They need my imagination, my temperament, my allergies, my intuitions. They finally figured out that I myself am a special case. Just like Sia Strihan. We two . . . But probably not as exceptional as the comrade who's so often in your thoughts, whom you miss so much.

Now him, he's definitely a special case, absolutely special
. . . Of course, I do have my successes. I do fairly well,
actually, fairly well. Otherwise, I wouldn't be here now.
That's why they keep in touch. They see me as a kind of
magician! Loathsome, sickly, cowardly, forgetful, eccen-
tric. But the man gets results! My reports come to an
optimistic conclusion, the compulsory optimism, the institutional optimism, so to speak. Institutional optimism
in the kind of institution that provides a 'self-invented'
man like me with enough illusions and occupations to kill
some time. In this way, a case that's been giving them
headaches for three months or three years is as good as
taken care of, so that the optimists can go back to enjoying
their idiot profession . . . However, I don't always succeed.
I lose some matches, too. Enigmas or geniuses. Or again,
quite simply, my laziness is to blame. My lethargy, my
distraction, and even, yes, yes, my generosity or my aver-
sion, sometimes both, yes, both at the same time. I am
only human, believe me, little lady. I'm only human and
I have occasionally been defeated. Often by myself. Nar-
row-minded people don't understand that failure is natural,
that it can even be delectable, like everything human, and
marvelously melancholy . . . Even temporarily appropriate
solutions contain a goodly proportion of failure. There's
no use in trying to explain to them that in reality everything
is failure! Except that some failures are less obvious than
others. Disguised, misleading, they pass for successes.
When I don't reach my goals, their goals, they forget all
my previous triumphs. And of course they also suddenly
forget their own impotence. Their confidence in their

clumsy, stupid arguments is renewed. It's not surprising that a person of my sort, a useless idler, a disgraceful loser, would be unable to get even the simplest job done! That's what they scream at me. At last they've got a chance to insult me. To spit their hatred in my face, a hatred born of vanity, folly, and rancor. To shout that they don't trust me. It's hard to take. Especially for someone like me. You understand, I hope . . . Lack of trust is my daily bread. Dry bread, a huge lump of chalk or ice crashing noisily down, trying to crush me. Or, on the contrary, bread dipped in vinegar, in poison. In a daze, I suck for days and nights and weeks at a time on a poisoned sponge that never runs dry. My lack of self-confidence . . . So, if others start showing me that they don't have any confidence in me, either, well! They just destroy me, I'm not able to think anymore, believe me. I become blind, dumb, paralyzed, I'm lost. I'm thrown back into my own misery and mess. Because of those idiots, I'm no longer good for anything here for months on end. They are the ones who should be dumbfounded whenever I appear! But in the end they call me back, those wretches, when they get a case that's beyond them, one they can't fathom despite all their efforts. That lunatic, they tell themselves, that weirdo might find the key, that's what they hope, poor jerks. And me, after such a depression, I don't have any idea where to begin. It takes me a long time to finally buckle down. I lack assurance, faith in myself. Without confidence, even for just a little while, even if it's only illusory, nothing works, my dear artist. I can feel them encircling me, those brutes. Silent, all of a sudden, but they're oppressive, stifling. They spy on my thoughts, my every move. And then something gets me going. A bottle, a woman, a book, a vacation. Or even a poem, don't laugh. Music, sometimes . . . I enjoy a renewed sense of vitality. Spurred on, champing at the bit, I'm raring to go. The facts, the hypotheses, the solution!"

It had grown dark outside, but he didn't turn on the lights. It wasn't yet completely dark, or was it? Although the prisoner didn't see him, she could tell he was now standing up behind the desk.

"I could work miracles for an intelligent boss! Someone who would know how to exploit my faults. Yes, my laziness, my carelessness, my absentmindedness. There's so much room for imagination in these little failings! You can make your moves without anyone being able to anticipate or foil your intentions. But how can I find a superior mind among these peons? It took them years to recognize my talents—even then, only grudgingly—and to learn how to use them. To show some degree of comprehension, providing me with favorable working conditions. A stimulating environment. Putting up with my whims. In other words, nurturing my talents. Which are few, perhaps, but very special, requiring equally special care. It would take them a hundred years to understand that my faults open up a whole new approach to the game!"

He was nervously rubbing his hands together, crossing and uncrossing his index fingers.

"A dilettante, naturally. Neither a professional nor an official. A dilettante, unused to the job, the bosses, the schedules, the plodding, methodical, forced labor. Work-

ing infrequently, but with pleasure. For money, for the
fun of it. Only when the offer is tempting, intriguing,
believe me. When he has the chance to come up against a
riddle and solve it. Without ever letting his intuitions, his
enjoyment of the game, be spoiled. His passion for inventing, for expanding the realm of possibilities provided
by chance. You see . . . whatever you could confess doesn't
interest me. I know everything about you. I'm the one,
rather, who could tell you things, if you like, about anyone
at all. Myself included. So that you might come to know
better both your comrades and your adversary.

"In actual fact, I must admit, we play as adversaries. It
means we are adversaries. If we dug deeply into our in-
nermost thoughts, we'd probably find that the situation is
more complicated. Knowing all that I do, knowing what
crimes you've committed, crimes that are real, but not
relatively serious, I'm perfectly justified in telling you that
your importance is entirely a matter of my opinion . . .
Ideas set people's hearts and minds aflame in no time.
Particularly if they're young. Taking power: how fasci-
nating! Afterwards, it's not that simple. Once power is in
your hands, things get a lot tougher. I've been around in
this business, believe me, sweetie. I know how it works."

The prisoner waited. Was he going to continue this
informality?

"You're hardly the most interesting case, little lady, you
must have realized that."

"But you have a certain correlative importance for me.
Because I found a correlation. Your friend, now he really
interests me. He deserves particular attention, I confess.

What do your comrades think about the fact that you were late on the very day they were arrested? You don't know . . . We haven't told them that you were arrested as well. I'll think about that later. Perhaps I'll request that you be released soon. Which would reinforce their distrust, wouldn't it? That man who so fascinates us both, you and me, would he defend you against the others' suspicions, against his own? I understand him, I even like him. A kind of cruelty, typically intellectual. Strength and vulnerability. That last counterbalanced by an even greater strength. Great strength that is at the same time a great weakness. An added attraction, don't you think? Vulnerable . . . therefore liable to fall into a fatal trap. And yet, as I was telling you, I understand him, I really do. The most dangerous excesses are those of the intellectual. The intellectual determined to conquer his weaknesses and hesitations by exaggerating his 'loyalty.' I've been watching that one for a long time, believe me. Ten years. I already know him well. Constantly threatened, not only by us or by others, but by himself. Let's let him struggle with himself, I told my bosses. That's enough, if you ask me. But no one understands me. Those idiots are blind to my powers of insight."

The little fellow had become so worked up he was panting. And there was something, at times, not quite right . . . The prisoner waited, unnerved at the idea that he might be coming closer to her.

Instead, he began screaming at the top of his lungs. "No, this isn't some kind of joke, and I'm not fucking around! Wipe that silly smile off your face! Perhaps there's someone paying me to play this double game, paying me for my double-triple-multiple role, what would you know about it? What gives you the right to despise me?"

Still yelping, he abruptly turned on the desk lamp and peered suspiciously at her. He stood there trembling, banging his small fists on the glass. He was completely flushed, his shoulders twitching. In an utter paroxysm of rage, he glared pop-eyed at the prisoner. He flailed his arms in all directions. His body began convulsing in a violent fit. He sneezed . . . yes, he was sneezing again, the little rabbit . . . couldn't stop sneezing . . . The irritation and weakness that had overtaken him seemed to have sensitized all his membranes at one stroke, for they now quivered under attack. The pleasure of sneezing! As though it drained and revived not only his mucosae but also his soul, his delicate sinner's soul. He moaned, purified. Rejuvenated, cleansed. Unable to recover, exhausted. At last he collapsed on the desk, all in. His trembling hand fumbled across the glass, seeking the switch. The light went out.

After a long pause, the voice rose once again into the darkness, hesitant, obscssive.

"The game I'm playing is more dangerous than you think, my dear. Much crueler than you suppose . . . A mind-game. Calculation and imagination. A restless mind, a subtle, delicate mechanism. It's true that I lack character . . . but not cruelty, not ferocity, believe me, madam. A worthy opponent for you. You'll understand this, you'll understand this, too, later on."

The room was steeped in darkness, immersed in dense shadows. The prisoner couldn't see a thing, not a thing

. . . except the tortuous trajectory of his words, his voice thickened by drink, hoarse, even vitreous at times, even moist, emerging between sneezes, swelling, filling the air, suddenly bursting, blown out, like a thin balloon touched by a knife blade.

Perhaps she shouldn't have listened to him. The preparations, the last few days of softening her up, the meals, then the shock caused by the beginning of this interminable interview . . . Instability, a kind of working premise, without which this dangerous clown could neither think nor breathe, a fragile, deceptive mechanism that probably becomes effective only in the end, when you add up all the bizarre elements . . . A permanent oscillation and vertigo maintaining each other on their own, functioning through trapdoors and falls and even more desperate recoveries . . . Oh, all that had worn her out, beaten her down. Little by little he'd succeeded in instilling a continual tension in her, and in sensitizing her to its different gradations . . . She knew that anything could happen and she couldn't have cared less, no, she'd run out of strength, she had none left, none at all, none.

She was sliding down into her armchair, into sleep. She thought at some point she'd heard the words "my dear." She was losing it, letting go, falling asleep, ready to drop with fatigue, slipping away into sleep, and he, he was watching her, on the alert, like a huge misshapen rabbit.

She clenched her fists to keep from giving in. She was sliding again, though, drifting lightly into the armchair's sweet softness. Her body was spreading, overflowing. She shouldn't give up, she mustn't; she tensed the muscles in her calves to keep herself awake. As for him, she no longer heard him, she hadn't heard him for some time now, perhaps he wasn't talking anymore, perhaps he didn't even exist any longer, long gone. No, she wouldn't listen to him anymore, she'd put her fingers in her ears, and anyway, he no longer existed, long gone, all gone, nothing left.

She raised her arms awkwardly. Slowly, because the slightest current of air could tip him off. He'd already proved several times how keen his senses were, the poor bastard. Even when he seemed to be absent, obliterated by the darkness, he detected every movement. She leaned over one of the armrests on the chair. She covered her ears with her hands. But she didn't want to fall asleep. She had to remain awake, attentive, at all costs.

The Plenipotentiary was often shaken by real moments of collapse; he disguised some of these episodes while flaunting others, or even cleverly mimicking a state of absolute prostration, and it was difficult, impossible to tell which was which. Anyone who could do so and thus avoid being fooled by him would unquestionably have a chance at foiling his plans.

At all events, he'd managed, she had to admit, to make her doubt all arguments and judgments—her own as well as his—and ascribe to that interminable monologue, despite everything that was dubious about it, a secret but very precise purpose, not yet clear to her, toward which he was doubtless directing her, imperceptibly, and thus he

felt free to indulge, among other things, in the most unexpected maneuvers on the side, forays well off his chosen
path, often inspired by a sudden whim.

Was it worth trying to figure out, wondering, for example, why he'd spoken of the engineer Mateescu and not
of the Mateescu brothers, who were engineers? As for
young Patraulea, it never would have occurred to her to
speculate about his peasant origins. An interest in the arts,
yes, that she would eventually have wondered about. But
not any problems with his health, certainly not. She'd
never heard any mention of ill health, she didn't see the
connection. When she thought of him now, however, anything seemed possible, everything became more or less
plausible.

Had he stopped talking? Was he tired, too, drowsing
quietly just as she was, the poor man, the creep? He was
silent, and she hadn't heard him for some time now. Nor
had she been in any way aware of his presence. She'd been
waiting the whole time, even when trying to think about
something else, she'd kept her eye on him, thought she
could feel him waving his soft, weak arms around, quite
close to her, flitting about the room like a bat, she'd waited
for him to draw near, to awaken her, to punish her for
not listening all the way through with more interest and
respect, to hit her, undress her, or who knows what, in a
frenzy . . . Yes, he would have been capable of doing
absolutely anything. A few times, behind the apathy and
timidity he made such a show of, whether real or affected,
she'd glimpsed an unsettling mixture of desire and hatred
and pleasure, still perfectly controlled, held in check, but

directed toward her, touching her briefly, like an invisible arrow. She'd pulled herself together, feeling vulnerable and afraid.

She raised her head, threw back her shoulders, stopped leaning on the armrest. She listened carefully. Faint, even breathing, the breathing of a spoiled little rabbit. So he'd fallen asleep, too. This interview certainly seemed to reveal a ridiculous complicity between them!

"No, I'm not asleep. I was letting you rest for a moment. You seem tired," he murmured.

He'd hardly spoken when they both started and looked up sharply. The telephone was ringing! Even he was surprised. Now what were they up to?

The racket was horrendous, and in the dark he was having trouble finding the receiver. Finally, he picked it up.

"Yes. It's you? What's gotten into you? . . . Not yet . . . No, a little more . . . You can relax, no, I haven't done a thing to her . . . A wig? Ha ha! No, I swear."

His laughter was forced, he seemed fearful, uneasy, irritated. But also furious and delighted.

"More or less . . . No need for you to worry about it. Not over that . . . Yes, just to keep my hand in, it wouldn't hurt me. Don't fuss over nothing . . . No, don't call back. That's an order. Do me a favor, let me handle this, no, please . . ."

He was begging her in a subdued voice, whispering more than speaking, ashamed of himself. Dominated by a woman, but feared by her as well, he was twisting around on his chair like a child caught doing something wrong.

———

His caller also seemed to be speaking in an undertone, without raising her voice at all. Complaints and treacherous entreaties at both ends of the line.

Had he hung up? She hadn't heard a click. But the voices had been quiet for a while. Perhaps they were listening to each other breathe . . . Then a slow half-turn. Waiting. Silence.

Finally, he switched on the lamp. Both of them rubbed their eyes; their faces were drawn. After so much darkness, the light was blinding.

"Yes, it's rather late. As you can see, I didn't try to drag all your secrets out of you."

The prisoner looked at the clock over the desk, but she was dazzled by the light and couldn't decipher a thing. Everything looked the same, all white.

"You'll have to learn to deal with your friends' distrust, I suppose. And I should let you know that you won't be charged along with them at their trial. We might decide to release you. We might just as well decide, after all, to condemn you. Not necessarily for any political crimes. We'll look for something else. Haven't found it yet. I've been frank with you. Don't kid yourself. I'm not always like that, but this time I chose to be. It's part of my plan. Don't get the idea I've been faking all this sincerity. In time you'll discover just the opposite. No, I haven't cheated. I was trying to be open, aboveboard . . . Whatever happens to you from now on—I'm being sincere right to the end—will be connected with Lucian Hariga, your beloved, as they say in melodramas. Even when you'll no longer know anything about each other, when

he won't have seen you or thought of you in a long time
. . . The freedom of work, the freedom of love, the freedom of creation! Wonderful, isn't it? Artists become rebels, because of everything they are and especially because of everything they're not. Art certainly seems, at
first, like dislocation, deracination, inadequacy. Nourished, enhanced—I'm repeating a quaint aesthetic cliché—
by an obsession? Weakness can give rise, let's not forget
this, to a formidable strength. We've seen this time and
time again. It's only natural, that's what I'm saying, for
you people to be always on the side of the opposition. To
end up championing the downtrodden. And those rare
prophets who still come along now and then . . . I'm
familiar with such pastimes. I had my own fling with them
at one point. Don't think I don't know what I'm talking
about. I dabbled a bit. Even I was a firebrand for quite a
while. Yes, me too. Perhaps there's still a fire in my belly,
but it feeds on a colder, more artificial fuel. That's why
my employers consider me skilled at handling special cases.
Because, as I told you, I once was one myself. I was even
becoming especially special. I was done in by laziness, my
little vices. Perhaps by my intelligence as well, I'm not
very modest, as you've noticed. In other words, I'm the
product, some would add the symbol, of corruption . . .
I certainly couldn't discourage you personally by claiming
that you people, our rebellious fringe element, haven't got
a secure, safe place even among those with whom you
naturally belong, as I was just saying. One senses this cruel
quirk of fate rather quickly, but understanding it takes time
. . . You, Miss and Mrs. and Comrade Strihan, you've

loved this exceptional man. An intellectual with a solid education, and a fighter. To all intents and purposes, a leader, that's Comrade Hariga! You're younger than he is. Which made the attraction, on both sides, all the stronger. You had a part to play in his life. Although he is or might readily be taken for a hedonist, I ought to tell you. He's fascinated other women besides you, become close to them, then drifted away without any useless complications . . . Your grades at the School of Fine Arts were not outstanding. But I saw every picture of yours that's still there. I was able to understand who you were, what you were after, I could see the truth in those paintings. A truth still nebulous, seemingly chaotic. The truth of art, of your art, for example, is not something obvious. Perhaps truth is too big a word, a balloon of hot air. Hmn . . . The money I receive—grossly inadequate compensation, when you consider how much they get from me—would be even more degrading if it didn't allow me, at least occasionally, to indulge not only in the pleasures that money can buy but in others as well. Not simply fleeting ones. Pleasures of a more lasting nature. I hope that you'll be one of them, Sia Strihan . . . Please excuse me for having used the familiar form of address with you now and then. I'm a little drunk, and I don't feel well. Nevertheless, perfectly lucid, I assure you . . . It would be pointless, anyway, but even if I wanted to, I couldn't keep them from continuing to interrogate you. To shock and offend you, sometimes to torment you. They like driving things into the ground, there's nothing I can do about it. They think the whole apparatus will get rusty if it isn't constantly at work, that's their rule. I have only limited power to change their methods. What's more, they claim, and sometimes prove, that they get results. It's not my department. But even so, there are certain things I can do."

He stood up. Ever since he'd turned on the light, after the episode or the dream or the nightmare of the low, feminine, feline voice on the telephone, his words and actions had lost some of their uneasiness and elasticity. In a single instant, some chill wind had frozen his mobile, human features. It would have been hard to tell if this new posture or imposture hid something even worse, even more unexpected. He seemed abruptly conscious of being less interesting and mysterious than the character he'd portrayed until that moment. But at present he was indifferent, agreeing for who knows how many seconds to play an official, aloof, and boring role. A sacrifice he certainly would never have made without knowing that it had become opportune.

"As you saw, I brought a great many packages, both large and small. I made sure nothing was left out. And that nothing got lost. I brought them here personally, after checking to see that I had everything on my list. So as not to forget, through carelessness, a single one of my presents. I'm courting you the old-fashioned way, so to speak. Being considerate of ladies who honor me with their kind attention."

A smile was appropriate here. A brief smile, the barest hint of a smile, after which he immediately recovered his neutral expression.

"Brushes of several sizes. Pencils, drawing charcoal, India ink. Watercolors and oil paints. Best quality. I wasn't stingy. I chose carefully and paid without hesitation. Various kinds of paper, of different weights. Even canvases. If you're really set on it, you'll eventually be able to do etchings as well. Sometimes art arises out of tragic ink blots, like the ones published almost a hundred years ago during the period of German Romanticism. But perhaps you won't need to go that far. Personally, I prefer drawing. Unless all that black and white becomes tiring for you, too ascetic in the long run. Besides, a bit of color would be acceptable in the drawings, if it's done with colored pencil. Pencil or charcoal drawings. Chalk, pen and ink, brush, whatever you like. If you feel the need to paint, at a certain point, in oil or watercolors, feel free to do so. Along with all the supplies I got for you, I even brought varnishing materials. What's called, at least that's what's written on the box, *mastics in lacrima pura* . . ."

He was using a normal tone of voice, as though he hadn't noticed that the prisoner was both dismayed and alarmed. And suddenly she spoke.

"Fine, but . . ."

That was all she mumbled. Considering her previous stubborn silence, however, it was enough. He noticed discreetly how she kept gazing longingly at the packages piled in their corner.

"I've brought you everything you need to draw and paint. If you're serious about wanting to do etchings, perhaps at some point I'll be able to obtain the necessary authorization. Accordingly, we're going, that is, they are going to hold on to you a while longer. Perhaps they will keep you here. A few months, a few years, hard to say. We're a small country, we're affected by what goes on in the world. If you want my opinion, I don't think it can last much longer. Things are beginning to move quickly . . . Whatever happens, whether you remain in custody for a long time or not, you must finish one drawing every day. Of the house, the exterior or the interior, the exterior and the interior of the house where Hariga, Kahane, Vaduva, and the others met. Too much like an assembly line for an artist? That's what it seems like, at first, but only at first. You'll work every day, without laboring over details, simply putting down what you remember. The drawings will probably repeat themselves, with a certain accuracy and frequency. Later you'll be able to spend more time planning and working on each piece. They'll become more artistic that way. More inaccurate, or accurate in a different way, a bit 'off' from reality as it is in your memory. Useless to explain this to you, you're familiar with psychology and aesthetics. Memory, in the last analysis, will in turn find itself serving the obsession. As well as joining in the game. I told you that you could choose your medium. I've brought everything. But I wish you to begin, as in art school, with drawing. Of course you'll be allowed to switch from one medium to another, if you like. But to begin with, and for a certain time, only drawing. A few hours will be reserved for this activity in your daily schedule. I'm sure you're well aware of the importance of this privilege. You'll have to work conscientiously, however. To get used to this obligation. You'll be reluctant, at first.

Then, little by little, you'll come to enjoy it. You'll look forward to it. Let's hope that you'll get more and more caught up in the game, that you'll become increasingly intrigued, fascinated. It's the same way with depravity, the same with love. Now, art . . . depravity and love, right? . . . These drawings will describe explicitly the topography of the place. The disposition of the building, your own place in the composition. I know exactly how many times you went there and whom you met there. A dozen times. More precisely, eleven times. Admit that the real purpose of this task—which will, I hope, become increasingly pleasant, increasingly useful for the artist you are or will become, leaving aside its therapeutic aspect—admit, as I was saying, that the purpose of this activity or this ex-periment escapes you. What can I tell you? Sincerity has been a constant part of my plans, in your case. This detail, however, I'm going to keep strictly to myself. Not even to myself, I might say. In fact, here's another hypothesis: even I don't know exactly why I've started down this particular path, or where it will lead me, and us. Yes, why not? So, now everything seems coherent and explicable again. I know you've been taught, and that you need to believe, that there's a reason, an explanation, for every-thing . . ."

Her impression was confirmed: the fellow's words, but also his voice and rigid countenance, had taken on a certain assurance, a certain indifference.

He was drumming his fingers on the desk, glancing only rarely now at his prey. He was still standing. He'd emptied his flask; he spoke rapidly, coldly, and with determination.

"The fairy story about the marvels that might be revealed by studying a complete series of your drawings or paintings of the house or, rather, the former house of Comrade Lucian Hariga turned out to be a convincing argument to my employers. My good sense—my relative good sense—and, in addition, this vague fantasy of mine, seem so crazy to them that, as time went by, I watched them become self-conscious in my humble presence. Whatever I suggest to them, everything I say to them, makes them hesitant, unsure whether I got it from books, or made it up myself, or even whether I made up the books . . . In any case they have no way of knowing. They are possessed of a sort of humility—which is related to respect, let's not forget—that constantly increases, of course, along with their hatred of me, of you, of anyone connected with books, of anyone who believes in books. Contempt, superstition, and hatred, whether the books are real or imaginary . . . They wouldn't be capable of understanding how unreal a real book can be! How real a still unwritten book can be, as long as its contents exist—virtually—in the mind of at least one person . . . Anyway, as I see, my speculations haven't disturbed you too much. To conclude, let's agree specifically that you'll be required to execute drawings on a given subject. We'll just call it one of my whims. You've noticed, I'm sure, that I tend to be capricious. As long as you go along with me in this fancy of mine, admittedly a rather unusual one, I don't see why I should deprive you of the attendant privileges that will be granted you from now on. My promises will be carried out scrupulously. You'll probably be spared, as I mentioned, the rigors of a political trial. Which will perhaps fuel—at least I hope so—your comrades' suspicions regarding Sia Strihan . . . Now we'll turn out the light. We don't need it anymore. You see, dawn has crept up on us. We can say that we've spent the night together. A gorgeous morning, look! Boundless, clear sky. Misfortune, unhappiness, prison, these things belong, like the sky, like all joy or sorrow, to the life we've been given. We should welcome everything that belongs to life with joy and astonishment. We won't get to enjoy anything else . . ."

He was right. The finite earth, subject to its unchanging rotation . . . The night that had united them now cast them up, together, on the cold and glassy shore of day.

He smiled, like a dead man. "Open the window, please."

The prisoner stood up clumsily. She was pale; her eyes were bloodshot, with great purplish circles under them.

She pivoted and took a first, slow step toward the window. She took another, leaning on the arm of the chair. She kept going, stretching out her left hand, with nothing more to lean on. She took one last, big step and reached the window, almost collapsing, holding both her hands out in front of her to grab the window frame, just in time.

She breathed deeply, with slumped shoulders and downcast eyes. Then she tried to straighten up. Her left hand clutched at the windowsill, her right slid across the casement, fumbling for a moment before reaching the cold metal of the window fastening. She tightened her grip, attempting to open it. She couldn't. She stood on tiptoe, reaching up with her left arm as well to grasp the handle of the casement bolt with both hands, to wrench it free.

Her forehead was damp. She struggled with the bolt, again and again, until at last the two sides of the espagnolette window parted gently. Her arms fell limply to her sides. She leaned on the sill for a moment, then grasped one of the casements and swung it completely back against the wall, doing the same with the other side as well. She stood awhile at the open window, her eyes refreshed by the cool morning air.

She gazed at the downy white sky, the rows of dawn-blue houses, the glistening wet ribbons of the streets, along which raced a few cars, vanishing like insects in a hurry. She placed her hands flat against the sides of the window, which in this room as well was furnished with thick bars. A sky streaked with clouds. Still white, though. Serene.

Prison, illness, solitude, the misfortunes of this singular life. Brief, of unforeseeable duration, let's enjoy it while we may. If I weren't revolted by hearing those words from his lips, I might well have spoken them myself, who knows?

Behind her, nothing stirred. Had the little rabbit fallen asleep, with his head on the desk? Or was he still watching her, holding his breath? There was no longer the slightest sound.

She listened intently; no, nothing. Some time had probably passed. She'd opened the window, had rested for a long while, contemplating the sky above the deserted city. She'd forgotten the man who'd shared her night. After all, he'd only told her to open the window . . . She turned her head slowly toward him. To indicate, quite properly, that she was entirely at his disposal.

———

But he was no longer in the room. He'd probably slipped out while she was wrestling with the window.

The chair was in its place behind the desk, as though no one had ever sat there. The telephone, dead. The thin flask and its metal cap that had so often brightened the room during the night, like a tiny sign of life, were gone.

She had such a longing to stretch her legs, get the stiffness out of them. To relax into oblivion, her head buried in a soft pillow. She wasn't strong enough yet to remember everything, to start putting her thoughts in order.

She gave up the idea of going back to her armchair. Exhausted, she leaned her elbows on the window ledge. Until they came to drag her off wherever they wanted, she was staying right where she was. The door was closed, however, and no one was calling her. *They opened the door for barely a second. To keep an eye on me: I could have broken through the bars and escaped by jumping down from the second floor. They saw me and closed the door, reassured. Or perhaps it was him again, taking one last look, between two swigs from that flask.*

She felt a light hand on her shoulder. She shuddered; the serpent glided across her shoulder, and now she felt it slithering down her back, cold and damp.

So it wasn't finished; it was just beginning. The hand pressed softly on her shoulder. Everything was starting all over, and even worse, picking up from the point she'd always dreaded the most. He had unbeatable endurance, that feeble wraith! Strength and inclination had returned, he'd emptied another bottle. He was off and running again, daisy-fresh. It would never end, he'd figured correctly, right on the button, his victim wouldn't put up a fight, wouldn't be able to hold out.

"Relax. It's not starting up again," murmured a woman's voice, apparently quite close . . . right next to her . . .

The slim fingers seemed to grip her shoulder, turning her gently around. The woman from the day before perhaps, that stern, delicate brunette, so familiar, like a colleague . . . There was something both lewd and maternal about her. Her hair mussed, her face pale and sweaty, her skirt twisted, her white blouse partially unbuttoned, as though she'd just been unexpectedly rousted out of her lair, after a nap or a night of insomnia or after . . . after anything at all. Her breasts, naked and dewy with perspiration, quivered in the plunging neckline of her blouse.

"Thank you. You behaved very well, you didn't provoke him . . ."

The words were barely audible, whispered too softly.

The hand on her shoulder kept creeping, it seemed, serpentinely, toward her neck. The apparition tried to caress her cheeks, ever so gently? The prisoner moved away.

"Who tossed your cap over there?" she heard, far away, or was it close by?

The woman bent down, picked it up. Looked at it with a kind of tenderness, thwacked it against the windowsill. Flicked off the last specks of dust with her hand. Then placed it, slowly and carefully, on the shaved head, and came even nearer to the window.

The wretched prisoner leaned her forehead against the bars, drinking in the cold daylight and fresh air, fleeing the voice that pursued her. Sirens wailed, one would have said, all of a sudden; she heard them and didn't hear them, perhaps they'd been shrieking all night long, just for her, and she hadn't heard them.

"You behaved well. You can rest a bit, even sleep . . ."

Someone, somewhere, sometime, had murmured these words slowly, too slowly, as though talking to a sister. Was the woman barefoot? Was that why she hadn't heard her come in?

At some point, the door closed again, quietly. A breath, perhaps a trace of scent, a blend of new odors, difficult to identify. She stared at the door a while longer before turning back toward the window.

She stood motionless, her temple resting against the chilly window frame. Her weary face seemed to glow with the light of dawn. She appeared to be asleep.

COMPOSITE
BIOGRAPHY

FOR A LONG TIME NOW WE'VE BECOME UNABLE TO UNDER-
stand ourselves except in relation to others. Only this approach,
apparently, can lead us to any meaningful conclusions. In the
same way, we cannot look to the future before learning who we
are.

Perhaps what the eager originator of the project had in mind,
essentially, was a portrait of his time. Individualization, or what
would remain of it, would once again result only from comparison
with a frame of reference. Anyone bothering to consider in this
light the personal data sheet (to be handed in the following day
at the designated political department) would have no difficulty
understanding that he is participating, willy-nilly, in this sum-

mation, or synthesis, and that his life, as singular as it may seem to him—a somewhat elusive and astonishing mystery, in his own eyes—would be discernible, if only as an extravagant detail, within a range of collective data.

So it's easy to understand why the new Director of the Institute of Futurology would prefer to diversify the pool of participants in the study rather than adopt new techniques. As a result, not only the usual mathematicians, physicists, psychologists, doctors, and lawyers will be invited to the first of those lively Thursday conferences, but others as well, strange categories outside the norm.

Thursday, six o'clock; the serene light of a late afternoon in July in the 1970s. In the gleaming auditorium of Orlando Street, the guests will include a typist, a taxi driver, a restaurant manager, a kindergarten nurse, a novelist, a personnel director, a gym teacher, a customs officer, and a National Savings Bank employee.

The introduction of these new guests to their colleagues will form the sole agenda of this first session.

Without rising to address his audience, omitting the usual "Silence, please" or "Dear comrades," the director will begin with someone he will have, let's say, noticed by chance, in the third row, near the window. A nondescript young man, a taxi driver, smiling patiently in the peaceful light of the room . . .

"Comrade Voinea belongs to the taxi drivers' union and works in the capital. A young man, as you can see: only twenty-one years old. An excellent driver, I'm told. And what's more, I've had occasion to learn this firsthand before asking him to join us here today. In school, he showed promise in mathematics, although he eventually decided to study ballet, taking courses at the Conservatory of Choreography. I trust I'm not being indiscreet, nor overdoing this introduction, my dear Cristian . . ."

Cristian Voinea will merely bob his head in acknowledgment. A blond, with a pale forehead and a strong torso, he will wear a checked shirt of a sheer material. The future participant will listen impassively to the résumé-spiel, as though the director were speaking about someone else.

"An unfortunate accident led him to abandon his ballet studies. Cristian was too old to return to mathematics—a vocation that demands, like the piano, both precocity and serious groundwork at the earliest possible age, as he likes to say. But I wouldn't like to reveal all the surprises in store for us from Comrade Voinea, who comes to us from the taxi garage on Rosetti Place in Bucharest."

The silent audience will then learn that the typist, a youthful fifty-year-old lady, is not just any typist, although that is her profession, but the daughter of our ambassador to Great Britain during the inter-war years, and a recognized expert on the decorative arts. Before her biography was distorted for political reasons, she was an important consultant on antique Oriental ornaments. The gym teacher, a former military man and famous jockey, was involved, unfortunately, with mystical sects. He is well versed in heraldry, a fact attested to by the many diplomas he has received, while the affable aristocrat with the white thatch of hair and imposing double chin, presently employed as a restaurant manager, has unique experience in the pre-war world of finance, but has also won numerous prizes for the experimental varieties of grapes he grew and the wine he used to produce on his small but no less exemplary estate.

These intriguing characters will have what it takes to arouse the interest of the listeners, who don't often get a chance to meet such exotic fauna.

One may therefore conjecture that at a certain point the participants begin wondering vaguely about a stranger whom the director does not seem eager to introduce to them.

Sure enough, when this first meeting comes to a close, the elegant master of ceremonies will have passed over in silence the adolescent who seems completely out of place in this distinguished company and who follows the proceedings intermittently, sitting in the first row, engrossed in a magazine from which he now and then looks up nearsightedly, as though awakening from a deep sleep.

The sixteen- or seventeen-year-old young man doesn't seem to belong in this weighty atmosphere of projects, research, surveys, and studies of the future. What is also puzzling is his own seeming confusion, as though he were frankly uneasy surrounded by all these serious and hyperspeculative scholars. A plump boy, with thinning hair, even a few gray hairs. Little wire-rimmed glasses. Relatively short, relatively shy. In brief, in a word, relatively . . .

It isn't until the next week, on a rainy Thursday, that the discussions will continue almost until midnight. All sorts of rumors will begin to circulate about the stranger's identity. A young mathematician of genius, an incredibly gifted although as yet unknown poet, discovered by the comrade director himself! Such hypotheses would be at least compatible with the intruder's age and appearance. As for suggesting that he might be an engineer who'd studied in the United States or a former escapee from a Nazi camp, or, as someone will insist, the lover of Madame, the singer, the comrade director's wife, or even an important political personage—these speculations will seem like pure aberrations, given the youth's age, for one thing. An uncertain age, it must be said, only a mask, as many are thinking. Be that as it may, these rumors will naturally arouse curiosity, since they will jar with the youth's comments from the floor, delivered in a hesitant and slightly feminine voice, comments that might best be described as a series of dots on i's.

In any case, everyone will agree that the adolescent brings a welcome stimulus to the polemic. Such ideas as "The future is in the present," or "Hazard is the enemy of Authority," or "Time subsists only in writing," or "Gas is the blood of the future," or "The typical day contains an entire biography of an age," or "Our biography means our political dossier," will be ascribed to that strange and seductive child, even though, according to some participants, they were actually proposed by other speakers. Nevertheless, these ideas will appear to be "provoked" by his fresh impetus, which is, moreover, the reason why they will be attributed to him in the end.

Many of the questions and mysteries swirling around the young man will probably be swept away in time, perhaps along with much of the admiring interest that greeted his first appearance. But it will no longer be possible purely and simply to forget him, to omit his name from the ranks of those collaborating on the final, future synthesis.

I.1.

SEVERAL YEARS EARLIER, A THIN LITTLE MAN HAD AP-
peared at a branch of the National Savings Bank. The
young employees there had gradually grown used to seeing
the auditor, Comrade Scarlat, turn up every year shortly
after the summer holidays, in September or October,
wearing his glasses with Coke-bottle lenses. The desk he
had chosen for his own was right in the middle of the floor,
in the center of all the conversations circulating freely
among the other employees.

Comrade Scarlat had never stuck his nose into anything—no complaints on that score—but it wasn't very
reassuring to have that extra pair of ears in the neighborhood, not to mention those enormous glasses, dark glasses,
which meant you could never tell if you were being observed from within their smoky depths. A typical bank
inspector, a dull creature of routine, sent by management
to take one last look at the year's transactions. He showed
none of the easy friendliness of a fellow worker who was
an old hand at everything involving figures and accounts,
and none of the snotty superiority of a wimpy pencil-
pusher promoted to supervisor.

Mr. Victor, sir, as the girls called him, had remained
barricaded behind his stiff manner. A loner, he was always
buried in his papers. He listened to the employees' chatter
with a certain contempt. At least, that's how it seemed to
them at first, but now they never noticed anymore. The
man they'd grown used to having as their neighbor every

final trimester never meddled in their affairs. About once a week, he'd bring them some chocolates . . . And the time Viorica was in a jam, he'd intervened entirely on his own, lending her the money she'd needed. He'd given Geta the name and address of an excellent lung specialist, and he'd arranged to get Ina's little girl into a nursery school. As for Chickadee, his favorite, apparently he hadn't dared do a single favor for her. He limited himself to watching her sashay around the office, and he was particularly captivated by her phone conversations, when he could listen to her surprisingly deep voice. Comrade Scarlat invariably looked up from his account books during these phone calls. And then looked down again in embarrassment. It was obvious that he listened very closely, intrigued by the slightest word, or rather hopelessly seduced by the charming young woman's husky voice. Sometimes he ran his ballpoint pen repeatedly through his thick hair, quite unconsciously twisting and ruffling his white locks throughout the entire phone conversation, until he was completely tousled. He often wound up looking like a snowy-haired fuzzy-wuzzy. It would take him more than a moment or two to recover his composure. He would nervously pull out his comb and practically scalp himself trying to get his hair looking neat again.

I.2.

COMRADE SCARLAT HAD GOTTEN UP ONCE MORE AND was heading for the telephone on Geta's desk. Carmen had signaled to Chickadee to keep an eye on the Turkish coffee pot. The brown-haired young woman, lifting her delicate face from the black circle of the open pot, had intercepted, in some confusion, the fed-up-to-the-back-teeth signal from Auntie Carmen, nicknamed Lots More Fish in the Sea. Chickadee remained on the receiving end of this private message for a moment or two, not having the nerve to look away or ignore it. *Volens nolens*, she'd duly watched Mr. Victor—proof of consent—as he approached Geta's desk and leaned once more, as he'd already done twice before in the last half hour, over the telephone. Catastrophe! The coffee boiled over. Chickadee the Geisha, as her girlfriends called her, blushed and became too flustered to think of instantly removing the pot from the hot plate, so the coffee spilled all over it in a sizzling black mess. Carmen, in her role as the boss driven up a wall by the incompetence of youth, which she herself had long outgrown, flung up her hands in irritation and then simply turned her back on the whole situation. Luckily, Viorica, always ready to help, arrived in no time with a cloth she'd just happened to have in her drawer, and wiped off the edge of the chair. The hot plate was finally unplugged and left to cool . . .

The flurry of activity over the accident hadn't bothered Comrade Scarlat in the least. He'd given the same number and used the same words, pronounced in a serious and even tone, as he had for the two preceding calls: "Hello, Scarlat calling. Is he there?" He'd evidently received the same answer. Without another word, Mr. Victor slammed the phone down once again. He returned to his desk, treading heavily, looking straight ahead of him. Ina, his closest neighbor, smiled as she polished her glasses . . .

Comrade Scarlat hardly ever used the telephone. For the last few days, therefore, his colleagues had been understandably amazed by his repeated phone calls, during which he always asked the same question and apparently met with the same disappointment. The identical scenario had been played out the previous day, and the day before that.

As she was settling her big red glasses on her pale, thin little nose, Ina noticed that Geta was winking at her and holding up three fingers. Yes, Mr. Victor had called for the third time, just like yesterday morning, just like the morning before. Three calls, at relatively short intervals, early in the morning . . . Then, nothing, *basta*, no more calls for the rest of the day. Sure enough, Comrade Scarlat was once again bent over his long columns of figures, just as on the other mornings. No one would ever have believed that, barely a few moments before, he'd been so irritable and impatient. That meant things were going to follow the same pattern as before: he wouldn't touch the phone for the rest of the day! Mr. Victor had never called up a friend, or made any business calls, or even called anyone at home, just to ask his wife or mother-in-law or daughter or God-knows-who about whatever, like everyone else, to see if there were errands to be done on the way home, if the elevator was fixed yet, you know, the whole daily pain-in-the-ass grind of every honest and multilaterally put-upon citizen.* No, Comrade Victor Scarlat had never telephoned anyone, and what's more, no one had ever telephoned him, either . . .

So it was no wonder this business of the three morning phone calls had intrigued them: the old so-and-so was actually asking for an extension number, how about that! Which meant he was trying to talk to someone in the same building, a colleague, so to speak, a comrade working in a different department there, where, frankly, the girls know everyone, whereas Comrade Scarlat neither knows nor has ever shown any desire to know anyone, aside from his poor, chatty, perfumed, amusing co-workers, among whom—that's his bad luck—he has landed again this year to spend the autumnal season of balance sheets and pickled vegetables.

1.3.

THE SOOTHING SUNSHINE OF A BUCHARESTIAN FALL DAY had reached, in its expansive course, the large windows of branch 46 . . .

"Pass me a Kent, puh-lease," mumbled Ina sleepily.

Shading her glasses from the light that had suddenly

---

* A "multilaterally developed socialist society" was a favorite propaganda phrase under Ceauşescu.

flooded her desk, she'd leaned down to finish the last of her coffee. The red-polished nail of her index finger traced the cup's contour. A fond little mannerism, that's what it looked like . . . Ultra-thin Ina sometimes had these sleek, feline moments, as though to ward off the fatigue of her working day, or who knows what annoyance she could sense well before it actually turned up. She was bending over the yellow cup, she was smiling. Her finger caressed the outline of the cup, which still contained a swallow of coffee. She was leaning forward, languidly. She savored the fortifying beverage. Her scented, downy nape, the delicate curve of her neck, this charming scene of Chinese refinement . . . Comrade Scarlat, who had a view of the tableau, had timidly bent his thick glasses over his accounts.

"Haven't got any more," Viorica had snapped belatedly. "Everyone's been helping themselves all day long . . ."

"I've got zome," murmured Geta Sugar Candy, close by. "The guy with the zavingz bond at eight hundred zlipped them to me, about two hourz ago. Lord knowz, he zure zurprized me. Juzt when I waz about to write down hiz name and ID number, he handz over the pack . . . A zolid-gold zmile, from here to there! I'm telling you! . . . To get a bond, can you imagine! I mean, it waz the lazt thing I expected."*

* In a context of poor-quality products and widespread shortages, imported cigarettes became a standard bribe necessary to obtain the slightest service. Purchased on the black market at the cost of an entire day's salary, a pack of Kents acquired so much cachet that it became a cultural symbol of both Western comfort and a moment of relaxation stolen from the system.

And Sugar Candy smiled—radiantly, revealing the golden disaster areas of her lousy teeth—to indicate how tickled she still was. She delivered a Kent, clamped between two fingers, to her colleague, but her face was turned in the opposite direction.

"Can't you turn that zdupid thing off? I really don't zee how you can zdand it."

The blaring transistor fell silent, and Auntie Carmen didn't seem offended by her subordinate's impertinence.

Ina adjusted her blond chignon. She sat up straight in her chair. She lighted her cigarette, pushed her big red glasses up on her little white Oriental nose. She stared off into the distance, looking as though her thoughts were miles away. And was defenseless against the whispers flitting from one desk to another. Unfortunately, she identified them immediately, in a sort of uncontrollable reflex. Uncontrollable, yes, a sensitive receptor reacting to stimuli, so just try to keep your mind on something else—if you can.

"He said he'd had it. That he was sick and tired of the pregnancy and ready to give up. 'Do whatever you want, abortion, whatever,' he told me, 'I'll be back when you've figured out a solution . . .' So much for using the calendar. Proof that it's not very reliable! It doesn't work every time. Ever since the other two, I've done everything absolutely right. It drives you crazy, you can just imagine . . . And the business with the rabbit, that's not a hundred percent certain either. Without protection, nothing is certain. That's the thing that screwed me up the most. The test had been negative. I thought I had who knows what

---

other problem wrong with me! So I'm waiting. My mother-in-law tells me she knows someone . . ."

So it was the angelic Chickadee, with her torrid, husky voice. Flat as a board—wherever did she get that voice of hers? When she wasn't speaking, nobody noticed her. All she had to do was say a few words and everybody's eyes started to boggle. Then they'd really see her for the first time: what a fetching walk, she's quite a darling, how demure she is, all that stuff. Unusual, yes, what a babe. She turned everyone's head. You couldn't catch her, but she wasn't exactly running away, either. Soft as silk, the things she said, and all those pauses . . . so you could think whatever you liked.

"Last year, when Banu had to go with everyone else in his office to help with the potato harvest, he brought back two sacks. They didn't do a lick of real work, they just screwed around playing games. It was the farmers out there who told them to take some home, can you believe it . . . Now, when it's time to go back there, he's stuck doing military service. I called up my old aunt, I asked her to help us out with some food, until we get a chance to drive out to the country one of these Sundays to fill up the car, because we just can't go on like this."

Viorica, the fluffy little cloud, was softly pouring out her heart while she scribbled away and signed her name at the speed of light. A fast worker, Viorica, faster than all the rest, but she couldn't resist backbiting and telling tales out of school. She wrote, added, signed, stamped in the twinkling of an eye. Which was what she was up to at that moment, and she'd yakkety-yakked about this and that until Geta finally got up to get herself another glass of water from the sink.

"You know, I told you zis zummer that I had zome pillz. But you didn't want them at the time. Zo I zlipped them to a neighbor, a young engineer. She livez in our building on the ground floor, she'z zingle. She getz oodles of packagez from her brother, who landed up in Canada."

That was Geta, with her sweetly sibilant s's, so sweet they'd put you to sleep. Easy to recognize her. So it was Geta, not Viorica, to whom Chickadee was talking, with those long pauses between words and that look she'd give you from time to time—astonished or mischievous, an irresistible look that would melt all resistance. Men, poor things, such easy marks.

A metallic rustle nearby: the Lady Carmen, obviously! Ina didn't bother opening her eyes, she knew who it was, she knew what was coming, and she didn't feel in the slightest bit like getting ready for it . . . If Milady Carmen was busy using that horribly provincial aluminum comb on the tangles in her thick black hair, that meant she was treating herself to her oh-so-familiar break. Soon she'd bring her chair over to Ina's desk. Then she'd trot out the usual opener: "Well, what's new, my little Inouchka from Sevastopol?" And she'd begin to caress her hand gently: "What pretty hands and eyes you have, my sweetheart of the steppes!"

Comrade Carmen Petroianu, who was in charge of this group, clearly preferred Ina to all the others. She showed her that protective friendliness reserved for tourists, when one points out to them the location of such-and-such a street or hotel or museum, tells them when a shipment of shoes is expected, and suggests they try looking for a certain item in this or that part of town. Ina had been living in Romania now for many years, a good ten of which she'd spent working in the bank; moreover, she was better than Comrade Carmen at all the chicanery necessary to survive daily life, but she accepted her assigned role. A warm welcome, no rebuffs . . .

No, she'd keep her eyes closed, she wouldn't open them even when she smelled the hovering odor of Comrade Carmen's huge body, soon to be seated on her right.

"Don't forget, you're assigned to the art brigade, Chickadee! This afternoon. For the patriotic festival . . . Perhaps we'll get to see you on TV, who knows?"

Carmen's voice definitely had carrying power. She was probably putting her barrettes back in, before getting up to go visit her attractive colleague. She called her Ina Chatova, even though for a long time now everyone else had been calling her Murguleţ, naturally, as the wife of ex-Comrade Murguleţ, formerly an important corporate director and university professor.

"An art brigade—juzt what every pregnant woman needz," groaned Geta from her desk.

Chickadee didn't say anything for the moment, only for the moment, of course.

As might have been expected, there was the sound of a chair being moved. One sensed the approach, the breathing of the matronly Carmen's massive bulk. Ina waited another moment. Then she finally opened her eyes . . .

"What's the matter, Inouchka, you're tired?"

The sweetheart of Sevastopol had barely had enough time to recognize the beauty mark beneath her supervisor's thick and scarlet lower lip.

"A bit tired. Last night, uncle of Micha came and stayed long time. But he gave me pair errinks of, how you say, of the pearl. Very pretty, very very pretty . . ."

Carmen could just have eaten her up! Much amused, she lighted a Kent, placing the pack on Ina's desk so that she could help herself. Comrade Petroianu didn't need to depend on the baksheesh of savings-bank customers trying to open special accounts, or the retired people all clumped together in lines on the fifteenth of every month, waiting to get their hands on their meager due, or lottery winners exhilarated by the good fortune that's come to them out of nowhere . . . Obviously, she wouldn't have refused a pack of imported cigarettes, or a bar of Western soap, or her fair share from what was given to her girls, who passed her quota on to her from time to time . . . It wasn't much, of course; they didn't work in a clinic or a gas station, for example.

"Girlz, I've got newz for you. They've ztarted zmoking king-zize even in the bookztorez: zomething'z going on, they muzt have reduced the zize of their printing runz," Sugar Candy had announced at one point. Comrade Petroianu couldn't have cared less. As for the boxes of cookies and packets of sweets, they were a pain in the neck. She couldn't stand confectionery. Sweet things revolted her, she gave them away on the spot, without even opening them. And she wasn't putting on an act, either, because she really wouldn't have touched them for the world. It made you wonder how she hadn't managed to lose any weight. Actually, she didn't even try to diet, she hadn't the patience to deal with all those half-assed low-calorie recipes. Who cares about fashion? Why should she worry about her figure? She felt fine, she had no reason to get all balled up in that complicated weight-loss stuff. But she really and truly did not like sweets. She wouldn't have anything to do with them, period.

"Forget about your 'earrinks,' or whatever you call them, let's talk about boots. Won't be any this year, not a single pair. Everyone's going to find themselves with their fingers up their . . . Wha? I heard it from someone at the top who knows, believe me. If you want, I can get you some in our special store. For eight hundred, Italian, with heels. And I asked Bebe to put down Chanel on the list, too. Only a hundred bottles are supposed to come in this year. We ought to be able to get two of them."

Ina had grown used to these periodic favors, she didn't even say thank you anymore. She waited patiently for her loot, as instructed.

"You don't have to thank me," Lady Carmen had once stated firmly. "Me, when I do a favor, it's 'cause I like the person. After all, what's the big deal? If you knew how much others take . . . I asked him, too: Do you think it's the same in the afterlife? Now he's off to Brazil, my sweetheart. And me, I'm stuck at my desk, like an idiot. But he absolutely promised me a vacation in Italy, my dear Party member. As it happens, he's already busy pulling strings for that one."

Comrade Carmen's husband held a mid-level but useful

position: he traveled, had lots of connections. His wife had jealously clung, not only to her mistakes in grammar and spelling, but also to a certain good sense that kept her from turning her nose up at the often-aired problems of her modest fellow workers, while preventing her from getting involved in petty intrigues or inappropriate gossip. She listened, didn't dodge the bittersweet stories or the constant grumbling, never interrupted, even chimed in occasionally with a snippet of information or an example, but maintained a consistent outlook: "I won't spit in the soup I eat. If I eat it, then that's what I eat, and that's that." Her unique and secret revenge, so to speak, against the privileges she enjoyed—privileges that were welcome but also faintly despised, and properly so—seemed to be precisely this fondness for Ina, a pleasant enough colleague and one who never caused any trouble, but who was treated with noticeable coldness by her superiors, for her Russian name. Of course, Milady Carmen didn't have any children . . . However, Ina wasn't all that young anymore, either. Be that as it may, Carmen made no effort to hide her affection for Chatova–Murguleț, yet she didn't favor her in any way in office affairs, treating her exactly like the others. Personal gestures, though, were saved just for her. A kind of affectionate mentor relationship, geared to making life easier for Ina and obtaining certain things for her outside of work. The most astonishing part was that they didn't visit each other: neither had introduced the other to her family, or invited her home, the way most people do. They didn't even call each other on Sundays. The sweetheart of Sevastopol acknowledged the special

nature of their relations only on the occasion of Comrade
Petroianu's birthday. Her fellow workers had long stopped
being impressed by the lavish presents she inevitably be-
stowed on their supervisor. Still, the gift represented the
barest minimum in the way of a return gesture, and was
far from equaling the advantages accumulated throughout
the year thanks to the wife of Bebe Petroianu, an official
who managed very nicely in his job at the Ministry of
Foreign Trade.

"Sooner or later, everybody winds up giving in to temptation. Who knows where my husband will be posted tomorrow, so why shouldn't we take advantage and pick up
a few trifles in the meantime?"

Just when Carmen was about to make it clear that "we"
meant herself and her friends, she heard Geta Sugar Candy
twittering, " 'Rade Carmen, telephone!"

Hefty but light on her feet, Carmen Petroianu was in
no time reaching for the receiver, signaling to Ina that she
would be back shortly.

The conversation was brief, as was the explanation offered to Ina. "The bosses want to see me. With any luck,
it won't take too long."

Comrade Scarlat looked up abruptly from his accounts.
After Auntie Petroianu had left the room, he hurried over
to the phone. It was after noon; the lines became very busy
as the day wore on. So Mr. Victor, sir, was going to try
again—for the fourth time! Well, how about that: little
Scarlat was just full of surprises today.

"Hello, Scarlat speaking. Is he there?" He didn't slam
down the receiver this time, but replaced it carefully in its

cradle. Now Mr. Victor was really ticked off. He returned
slowly to his desk, looking most annoyed.

*It will become harder and harder to determine whether the
young protagonist of the Thursday conferences has been a constant
influence during these weeks of preliminary discussions. Because
of this uncertainty, no one will be able to state positively that
the young man's remarks have indeed determined the direction
matters will take. And nobody will say how young this ageless
old-young man was.*

*Imperceptibly at first, then more and more clearly, these dis-
cussions will begin to focus less on the future than on the present
and the past—a surprising development, given the nature of the
institute in question.*

*One could maintain that this unforeseen reorientation is due
to the young man's interventions. The initial criticism of certain
conjectures and approaches bearing no firm connection to the
"working data," namely, the "human element," that is to say,
"the constituent factors" or "the collective biography" or the
"meaningful coefficients"—this critique might, of course, have
been made by him. It might just as well have been offered by
some other speaker, or represent a synthesis of several viewpoints.
The temptation to attribute such a major revision of the inves-
tigative process to this seemingly youthful participant would stem
from the interest aroused by both his startling appearance and his
unexpected, cogent, and always convincing remarks.*

*In the end, it won't much matter who set this course for the
group's future research, and how it was done. Not many weeks
would pass before the collaboration of the participants would foster*

a receptive familiarity, a frank exchange of opinions, reconciled by the conclusion that before seeking to envisage the future, one must know who will help to shape it. Only then can one attempt to define this impact . . . The future would thus belong to the present, and to the recent past that has formed us. There will be unanimous agreement on this point, for only on this basis will the necessary controversies be free to flourish.

Many of these meetings will be spent trying to define the requisite terminology. The audience will frequently linger late into the night, wandering through the nebula of those peripheral sequences called parables—a psychological test, sociological statistic, criminal trial, or case history offered for consideration by one or another of the participants.

One might mention, for example, that July evening when the subject under discussion ("The Pleasure and Quality of Work") will be illustrated by a vignette presenting the image of a world mired in a syndrome of generalized renunciation, referred to by the speaker as "the fed-up syndrome." Offered as proof will be whole groups of people who retire at an early age—a psychosis of mysterious evolution affecting quite diversified professional categories: construction workers, airline pilots, circus acrobats . . . Early retirement, motivated by the most unpredictable reasons, will spread slowly but surely to the bureaucracy and the military, finally paralyzing the health sector itself and leading to catastrophic peacetime annihilation. Sudden outbreaks of violence, rapidly subsiding without outside intervention into tacit lulls, will reappear periodically—new and paradoxical explosions of seemingly extinguished but still smoldering despair. Simulated behavior, the discrimination of values, sexual oppression,

---

parochialism, duplicity, data distortions, the half-truth as slogan and motivational factor—these are only a few of the topics that will mobilize strongly divergent opinions.

On September 26, for example, the Thursday session will be held at a psychiatric hospital, where the participants will be astonished at the good sense often displayed by the patients in their remarks. This challenge to any strict demarcation between mental health and insanity will suggest that illness be viewed as a more profound, subtle, authentic way to perceive reality. Would the afflicted actually be more adept at coping with unforeseen circumstances? Would so-called healthy minds be the cynical and indifferent mechanisms of a self-regulating routinism?

On other evenings, the subject of debate will be the quality of life; namely, the quality of shoes, bread, printing ink, books, movies, buses, hotels, prisons, tobacco, wine, perfume, the daily life of the average citizen. Other topics—not necessarily the most important—will be broached as well, such as suspicion and sur- veillance, sports as therapy and diversion, the lottery and ide- ology, the management and manipulation of discontent, the loss of quality in food and its increasing scarcity, heart attacks and the oil crisis, communal apartments, the manager-typist-chauffeur relationship, heart attacks and the oil crisis. On October 9, the Thursday speaker will read a paper entitled "The Synopsis of Captive Happiness: A Day in the Life of a Working Woman."

This excessive emphasis on details and preliminary activities that would delay work on the project itself will finally be abruptly brought under control by the comrade director, who will probably have to report to his superiors who initiated this strange trap.

The participants will therefore proceed to individual brief-

ings, the setting up of schedules, work groups, and inter-group meetings.

And only then will they realize that nothing was left to chance in the selection of their fellow workers. The plenary sessions will prove all the more interesting, since the delegates' diversity of background and interests will be reflected in their wide range of remarks and confessions.

II.1.

IN SEPTEMBER OF 1945, A SKINNY, NEARSIGHTED YOUNG man set out for the big city, determined never to return to the drab provincial town where he was born. He intended to join the Foreign Legion . . .

The train to Bucharest left at noon. The young man had forbidden his parents to accompany him to the station. Which meant, quite obviously, his elderly mother, since it would never have occurred to his father to be so foolish as to leave work in the middle of the day. His mother, however, seemed truly crushed by the absolute intransigence of her taciturn only son, who had obstinately refused to listen to her tirades and supplications and wouldn't even let her go with him to the station. How could God have done this to her? She'd never see her boy again. That was all she could understand of the laconic explanations her darling condescended to grumble now and then. The Evil One had turned his head! Why did it have to be this way,

why didn't she have the right to show how she was suffering? Poor woman, it was all quite beyond her.

On the morning of her son's departure, the unhappy
woman found out that the impatient fruit of her womb
didn't even want the food parcel she'd so lovingly prepared
for him. The wretch removed carefully folded garments
from his suitcase, tossing all over the room ties, gloves,
slippers, everything that his mother had secretly gathered
together for him. By the time he was finished, he was
down to one pair of trousers, a sweater, two pairs of shoes,
a towel, a shirt, some underwear, and a beret.

The young man's farewell to his mother was brief. He
made her swear she wasn't going to start crying, or be
silly enough to discuss his departure with the women of
the neighborhood, lamenting what was definitely over and
done with. He promised to write her regularly, not very
often, but regularly all the same. He wanted her to have
confidence in him, just as he was confident that the bereft
woman would keep her word and neither show nor read
to anyone the letters she might receive from him. He
hugged her tightly and kissed her damp and mussy hair,
refusing the sentimental gush traditionally displayed on
such occasions.

The woman stayed obediently at her window, gazing
after the scrawny, myopic lad going out into the wide wild
world, never to return. She watched him cross the long
courtyard with his quick little step, slamming the wooden
door behind him. Gone, the child she'd raised so devot-
edly, for whom she'd struggled so stubbornly . . . Petrified,
she imagined him climbing aboard the train, jammed into

one of those dirty, overcrowded, postwar cars. She saw him huddled on the wooden seat, glowering fiercely in a corner, oblivious to those around him. Night was falling. She remembered his bout with pneumonia, and the time he ran away from boarding school many years before, a sickly, surly brat, roaming around like a madman from morning till night. And she remembered the day she'd taken him to see the oculist. It was getting late; her husband would be home soon. An empty house, in the failing light. The woman turned away from the window, withdrawing deeper into herself.

The kitchen: the kerosene lamp, the matches, the wick. A gentle, timid light filled the room. Near the lamp, the open Gospel. So he hadn't taken it with him, after all. Even though she'd buried it all the way down in the bottom of the suitcase, he'd removed it and left it behind. He'd refused to let her have even this small satisfaction. It would've been better if he'd thrown it out somewhere along the way—God knows he was capable of it—instead of leaving it there, like a sneer, rubbing her face in the fact that she hadn't the slightest chance of affecting his decision.

The woman picked up the book, which smelled of old, much-thumbed paper, and went to slip it back into its usual spot in the cupboard. A photograph fluttered out.

She knew what it was, and the blow was too much for what little strength she had left. A picture of herself and her husband, a picture she'd given their son to take with him and which he hadn't refused. He hadn't been able to speak a word in protest, and yet he hadn't wanted even that, he hadn't wanted anything at all. The lamp still burned, shedding a calm, flickering, useless light. Later her husband came home from work and never once mentioned what had happened only a few hours before. The next day, things returned silently, monotonously, to normal.

III.1.

COMRADE VASILE COTIGĂ, BORN JANUARY 26,* 1925, TO a poor family. Attends elementary school and trade school, despite occasional interruptions. During vacations, finds a job unloading wagons and also works at a nearby brickyard. Does fairly well in school. Twice he is almost held back a year because of poor grades in mathematics. Sent home from school two or three times for fighting or for talking back to his teachers. Even as a student, his combativeness is already apparent, although poor health leaves him somewhat at a disadvantage. Turns out to be a natural leader, and organizes student opinion in opposition to the excessive harshness of some of the teachers. During penultimate year of school, undergoes a spiritual crisis. Temporarily abandoning his studies, he takes refuge for a number of months in a local church, where he works as a handyman. In the opinion of some, including his father, this behavior reflects, not a deep religious conviction, but a desire to alleviate his family's financial difficulties. Interpretation supported by the fact that despite his zealous

* January 26, Ceaușescu's birthday, was celebrated in the 1980s as a national holiday in Romania.

show of devotion at the Church of Saint John, on the outskirts of the city, he abruptly stops attending services when he loses his job there and must seek other kinds of employment; some turn out to be unsuitable for anyone of a religious temperament, working as a night watchman in the town's red-light district, etc., etc.

One of Comrade Vasile Cotigă's jobs while he is still in school is that of printer's assistant. Starts off by filling in at night for a sick apprentice. Ends up staying at the printing plant for a whole year, then goes back to school. When he returns to the printing plant, takes part in protest meetings and attempts to become a union delegate, but falls ill and must be hospitalized for several months.

In addition to work as a printer's assistant, becomes liaison between workers and staff of local newspaper, *The Bugle*. Demands and obtains a permanent column for the workers who publish the newspaper; contributes regularly for several months, initially signing as "Staff Printer," although eventually using his own name, Vasile Cotigă.

In 1944, promoted to assistant proofreader on the newspaper. He gives up his column, but occasionally publishes articles on current political issues and even a few poems, which he signs with a pseudonym. During this period, apparently, he also meets Valentina Vrînceanu, a student and the daughter of a well-to-do local forestry engineer.

From the political point of view, Comrade Cotigă expresses revolutionary leanings rather early, although in a somewhat confused manner. Spends a long time wavering between extremes, going from the far right to the far left and back again. As the country's political situation evolves and he himself matures, Comrade Cotigă chooses the only truly revolutionary path—that of the Party. Toward the end of 1944, he participates in left-wing activities on the local level. It is also around this time that Comrade Valentina Vrînceanu officially joins the Young Communist League, despite the opposition of her bourgeois family.

In early 1945, Comrade Cotigă holds first positions of real responsibility. Valued for his intransigence and industriousness, he works day and night, never shirking the most difficult tasks. At the same time, he strives to bring *The Bugle* into line with revolutionary objectives. Due to the presence of certain reactionary elements on the newspaper staff and even among the workers in the printing plant, the paper continues on its so-called neutral course regarding current events. The Political Opinions Page, a forum offered twice weekly by the newspaper to the major parties, is finally opened to the Communists. At that time, the Communists had few members in the city and surrounding region, unlike the reactionary "historic parties," as they were then called.

This political-opinion page is at the root of a dispute that arises between certain comrades on the editorial staff and Comrade Cotigă, who wants to be put in sole charge of this feature. Not much is known about this incident; the little information available is too vague. The conflict is resolved by the establishment of a collective committee that includes Comrade Cotigă, who collaborates on the political-opinion page during the following months without neglecting his other duties.

We do not know why Comrade Cotigă decides to leave

his native city. No definite proof that his departure is due to the dispute at the newspaper over the political-opinion page.

Comrade Cotigă turns up later in the port of Constantsa, working first as a longshoreman, then at an office job. We have in our possession the articles he wrote during this period—as well as a poem, all published under a pseudonym in a small local newspaper. They refer to a kind of fellowship among "loners"—the seafaring men of the port. Nothing political about these articles, which may even seem naïve. The poem is a call to never-ending struggle against "barbarous good manners" and the "self-satisfied hypocrites" of the whole world.

All available information about Comrade Cotigă's brief stay in Constantsa confirms his upright character and capacity for work. Close-mouthed, extremely punctual, he despises comfort and has only modest needs. He refuses to go out drinking, and wears plain, clean clothing. Has few friends and is not well liked by his companions. Some even claim to be afraid of Comrade Cotigă, because of his incommunicability; others say it's "impossible to figure out what his game is." There is no record of any immoral or reprehensible conduct on the part of Comrade Cotigă.

In June 1946, Comrade Cotigă arrives in Bucharest. First known address is 38A Buzeşti Street. He works at the Bucharest Streetcar Company (BSC) for a month before moving to a job in the printing plant of the newspaper *Justice*; then hired as a proofreader on a magazine.

At the end of 1946, he becomes a proofreader, then a staff writer in the agricultural department of the Party

---

newspaper, thanks to a recommendation from a former employee of *The Port Gazette* in Constantsa who is now an important official in the Arts Council. Comrade Cotigă enthusiastically carries out all tasks assigned to him, touring the countryside to counter the effects of reactionary propaganda. He is disciplined, hardworking, and combative in the campaign for the collectivization of agriculture. During this period he lodges at 27 Mihai-Vodă Street, a public-housing project, where he rents space in the kitchen of an elderly woman. The neighbors' reports indicate that he is often out of town for weeks at a time, generally comes in late at night and leaves again at dawn. He does not own many clothes: a single spare outfit, which he keeps in his suitcase. He sleeps in the kitchen on a camp bed he sets up at night and puts away before leaving in the morning.

Does not speak to his neighbors, and talks hardly at all with his landlady. He pays the rent regularly, with the exception of March 1947, when he refuses to pay more than half the sum due, citing the fact that he had not spent a single night in the apartment that month. The landlady's testimony is confused and unreliable, since it includes ill-considered political remarks and gossip about other lodgers.

In November 1946, Comrade Cotigă returns to his home town on official business. He refuses to stay in a hotel with the other comrades, preferring his extremely modest family home: a single room in which live his mother, his father (bedridden as the result of losing his left leg in an accident), and a niece from the country who is living there while attending school.

Comrade Cotigă stays busy in the surrounding villages

in the struggle for collectivization. Although he originally planned to remain in the city for only four days, he stays for two weeks. During this time the house of the Vrînceanu family is searched; the engineer Mihai Vrînceanu is arrested and made the object of an investigation. Comrade Valentina Vrînceanu, summoned from Iaşi, where she is a student at the medical school, confirms the accusations brought against her father and reveals the hiding place of the family's valuables. In January 1948, Comrade Vrînceanu moves from Iaşi to the medical school in Bucharest. Comrade Cotigă, who had been promoted deputy director of the agricultural department, informs his superiors of his intention to marry Comrade Vrînceanu; he furnishes a detailed description of the Vrînceanu family's bourgeois origins and education, as well as the reactionary ideas and contemptuous "kulak" attitude displayed by the engineer Vrînceanu, who has been sent to prison. In support of his request, Comrade Cotigă points out that the behavior of his future wife, Valentina, has been worthy of a true revolutionary. They are married in June 1948.

Comrade Cotigă continues his energetic political activity. With even greater frequency, he writes articles espousing the official Party line and scathing critiques of those who oppose our ideology or hesitate to step to the forefront of revolutionary activity. His devotion, vigilance, and ideological correctness are valued by those in leading circles of the Party, with whom he has close dealings, given his responsibility for the creation of the new socialist agriculture. All reports from this period praise his fearless service to the cause. The tone of his newspaper articles is staunch and rousing, while their language is simple and accessible to all. After 1948, his articles achieve considerable fame, and his name—the pseudonym under which he published his first poems—becomes an important byline in the Party newspaper. It is at this time that he permanently adopts the name with which he signed his first literary efforts, the name already written on the birth certificate of his daughter Dolores, born on April 23, 1949. The family's address during this period is a furnished room at 25 Transylvania Street.

II.2.

THE WOMAN HAD BEEN WAITING BY THE PHONE FOR SEVeral hours. She wasn't really sure what she was expecting to happen. Her mind was emptied of all thought as she watched the glowing minute hand of the clock coursing by, number after number. The hours ticked away: a hard day, a decisive night in those decisive years of the early 1950s.

"I'm sure he'll do the honest thing and side with me," said Petru, the family's friend. "He just can't do otherwise, we're old comrades. You've got to speak to him, convince him. There's something inside him I can't ever be sure of. You can imagine the consequences if he were to . . ."

But that conversation was from a long time ago, yesterday or the day before . . .

The evening had slipped into freezing night. A huge living room, stylish furniture: the woman sitting motionless in the depths of the armchair was almost invisible. From time to time she simply looked up at the clock. The telephone was next to her, close at hand to the leather nest where she dozed, waiting for her husband.

"Comrade Petru isn't here. Comrade Petru has no more meetings. Comrade Petru doesn't live here. Comrade Petru doesn't exist. He doesn't exist—and now what?"

That, that was yesterday. Suzana's voice, the wife, hysterical, whimpering, unforgiving. So Petru already knew everything yesterday . . . Perhaps he'd even left home by then. But that was yesterday, before the verdict. Now it was nighttime, the meeting must be over. One, two o'clock in the morning, in a silent, ice-cold, shadowy city where rats scurry and the wind grates against the stores . . .

"It's not a question of individuals. It's not men who count, but principles. There's no room for emotions here. What's important is not explanations or excuses or regrets, but standing firm. The only thing that matters is what course we choose to take."

That was this morning, in front of the bathroom door. Her husband's face distorted by fear and fatigue, a stubborn phantom in sagging underpants, with tousled hair and empty eyes.

Dead of night; the luminous hand sailed around the cape of two o'clock. In the little alcove on the left burned a bulb on a dimmer switch, shedding only a tiny oval of light. Long, very long shadows flickered uncertainly in the far corners of the room.

The woman wandered listlessly among the armchairs

———————

and slender vases, skirting the huge desk, oblivious to the statuettes of bronze and ivory. She went toward the door, toward the bedroom, walking as though she were blind.

"Comrade Director! They phoned you about an evaluation meeting. You also had calls from the ministry, the airport, the institute, your country place, and the foreign-press subscription department."

That was at noon—no, in the afternoon, around four o'clock.

"I just don't feel like practicing now. Really, piano is absolutely the last thing I feel like doing. *Je regrette*, but I'm off to basketball, so *ciao*!"

It was her daughter, around five or six o'clock . . . Then the secretary, the long-distance call, her mother's usual complaints and insults aimed at the son-in-law and his comrades.

And now the squealing of car brakes, yes, an unmistakable sound, at just past three in the morning. She got a grip on herself, hurried toward the bedroom. No, their daughter's room instead. He'd never look for her there, that was better, he'd never think to check in there. Tomorrow, not now, it was better to forget for the time being, simply sinking down into the comfortable sofa, so welcoming, as though no one, as though no one had ever, no one had ever gone through this ordeal. It was better, like that, collapsed on the sofa, no one, not the slightest idea, nothing, no one would ever awaken her again.

During one lively Thursday afternoon session, someone (no one remembers who, and in any case it's no longer important)

seems to have suggested, doubtless as a kind of extravagant gesture, this little trap: a discussion of purgatory and hell. In other
words, Dante, obviously. Without whom, get this, we'd have
no frame of reference from which to evaluate different perspec-
tives . . .

Such a farfetched idea to provoke debates, when so many ears
are listening. Someone will happen along who can tie the whole
question into some sort of structuralist analysis of biography.
Eager to broaden such an approach, this someone will finally
focus all commentary on a single point: the identity of those who
inhabit purgatory or hell. As for paradise, it will clearly be wise
to say nothing about it.

The consensus will be that purgatory doesn't matter, since the
whole thing will wind up in a shabby mess of details so entangled
they'll never be sorted out: vain hopes, weeping and wailing,
ersatz. Because of its vague and transitory nature—a kind of
indeterminate continuum—such an existence could not be con-
fined within any clear, succinct definition. Since this viscous and
heterogeneous matter would hardly lend itself to tragedy, it would
spoil all attempts to give it the epic treatment, dribbling along as
a minor perpetuum. Stupid suffering and anxious expectation,
reduced to the same average level, canceling out all individuality.
Just an inexpressive, immature mediocrity. As a result, expression itself would be impossible in this type of life, as would all
potential spirituality. Some of the participants, moreover, will
be quick to point out the connection: of course, tragedy is impossible in purgatory, since expressiveness has been nullified from
the outset . . . And, at that juncture, someone will inevitably
assert that the devil, who signifies mediocrity ("The devil signifies
mediocrity!" several participants will shout excitedly), actually

rules over purgatory. Hell would thus be only his secondary residence. A pseudo-home. A diversion! A kind of noisy cabaret serving to mask the true, wide-ranging, and incomparable activities in his real property, purgatory.

What about the collective biography in hell? Rich though it might be in spectacular events, it would in the end boil down to monotonous banalities, largely similar tales burdened with commonplace incidents. Violent and caricatural idiocy, recycled paper, dizzying cacophony! A rudimentary, mechanized product. A bestial joy nourished on blood, rictus, and rhinestone. An automated floorshow: pop a coin in the slot, and hurry hurry hurry —freaks on parade!

The controversy will finally be resolved with the suggestion that within the next two months each participant should bring in his or her autobiography on a few typewritten pages. This biography, real or invented, might also be the life story of the author's bed, fountain pen, or favorite tie, to be enriched with a succinct curriculum vitae of the author's parents, goals, and dreams. An epic, a collection of story lines that will meander off on their own or converge in patterns of the author's choosing. This text will be read and discussed in the light of what has been said regarding the Dantean versions of purgatory and hell.

"We are here to envision the future—in other words, something that does not exist, at least for the moment. So what we are concerned with here is paradise, and that is why the minimum biography must deal with purgatory and hell." With these words, the debate will be closed.

Words that a rather shy and starry-eyed ageless interloper would repeat to himself for nights on end. Unhappy at not being able to write his biography clearly and concisely, humiliated by the lack of imagination that hampers his attempts to set down the story of the armchair where he so often daydreams, or the story of the suspenders that hold up his pants. Too scrupulous to borrow the biography of some cousin or aunt, whose real lives, he feels, are hidden from him, leaving only innocuous banality on view. Keeping eyes and ears wide open in his tireless, frenzied search for something—anything—worthy of consideration, constantly taking notes on some new trifle that will seem like a good point of departure, only to prove dissatisfying when he takes another look at it, later in the day . . . This ageless adolescent would be absent a good long while from the Thursday meetings where he had once figured so brilliantly.

I.4.

ON THE STROKE OF NOON, WHEN THE WOMAN HAD BURST into tears, everyone else in the office had gathered around the chair by the window.

"No, really, can you believe it, she'z been calling an ambulance for two hourz, and they don't give a hoot. They zay they're out of gaz. They've uzed up their daily quota! The old lady'z got azzma. Maybe she'z even dying . . ."

Geta had wailed on and on, pouring out her sorrows in front of everyone, and the girls had listened to her sympathetically. The same old story: bribes and connections, under-the-counter deals and the black market. Naturally . . . Can't find any paper clips? Bingo! A pack of Kents! Nobody takes an old woman to the hospital these days. Only with bribes, only with baksheesh. I'm telling you,

---

we're going to wind up using Kents to wangle even a lousy handful of toothpicks . . . Everywhere you go, people say one thing and do another, they're all on the take. A golden age for every petty crook willing to sell any old junk! No matter what you want, they'll get it for you, if you can grease the right palms! Every attendant and caretaker, porters in fancy hotels, obviously! Same thing in the hospitals: nurses, doctors, all of them! Plumbers, of course, and dentists and taxi drivers and restaurant waiters, they're the ones in power . . . The flashier the façade, the more rot there is to cover up. Take a good look at them, you don't hear a peep from them, they know, all right, but they keep their traps shut or parrot the usual drivel. So once again the wheeler-dealers wheel and deal, while the rest of us get left out in the cold like fools, struggling with the first of the month and the long lines and the health problems and the mindless jargon . . .

The girls had listened to her indulgently; it was only natural for Geta to be upset, she was very fond of her aunt, who'd raised her since she was tiny.

All people think about is getting their hands on as much as possible of anything at all as fast as they can, and they don't care if there's none left for tomorrow . . . The setup's just perfect, have you noticed? Charlatans of every stripe, all the thugs and crooks—the trash can of the universe! You can look high and low for an ounce of honesty, but you won't find it. They're all thieves, every last one of them!

Sugar Candy was off and running on her favorite subject; she'd turned as red as a beet. She waved her plump little arms around like crazy, so pissed off that her rather low-slung rear end seemed even more droopy than usual.

"Try calling again," Chickadee had murmured.

"Vy don't chou go out to your aunt's place?" had been the contribution of Tovaritsna Murguleţ.

"Here, you can take the afternoon off, if you want," added Boss Lady Carmen. Like talking to a wall!

"But what am I zuppozed to do, where can I go?"

"Get a taxi and take her to the emergency room," urged Comrade Petroianu.

"Come on, the emergenzy room? Zo they can let me wait around for hourz or tell me Comrade Zo-and-zo izn't in today or haz already left or maybe that I need permission from my neighborhood committee or zomething? You know perfectly well what they're like," said Geta, brushing aside every suggestion.

They finally caught on. Even Viorica had figured it out, because she didn't say a word. She scribbled/signed/stamped at top speed. All sorts of papers, figures, clearings of accounts, but in absolute silence—Viorica, who would have kept chattering even in the electric chair . . . She was silent, that's all there was to it. Everybody knew: Amazing! Viorica had a brother-in-law who was a doctor. Some time ago she'd asked him to help out Comrade Petroianu and Chickadee and Ina Nikolayevna. Even Geta, too, of course, before Viorica fell out with her because Sugar Candy Geta let the cat out of the bag. It was when Viorica, the betrayed wife, had told Sugar Candy in confidence about her husband. Sugar Candy Geta, in turn, had gone and told Comrade Carmen. How could you keep this one under your hat! Then it had been Kamaradnaya Inouchka's turn to be brought up to date on the country weekends of Comrade Captain Voicilă, Viorica's husband. Which meant that Chickadee was then let in on the secret, and Chickadee wouldn't have breathed a word; she knows how to keep things to herself, that one, the kind that would rather have the goods on you than betray you, but she'd burst out laughing. She'd had a fit, pure and simple! Viorica had realized what was going on, obviously, how could she have failed to understand, it was the only thing that could possibly have made Chickadee laugh, that shtick, with her rumbling underground voice, taking everyone by surprise, making them turn around in astonishment to meet her wide-eyed, candid gaze, and I mean candid, guaranteed one hundred percent . . . Besides, who on earth could keep from laughing? Even a statue would have cracked up! So: Comrade Husband Don Giovanni goes off on a business trip, so he tells his wife, of course, with a suitcase and everything he needs—to shack up, in fact, with the little neighbor on the ground floor! He's holed up in there the whole time he's supposed to be away on this trip. He's got all the essentials: grub, mood music, a comfy pad, and coochy-coochy. I'm going to take out the garbage, announces Coralia, the mistress, one fine evening. It's like the North Pole out there, I'll go instead, the boyfriend, Don Juan, pipes up gallantly. What do you mean you'll go instead, chirps the floozy in surprise. It's late, no one'll see me, answers the poor bastard, picking up the garbage can. He tiptoes out. Complete silence, not a spy in sight. So our guerrilla, Casanova, in pajamas and slippers sneaks down to the trash bins without being spotted. He raises the cover and empties the garbage can, which he carries back to the elevator, this idiot, where he presses the call button. He takes the elevator . . . up to the fourth floor, where he lives! His apartment is right next to the elevator. Then the ass rings his own doorbell! As usual, to be let back in. There's the rub: instead of the adulterous ground floor, he's on the conjugal fourth! Memory can play these tricks on you, just when you least expect it. So the poor guy is standing there in his pajamas holding the garbage can, face to face with his own wife, our Viorica! I mean really, how can you not laugh? Even that goody-goody Chickadee, obviously! How could you not laugh, and how could you ever forgive the person who'd made you such a laughingstock?

That's why Sugar Candy had started blubbering when she'd seen that Viorica wasn't paying the slightest attention to all her complaining. Those tears were supposed to be her last resort, but even this final effort wasn't doing the trick: Viorica couldn't have cared less. She hadn't said a word; in fact, she was deaf and dumb to the moaning of her ex-confidante, now simply her fellow office worker Geta Muşuroi, whom she had no particular reason to help.

All the others were clustered around Geta when Comrade Scarlat returned from the manager's office. Ever since October, Mr. Victor had been summoned to the manager's office about twice a week. He never mentioned why, not one word. Even Comrade Pia, the manager's secretary, didn't know what was going on, because if she had, it would have gotten around. All of a sudden, sometime around September, Comrade Scarlat had started to use the telephone, like everyone else. Whereas, before, he wouldn't even have called home . . . Mind you, no one had ever called him, either. Then, in the same way, out of the blue, just like that, he'd started these little visits to the management, so who knows what he was up to . . .

This time Comrade Victor Scarlat didn't stick his nose right back in his papers the way he usually did. He'd been transfixed by the sight of the chorus of mourners. Impossible to tell whether he actually saw them or not. Behind the huge dark lenses of his glasses, it wasn't all that easy to tell what he was actually looking at. He seemed to be listening to the disconsolate mumblings of the women when Chickadee came over to his desk and leaned down, enveloping him in her musky, May-apple perfume . . .

That little hussy Chickadee had never done anything like that before. She never left her lair—she was always on guard, never springing to attack. If she was now launching an assault on Mr. Victor, it was because she'd carefully considered her chances and the possible consequences.

It didn't last long; in fact, it was all over very quickly. Comrade Scarlat got up from his chair. He dialed a number on Comrade Carmen's phone and spoke briefly, apparently unintimidated by the pouty lips, batting eyelashes, and soft cooings that formed the triple threat of Comrade Chickadee Moga, who was already modestly making her way back to her sanctum. Mr. Victor, sir, hadn't blushed, or blanched, or stammered.

There was quite a lot of activity around Comrade Mu-şuroi, plus the constant jabbering of her colleagues, as they tried to calm her down. Branch 46 wasn't much frequented by the public. At this hour, with the weather so variable and rainy, there wasn't a soul. Which meant that the voice of Comrade Scarlat, who was normally so closemouthed and only rarely used the phone, had registered immediately on all ears, despite the persistent noise. All ears pricked up, on alert, at the first words; by the second sentence, silence had fallen; at the third, the first chair had swung around. And so . . . well, in short, it was obvious, after all!

Comrade Scarlat had a wife who was a nurse, or a bookkeeper, or a doctor, or a switchboard operator—in a hospital, which wife had a friend: "your former colleague," that's how Comrade Scarlat had referred to Comrade Doctor Bretan at the hospital where the emergency room was ready to receive Comrade Bărbulescu, our Comrade Mușuroi's aunt, who had been suffering a severe attack of asthma for several hours, to the despair of branch 46 . . . "Oh, I see, directly to Spineanu. Fine, on your say-so, right," had been the conclusion of the miracle. Not even a trace of a smile had appeared on the face of Comrade Chickadee Moga, while Comrades Petroianu, Murguleț, and Voicilă, and even Comrade Mușuroi, were still openmouthed, as though hypnotized by astonishment.

So then . . . you had, or rather, your wife had . . . but really, once again, it's that dear little chickabiddy, quietly slaving away, she's really the one who got us all out of this fix . . . That adorable chickling who comes to our rescue when we're in need, as we so often are. We forget what our Comrade Chickadee can do, but she's always ready to remind us generously, including you, Sugar Candy, who are a mite too inclined to be careless and snooty about things, and you, peppery Viorica, always full of resentments and venom, and even you, Comrade Carmen, our fine matron, who've become rather high and mighty ever since your smooth operator managed to land himself such a cushy job at our Circus Cemetery.

They'd all come rushing over, except for Geta, who'd shot out of the office like a rocket. They'd crowded around the hero of the hour, who'd vainly tried to play down the whole thing, but it was no use. They showered him with questions and with thanks, in the hope of finally establishing—and it had taken long enough—the complicity they'd been expecting for ages, and which he'd always stubbornly and sullenly withheld. Now here he was surrounded in a flash, an object of unbridled interest, whatever you do don't let him escape this time, he'll have to listen to their stories, their complaints, their opinions on movies and children and recipes and America and condoms and horoscopes and washing machines . . . No, he was trapped good and tight, this time they'd really got him! One little emotional slipup had triggered an avalanche: now he'd have to listen day after day as one after another besieged him with her personal problems and hysterical crises and quotations from her favorite authors, until he was beaten, softened up, until he finally unlocked his own word-mill and started churning out stuff about his brother and his daughter and his mother and the comrade manager, whom he'd known ever since childhood, and the comrade manager's father, things like that, which he'd slip smoothly, discreetly, into future conversations, yes, they'd find out in the end what all those visits to the manager's office meant, what was going on in there, because there was something fishy about it all, they'd known something was up ever since those September phone calls, those pseudo-conversations, Comrade-Scarlat-speaking-is-he-there-he's-not-there wham goes the receiver . . .

For the moment, Comrade Scarlat was holding up fairly well. He'd exchanged only a few words with the noisy invaders, who'd relayed each other constantly around his desk, chatting among themselves—but for his ears—about this and that, about the same old daily grind. He hadn't started to frown or hunker down over his papers the way he always did. He'd listened to them, smiled two or three times, fidgeted a bit, cleaned his glasses per-functorily, blown his nose, straightened his tie. But he really had listened—benevolently and politely, if some-what vaguely—to the voice of the people, gushing im-petuously and tirelessly from all these mouths full of warmth and lipstick as they whispered, whirred, and cranked out, stitch by stitch, the soiled and rumpled ma-terial of the moment.

The day was approaching its soft, translucent edge, be-coming flabby, sluggish, ready to fall apart.

Two hours had quickly passed since Sugar Candy's de-parture and the shift in the current of office gossip. The conversational waltz was still going strong in the Scarlat orbit.

None of the women had deigned to glance, even obliquely, toward the one who'd made all this possible.

———

Their quiet colleague, sly Chickadee with the heart of gold, this hypocrite, was busy working, calmly, unobtrusively as always, aloof from the bustle of activity she'd set in motion.

III.2.

IN THE EARLY AND MID-1950S, WITH OUR PARTY PLAGUED by deviationism on the left and right wings, Comrade Cotigă remains steadfastly devoted to revolutionary principles. He distinguishes himself at meetings by harshly rejecting all criticism of the Party line, all indulgence toward the serious failings of comrades who may have once been examples of self-sacrifice and revolutionary fervor, but who are now plotters practicing splinter tactics. He leads an energetic campaign against decadent conciliatory policies, liberalism, and the petit-bourgeois tolerance of inefficiency. Doesn't hesitate to attack the reactionary tendencies of former comrades, denouncing their past political waverings as evidence of corrupt foreign ideas (c.f. the case of Petre Petru, his former friend, expelled with Comrade Cotigă's consent).

He is promoted to head of the industrial department at the Party newspaper, a key position in the organizational and ideological structure. In constant contact with important ministers, directors of the nation's large industrial concerns, authorities in charge of planning and statistics, and even members of the Politburo, whose decisions he implements and whom he keeps informed of developments.

Works steadily and selflessly from seven in the morning until ten in the evening, sometimes after midnight. Information from this period in his life emphasizes his punctuality, energy, peerless dedication, and strict discipline—qualities he demands from his subordinates, participants in a vital military campaign that must be carried out day after day. Failure to reach a determined goal is always severely punished. His colleagues fear his devotion to duty, his extraordinary capacity for work, his honesty, and his steadiness of purpose. They call him "the corporal."

In addition to working at the newspaper, teaches courses on topics of revolutionary interest, does propaganda work as well, speaking at political-awareness and self-criticism meetings.

Comrade Valentina Cotigă heads an important health agency in the capital; she also serves on numerous work committees, competently fulfilling the duties assigned to her.

During this period, the Cotigăs travel, as members of official delegations that often go abroad for conferences, congresses, missions of cooperation, or fraternal visits of friendship.

In 1959, during a campaign to fortify and purge the Party ranks of suspects and undesirables, Valentina Vrînceanu is expelled because of her unhealthy social background, which is discovered to have tainted her career. When called to account for her actions, Dr. Vrînceanu is unable to explain satisfactorily why she has allowed her reactionary mother to live with her for several years; above all, why she has allowed her—the wife of the engineer Vrînceanu, incarcerated as a known reactionary and rumormonger who ridiculed our socialist achievements—to supervise the education of Dr. Vrînceanu's only daughter, Dolores, ten years old at that time, an exemplary Young Pioneer in a special school for children of Party officials who should have been spared all contact with obsolete elements of the former social order. When asked if she knows about the packages her mother sends to Mihai Vrînceanu in prison, or if she has read the postcards her mother writes to this criminal, Dr. Valentina Vrînceanu does not provide clear answers. Ex-director Vrînceanu is also unable to justify the hospitalization for two months of the ailing Rodica Vrînceanu, her mother, who had no right—although gravely ill at the time—to avail herself of medical facilities not available to the general public.

In October 1959, the organization discusses the case of Dr. Vrînceanu's husband, the former head of the industrial department of the Party newspaper. Demoted to a lowly editorial position, Comrade Cotigă is reprimanded for his unworthy conduct toward his subordinates, for sectarianism, authoritarianism, and individualism. Moreover, he is condemned for the influences of his unwholesome family situation, discernible in the contempt with which he treated his fellow workers, and in the "kulak" arrogance he showed by making all decisions on his own and requiring that they be implemented without the slightest opposition, just as in the army of the discredited former regime. On this occasion, a letter of recommendation is read aloud, written by a certain Stamate, once an influential cultural representative of the Party. Comrade Cotigă had been hired by the newspaper in 1946 on the strength of said recommendation. The file on the man named Geo Stamate shows that this second-rate journalist, a well-known black marketeer in the port of Constantsa, turned out to be a clever impostor, an undesirable element of society, and a demagogue who had hoodwinked Party authorities for many years. He succeeded in attaining positions of great responsibility before his past was revealed. He was unmasked as a hateful agent of the interests of our formerly class-ridden society, and of enemy forces abroad.

Between November 1959 and February 1960, Comrade Cotigă is treated in a sanatorium. In April 1960, he is transferred to the Committee for the Defense of Peace, as head of the accounting department. His superiors have no complaints about his performance. In October 1960, he is promoted to assistant editor-in-chief on the Peace Committee newspaper. All reports indicate that he continues to provide satisfaction in this new capacity, just as he had in his previous position. He is conscientious and punctual. He keeps his relationships at work strictly businesslike. He does not drink. He is serious and disciplined. He works long hours without hesitation, often remaining in the office until late in the evening. He introduces measures intended to popularize the newspaper. He does not make his voice heard within the Party organization, however, preferring to keep a low profile, as though he'd never been a high-ranking Party executive.

Beginning with the academic year 1960–61, Comrade Cotigă takes correspondence courses in economics to complete his education. He passes all his exams, receives average marks. His diploma, like the rest of his personal papers, carries the name Victor Scarlat, the pseudonym adopted for his first literary efforts.

In 1963, at his mother's funeral, Comrade Cotigă meets Mr. John Lama, Smaranda Cotigă's brother, who left Romania in 1936 and became a Canadian citizen. Comrade Cotigă states that he was not previously aware of the existence of this uncle, which is why he never mentioned him on his personal data sheet. What is certain is that, beginning in 1965, Comrade Cotigă and especially his wife, the former Valentina Vrînceanu, correspond intermittently with the said John Lama of Toronto. Likewise, beginning in 1966, through letters sent via an intermediary, Valentina renews ties with the family of Marius Vrînceanu, who left the country in 1945 to settle in Milan, Italy.

In 1964, Comrade Cotigă petitions the relevant authorities to be reinstated at the Party newspaper, in the industrial or agricultural department, where he formerly worked. Receives no answer. Remains in his position at the newspaper of the Committee for Peace. When the newspaper reduces its staff, he loses his job as assistant editor-in-chief to become head of the public-relations department. When the newspaper ceases publication, Comrade Cotigă manages to find a position in the Ministry of Foreign Affairs. In 1971 he leaves this post, which is incompatible with his family ties abroad and with the fact that his daughter, Dolores Scarlat, foolishly succumbed to the siren call of capitalist decadence while on an organized tour in Turkey, and defected to Belgium, where she still lives in Antwerp.

On the basis of a recommendation from Comrade Petre Petru, whom he has known since his early years in the Party, and who has become, after his rehabilitation, a director at the Department of Public Worship, Comrade Cotigă obtains a position on a religious publication put out by the Romanian Orthodox Church (exactly which one remains unclear); he is quickly promoted to the protocol department. All reports state that Comrade Cotigă fulfills his obligations in this position, which he holds until 1973, as conscientiously as always. His colleagues are favorably impressed with him. There are indications that in addition to his duties in the protocol/public relations department, Comrade Cotigă is sometimes consulted, in view of his long experience, by the Most Reverend Metropolitan whenever the prelate is confronted with a particularly delicate political matter.

II.3.

THE GIRL HAD BEEN SPRAWLED FOR SOME TIME IN THE rocking chair, in front of the mirror; she was staring at her reflection, without really seeing it. She needed the calm of perfect concentration—at least that's the impression she gave, absentmindedly rocking for hours . . . In fact, she was more interested in simply staying right where she was, lolling in that red chair. Apparently she created this atmosphere of peaceful isolation, in which she'd been beginning her mornings over the last few weeks, in a highly original way, by starting a frenetic uproar with the radio, the tape deck, added to the constant ringing of the telephone—an uproar she then ignored . . .

She wouldn't make the slightest move to stop the noise, as though she couldn't hear a thing. Every once in a while, she tried to continue writing the letter she held in her lap, but the words wouldn't come to her, or else they vanished before she could grasp them.

The lovely spring morning was far away. The locked windows and thick curtains kept out the fresh air of the new season.

She was naked to the waist, wearing jeans, with her bare feet propped up on the huge bureau. Hair cut boyishly short, circles under her big, heavily made-up eyes, and ripe breasts, as mature as the rest of her solid, confident body. Her parents said she was a shy girl; her teachers at the Polytechnic described her as an excellent student; according to her friends, she was laid back and an easy lay.

A tape of Ray Charles, a children's program on the radio, and on the telephone, Sorin, who called her in a frenzy for hours on end every morning. She was writing to him, actually, to Sorin—one or two lines a day, tiny stories intended to make him understand, when he got them, the how and the why . . . It wasn't just a simple explanation of these past two weeks of absence and silence; she wanted to present him with a motive she'd discovered hidden away in the Technicolor folds of a privileged childhood, one that had given her, she had to admit, very precious advantages.

The words were accumulating rather slowly, just a few lines a day. And now she'd finally managed to fill two pages in a notebook, which she reread frequently, without enthusiasm.

"I was still in school when I got to invite my Swiss friend, Yvonne, daughter of a comrade, of course, to visit me over the holidays—one of the many special favors I enjoyed, thanks to Comrade Dad. I was all starry-eyed, as you can imagine, with shyness and admiration for the frail Yvonne . . . To me she seemed magical, like a fairy-tale princess, from that paradise in the West, spirited and gay . . . Plus all her clothes, her naughty little secrets, so important at that age! She had no doubts, no hang-ups, no apprehension. She knew what she was going to do, where she was going to travel, she was perfectly sure of herself and all that . . . and then I finally figured out she was a jerk, my dear Sorin . . . I mean, no, she wasn't a jerk, but I was simply smarter, prettier, more cultured, but timid and hesitant. I couldn't outshine her in anything specific, but I was better than she was, that's all. I say this quite objectively. But I knew perfectly well that if we were to meet again in twenty years this pert little bitch would have it all over me with her chic clothes and her fancy cosmetics and her trips abroad and her confidence in her 'personality.' Sure of everything she said and did, because, you see, 'each individual has something unique and worthwhile' to offer—that's the message she sent with every move she made. I've never stopped thinking about that, but at the time Comrade Dad didn't even bother to listen to what I had to say."

All this barely filled the first page. She was well aware

that there was nothing special about any of it, but she didn't feel able to explain why, in her particular case, this commonplace quality shouldn't be scorned; the fact that her reflections were as banal as the daydreams of a beauty-school student didn't make them any the less true, after all. Because that's it, kiddo, that's what the truth is, she would have liked to shout at Sorin, and there's no point in trying to see anything good in failure and helplessness and so many useless complications.

She no longer had any desire to reread the second page, to slog through another batch of worn-out platitudes. She could imagine Sorin's reaction and his grimace of contempt: "Well, well, so that's where the little darling's been hanging out, writing mushy women's-magazine stuff— the intellectual who couldn't be dragged away from her Einstein and Kierkegaard!" How could she explain to him that a woman feels things that her lover, who's still too young to have acquired an instinct for reality, won't understand for another twenty years?

Clack, the tape was over. So now here's our philosophizeress, yes, hopping over on one foot to flip the tape. The young woman glimpsed the curved nudity of her reflection in the mirror, and looked at herself. She saw her large, pale breasts, held them in her hand to examine them, first one, then the other . . . A year, five years, that's all you've got left, that's how long your short life lasts, her weary smile seemed to say as she reinserted the tape with practiced ease.

As she pressed the play button to restart the hurricane, the phone began ringing again. Sorin hadn't given up, poor guy. Our adventuress seemed to bow to the vague absurdity of the whole thing; she'd grabbed the receiver and was still holding it in the air, still making up her mind . . . It was, quite obviously, Sorin, that adorable Billy the Kid, that young scholar who wore his brooding expression as though it were a halo.

"Yes, it's really me, Dolores. Nothing, why would anything be the matter? Strange? My voice? . . . Nothing's gotten into me! No, I'm not pregnant. Sure I'm sure! It's just my period, that's all . . . Yes, you know, what that dumb author of yours claims makes it impossible for women to be judges in a court of law, or some shit like that. Not fit to be entrusted with the fate of men on those particular bloody days. Perhaps on other days as well, who knows? So that's it, pal, I'm on the rag, that's all there is to it!"

She replaced the receiver in its cradle, then buried her head in her hands. She seemed to doze, listening at the same time to the Beatles on the tape recorder, the farm report on the radio, and the phone. Because the phone was ringing again, ringing endlessly, for all the good it would do him! The Beatles, milk production, the phone, not her problem!

Interesting results for the synthesis will be obtained from a period of observation in a restaurant, a sports club, a taxi, a child-care center, a savings-bank branch office, a courtroom, an airport, or among streetcar conductors, newspaper vendors, traffic policemen, or in a hospital emergency room, a state manpower allocation office, a national housing agency, in a library or a

---

*hairdressing salon. These investigations will serve as prelimi-
naries to the regularly scheduled work sessions. The singular
young man who had so stimulated the participants' imaginations
and speculative appetites during the initial conferences will not
be on the list of drafting committees and work groups. The ageless
youth will probably be quite forgotten. Regrettable as it may
seem, the others will have lost him in some sort of nebulous
borderline reality; one day, they may well wonder who this
whirlwind was—if in fact he ever existed—who carried them all
away at those first meetings in a brief flurry of surprise and free-
ranging speculation . . . Sitting in their assigned places, they'll
barely remember their own youthful faces, thirsting for knowledge
and aflame with curiosity, at the moment when they recognized
themselves, so long ago, in the impatient eagerness of an unusual
and unknown young man. They will be all the more diligent
and methodical, persevering, step by step, in the competent and
laborious completion of their assignments.*

*They'll be unable to say whether the stranger remained among
them long enough to listen to those bold theories about the "Crisis
of Energy and Character in the World Today," or "Destructive
Intervention of Authority as a Denial of Chance," or many other
similar topics.*

*They'll be even less sure whether he was present for the very
informative movie to be shown by the director just before vacation.*

*A great film by a great film genius on the moral and economic
crises in Germany during the 1920s. Poverty, police, surveillance,
suspicion, growing discontent; the pressures exerted on the individual worried about losing his job, terrorized by increasingly
restrictive policies, dazed by the din of propaganda, dogged at
every step, constantly obliged to fill out information forms about*

*his life and his beliefs and his family, weighed down by fear,
curled up in a bed that grows more and more rickety as the film
progresses. The viewer will see how humor and art are punished
with a growing severity that leaves no room for doubt and irony,
how a Terror of martial enthusiasm and relentless unanimity
springs up, how the public begins to hound strangers, foreigners,
scientists, revolutionaries, prostitutes, artists, theorists, how dem-
agogues don pitiless uniforms, how useless failures, sadists, informers, and fanatics are promoted to positions of power.*

*"The victory of these diversionary tactics is the fostering of
aggression in human relations," the professor will say, turning
the lights back on. "Suspicion is so easy to manipulate," he will
say, as if not knowing how many strange ears are in the room.
"I think it's instructive to situate such deviationary factors between the real cause and its disastrous effect. The scientist studies
cause and effect, but also these filters of deflection. I thought that
a meaningful work of art would excite your imaginations before
this well-earned vacation . . ."*

*Because of the cold and the lateness of the hour, but also because
of this provocation, the witnesses will be pushing and shoving as
they leave the hall, so it will be impossible later on for them to
remember who was there and who was not.*

III.3.

AFTER THE DEATH OF THE MOST REVEREND METROPOLITAN,
Vasile Cotigă's situation becomes uncertain. Leaves his job
and finds employment for several months at a philatelic
publication.

Two months after the earthquake in 1977, Vasile Cotigă undergoes an operation to correct a detached retina. Spends ten days in a ward at the Military Hospital, where he makes the acquaintance of both an employee of Tarom, the Romanian national airline, and a little-known writer, the author of several novels. Reports indicate that this writer and Vasile Cotigă engage in lively discussions. After learning that his fellow patient has until recently been on the staff of the Most Reverend Metropolitan, the writer questions Cotigă about the prelate. Cotigă's description is that of a leader, not a saint. A resourceful man: intelligent, determined, concerned about his own interests as well as those of the church. Authoritarian and practical: his subordinates were careful to avoid making personal comments in front of him. A zealous manager, a good organizer, a hard and tireless worker, used to making all decisions—whether important or minor ones—on his own. A leader who stood out from his fellows through his energy and imagination, but who knew how to compromise opportunely with other leaders, and was willing to do certain favors for those in a position to shield him from various difficulties. This brief portrait devoid of personal details, sketched on a sultry night when the patients were unable to sleep, leads to a discussion that lasts several days. The writer, intrigued by what he learns, demands more information about the nature and values of religious work. Cotigă answers his questions with precision, without making any personal comments, which exasperates the self-proclaimed writer, whose name means nothing to Cotigă and the Tarom employee, since neither of them has ever heard of him before.

"You bother me, in a way," the writer confesses, "simply because I'm trying to see in you I don't know which uncle, or cousin, or perhaps someone I went to school with . . . unless you reflect a part of myself, some impossible, unsuspected face I'm just not able to recognize as my own! I'm looking for the faces of our time, by which I mean that I'm trying to understand what I've lived and what I'm living and what I'll live in the future, unless I can get rid of this clumsy need—and I don't think I ever will—to understand, to have standards of judgment."

The writer spews out such nonsense, probably in an effort to rattle Cotigă, who calmly replies that he feels it's important to do one's work well, whatever it is, and that's all. Reports mention the inappropriate attitude of the writer, who raises his voice; Cotigă answers him in a poised and good-natured manner. On the following day, or perhaps even that first night, the little scribbler, who is restless and suffers from insomnia, sets the following problem for his listeners.

"Let's suppose I know a young painter of genius. A kind of Picasso. Or else an exceptional poet, Lautréamont, for example, off living in a garret. Poor, ill, no resources. Let's also suppose that this person, without realizing it, is a perfect example of what a good Christian should be. He doesn't steal, or lie; in short, he doesn't do anything bad at all, a sort of angel. Rather difficult for an artist to pull off, and even harder for a genius, but let's just say it's true. Now, imagine me going to see your High Holiness guy to tell him the whole story, you know, the great man suffering in a garret and so on, a really gifted soul, also a political suspect, also a very lonely man who doesn't go to church, who never prays to anyone about anything, who bows down neither before the powerful of this world nor before the Guy Upstairs, a good Christian without knowing it. So, fine, he paints pictures nobody much understands, but myself and a few others who know what's good when it comes to this stuff, we guarantee that these works are outstanding and that one day they'll be worth outrageous sums. Okay, is your guy, the Most Reverend—that's right?—is he going to ask me if the kid paints pictures of the Resurrection? Or is he going to require that the artist insert a little cross, or something like that, somewhere in all his pictures?"

"Of course," replies Cotigă.

"Otherwise, he won't be interested? He's not inclined to help him out, just out of, you know, Christian charity?"

"Of course not," Cotigă replies again, "he's only interested in matters he's responsible for. Otherwise, it's none of his business . . ."

"Oh, right, so His Holiness is just your basic state employee . . . Give and ye shall receive, you fit the profile, you don't, first pay up, then we'll see . . . No difference, in other words . . ."

He goes on in the same idiotic vein, along the lines of: if you work for us, no problem, we'll let you play around at challenging authority, you'll even be able to tell the truth once in a while, what's important is that you remember which side you're on. Cotigă ignores these provocations. The other man isn't discouraged; he keeps mouthing off, a torrent of foul language, protests, ridiculous ideas. Finally, the two men become friends! There is proof that this hot-air artist stays in touch with Cotigă; he even visits him in his home.

When he leaves the hospital, Cotigă refuses to follow the suggestion that he retire. He spends several months looking for a new job. The report claiming that he is hired at the National Insurance Agency thanks to the influence of the writer he met in the hospital turns out to be false. The position of insurance investigator Cotigă obtains there, from which he will later be transferred to the accounting department of branch 46 of the National Savings Bank, is due, once again, to Comrade Petre Petru, his editorial colleague in the 1950s, now retired, whose son, Vladimir Petru, holds a managerial position in this same banking organization.

I.5.

"I REALLY DON'T KNOW WHAT TO DO ABOUT THAT SCHOOL anymore," Viorica had complained while settling the fate of a pile of printed forms. "They've gone completely crazy. The children have to sweep and mop the floors! They haven't got a janitor, imagine! But let me tell you the latest thing they've come up with: each child has to bring in, every month, five corks and I don't know how many kilos of recyclable paper! And bottles. Four bottles or jars, plus some medicinal plants! Where do they think we're going to find medicinal plants in Bucharest? No, I mean, come on! I asked the head teacher yesterday at the class meeting.

She was smiling like a total idiot! You'll have to buy some, she said . . . Buy some, can you believe it! We have to give them all this stuff so that the school can turn around and sell what we've bought . . . Just once, I'd really like to see teachers that would refuse to go along with this crap! Whatever they're told to do, they can't wait to say yes, we'll follow orders, no sweat. They're scared of losing their jobs, of getting booted out on their butts!"

Geta wasn't really listening, but she genuinely agreed with Viorica. She had a daughter, too; she knew what the other woman was talking about. Bundled up in her big woolen cardigan—there was no heat in the room and it was as cold as a refrigerator—she yawned, paying a bit of attention now and then, thinking mostly about the fact that there was only one more hour to go until their little treat. Just what they needed to liven up this cold, gray day! The plates, serving dishes, bottles, and glasses had been carefully stashed behind the cupboard. She'd made friends again with Viorica; the girls weren't really bad-tempered, these things happen, that's all. She'd simply gone to see Viorica one morning to talk to her, heart to heart.

"Come on, what do you zay, shall we make up? I've been quite upzet that you're not talking to me . . . Thingz just zlip out, you know how it iz. Onze it waz zaid, that waz it, I couldn't do anything about it. It'z true I should have kept my mouth shut, but you've got to admit, you're the one who told everyone about that buzinezz with the minkz. The ztory that I had a mink hutch in my garden and waz going to get rich. And then the fib around three yearz ago that I waz growing mushroomz in my zellar.

You know perfectly well it'z not true! Happenz to everyone, talking too much. Look, I've brought you a prezent,
zo let'z kizz and be friendz again!"

And she'd unwrapped a bracelet *Made in China* that she'd
slipped around the other woman's wrist. Viorica'd had
tears in her eyes. Because she wasn't a bad sort, Viorica,
just a bit touchy, always ready to fly off the handle, but if
you knew how to manage her, she'd soon be herself again,
sweet and attentive . . . Today, for Viorica's birthday, her
next-desk neighbor and gossiping companion had prepared
stuffed cabbage and a jellied meat dish. In other words,
the main course. You have to wait weeks and then stay in
line hours and hours to get some meat, but she did it! So,
in comparison with Chickadee's deviled eggs and Ina's
pastries and even Comrade Carmen's cake, Sugar Candy
had definitely proved she deserved her place next to chatty
Viorica, once more her friend and confidante. Nothing,
not even the worst blunder, would ever come between
them again! After all, that was truly something, that item
about the husband accidentally coming home unexpectedly
in his pajamas from his out-of-town business trip that was
actually just downstairs in the same building; and those
stories about the minks and the mushrooms hadn't been
easy to brush off, either . . . Well, all that was behind them
now, friendship had triumphed! And here was Viorica,
fresh from the hairdresser's, impeccably turned out in a
brand-new green dress, waiting to be feted by her office
chums.

They celebrated everyone's birthday, and their saint's
day, too: Saint George for Geta and Saint Gabriel for Ga-

briela aka Chickadee and Saint John for Ioana Carmen Petroianu. But Viorica's pig-out was even grander than Carmen's, because her birthday fell on December 25, so she was treated to the traditional Christmas dishes of stuffed cabbage leaves and jellied meat, with more wine and stronger brandy than they usually had.

Barely a week had gone by since they'd had their party for Comrade Boss Lady Carmen, who was also born in December. Here at branch 46, they had a special way of doing things: it wasn't the birthday person who gave the party—which was how it was done elsewhere—but everyone else in the office. The idea was that the star of the day should feel pampered, coddled, and enjoy being the center of attention without having to worry about waiting on line and slaving in the kitchen. Almost all of them lived in newer, outlying neighborhoods, far from the downtown area where they did their shopping, endlessly on line. Sweating, lugging heavy bags, they stood around for hours at bus stops waiting for broken-down vehicles to lurch into view, buses already stuffed to bursting with desperate commuters, more of whom still managed to shove their way on at every stop.

At branch 46, the birthday person truly was the star. All she had to do was visit her dressmaker and her hairdresser, as Viorica had done to get her new perm and that striped green dress.

On Wednesday, Ina had returned to the office after a bout of flu, so the gang was all there. The week before, Carmen's pet had been absent and had missed Auntie's birthday, so the girls hadn't had a chance to admire the extravagant gift with which, year after year, Ina Murguleţ made up for her relatively apathetic response to the office manager's daily show of affection. Naturally, they hadn't been able to resist quizzing Comrade Petroianu about it, and once again it was that little motor-mouth Viorica who'd dared pop the question they were all dying to ask.

"And Ina, what did she give you this year? Since she isn't here, we've no way of knowing . . ."

Carmen had replied without hesitation and with definite satisfaction. "As you know, girls, Ina never stints on my birthday present. She's just adorable, I'm telling you. Sweet, intelligent, discreet, doesn't shoot her mouth off all over the place. Which she's proved more than once . . . She called me the afternoon before my birthday. She could barely talk, because she was running a fever. After she'd wished me a happy birthday—she was quite upset that she wouldn't be able to be with all of us—she told me that in an hour she'd be sending me her present, something special, and that her son would drop it off. Because, besides her daughter, she's also got a boy who's still in school. Real cute he is, too. He was supposed to arrive with a van. A van! I couldn't imagine what she was giving me, my little sweetheart of Sevastopol—you know I call her that, she's just so adorable! I mean, it couldn't be a refrigerator or a washing machine, after all! Well, what do you think it was? A samovar! A real collector's item! Silver-plated, with loads of ornamentation, a superb piece!"

Comrade Carmen seemed truly pleased, and she really did love Ina like a sister, there was nothing suspect at all about her affection. She'd been very jovial at her own party and had joked around a lot; she was already a trifle tight, La Carmencita, when they started in on the traditional droll stories about the eminently subversive Bulâ, that foolish trickster and sexual maniac of Romanian folklore. That's when she'd taken a swipe at Chickadee.

"Well, girls, I had the feeling that cold fish they've been shoving down our throats for three months every year wasn't going to turn up today. He doesn't like this sort of thing. But he always used to come anyhow, when it was my birthday . . ."

True, Comrade Victor Scarlat had never gotten used to these office parties, and preferred to avoid them. In previous years, he'd come up with excuses to be absent, and over the last trimester he'd skipped September 18, when Sugar Candy had celebrated her daughter's birthday, and September 29, Chickadee's anniversary, and November 14, when Carmen had bought her Skoda. Of course, Comrade Scarlat would have been welcome to join in the regular or improvised parties of the last three months, even if he was only a temporary colleague instead of a permanent employee. He'd never shown up in past years for Viorica's birthday on December 25, which was an ordinary working day under our atheistic calendar, and sometimes he'd even found a pretext to slip away for a few hours on December 31, to avoid having to toast the New Year. But he'd always come into the office on Comrade Petroianu's birthday, even though he never stayed until the end of the festivities.

This December 18, however, Papa Victor hadn't shown up. Nor had he appeared the next day, or any of the following days. There was no reason to expect him now.

Inspector Scarlat's affront had not passed unnoticed by Carmen. She probably wouldn't have attached too much importance to it, however, if the alcohol hadn't gone to her head, prompting her to start talking about him.

"Hey, Chickadee, you always seem to know what's going on, whatever's happened to our little accounting expert these last few weeks?"

"I don't know much about it," Chickadee had replied evasively, to no one's surprise.

"Well, what I heard on the grapevine," Milady Carmen had continued as she set down her cracker spread with taramosaláta and turned to her audience (which was all agog at the idea that the Matron was going to break her long-standing rule of never gossiping about anything overheard at business meetings or in the manager's office), "what I heard from Pia is that our Comrade Scarlat submitted a proposal or a report to management, some idea that he's argued for a million times before the manager, Comrade Petru. Something really unusual! A bombshell!"

Carmen had glanced meaningfully at Chickadee, as though that was her cue to continue the story with a barrage of thrilling details, but the other woman didn't say a word and went on listening closely, pretending she was just as much in the dark as everyone else.

"I have to tell you, girls, because it's absolutely outrageous," Comrade Petroianu had continued, draining her glass of Bulgarian cabernet to give herself strength for the task ahead.

They were all in a good mood, although a bit tired. It was late. The news hadn't bothered them. A boring story, not very interesting, too serious, really twisted, something for loonies and crackpots running after heaven knows what lousy privileges, or nuts obsessed with some weird idea—so, big deal, everyone's a little strange about something, right? Comrade Petroianu hadn't been satisfied with these offhand dismissals, however, and had expressed personal dismay at the paltry level of the conversation.

"Come on, girls, we're not complete birdbrains here, you know, this is important! It's a question of principle! I spent an entire evening talking it over with my companion Comrade Bebe, and he opened my eyes on this, I have to admit. I mean, what is it with Scarlat and others like him, who have a certain way of looking at things—where does that come from, what does it mean?"

So the girls had realized they'd have to rise to this occasion. They'd show that they weren't airheads, idle windbags, interested only in foolish frivolities, no way, these girls had a lot between their ears.

"Obviously, it would seem like a fair solution, to do it like that. But that's where all the confusion comes in—Bebe explained it to me, Bebe knows it too well, he's been working for years with those guys."

Carmen had more or less led the discussion, which wound up confirming that yes indeed, this problem they'd been tempted to brush off as a minor one was actually quite important.

"Where he got this idea from I can't imagine."

Well, the others had seemed slightly overwhelmed, until Ina intervened. Briefly, with an unexpected pessimism that appeared deep and well founded.

"No, mustn't. Mistake, big mistake. They still getting to decide, always they decide. That words, just words. Mustn't let happen."

Ina Nikolayevna's replies always tickled Sugar Candy, who'd smiled and almost burst into giggles, so that a bite of pastry started to go down the wrong way, but she'd managed to recover and had wiped her little mouth quite properly before chiming in earnestly.

"But all that could be verified. There could be zupervizion! Perzonally, I don't think that idea'z zo ztupid. Viorica'z right. In my building there'z a guy who runz a kind of cafeteria. He had hiz certificate in metal ztamping. Then he huztled to get thiz job. Eight hundred lei per day. Eight hundred lei, can you juzt imagine, when the average zalary'z about two thouzand five hundred! Zo he became a cook. He'z got more money than he knowz what to do with! You should just zee hiz apartment. Porzelain and rugz and a family-zize refrigerator and all thiz zdereo zduff. Whenever I run into him, he'z won zomething elze. Zometimez at lotto, zometimez zportz lotto, zometimez the horzez at Ploiezti. Lazt year he won a car in a National Zavingz Bank drawing. With the dough he'z got, not zurprizing he feelz he can play. And zo he winz. Zo what'z juztice got to do with thiz? Luck'z alwayz on the zide of thoze who take life eazy."

Comrade Petroianu had spoken up here, of course. She'd related everything that Bebe, who was back from Brazil, had told her about the terrible danger represented by ideas like Scarlat's. Ones that "stopped up the last air vent," as he'd put it. Meaning, you shouldn't try to eliminate all traces of chance from life. Meaning, also, his chance, of course.

"If you try to control everything, then nothing will work," Comrade Carmen had declared, repeating word for word the speech her husband had made to her after his trip to Rio.

Then Chickadee had asked timidly, in a low voice, as though speaking just for herself, "Do you think that Scarlat really pushed this idea of his?"

Everyone had turned to look attentively at her delicate and impenetrable face, urging her to tell what she knew, because she'd given herself away there, she certainly knew something. But once again the little china doll simply said a few soft and hesitant words that could be interpreted any old way.

"I mean, it seems a little strange; at his age, you'd think he'd just be interested in his salary and his pension . . ."

They'd continued drinking and chattering for a while, but they simply weren't interested in taking the question any further, despite Carmen's prodding. Darkness had fallen . . . They usually held their celebrations during the noon break, but on Comrade Carmen's birthday, they celebrated after work. No matter how enjoyable it was to gossip and nibble goodies, the day was drawing to a close. The women couldn't face dealing with the evening buses, which were even worse than the daytime service, so they'd finally packed up plates, pastries, cakes, bottles, all the leftovers, wrapping them in plastic bags they'd carefully set out on a chilly window ledge until snack time the next day.

And now the birthday party for Viorica on Christmas Day had been planned for two stages, the first one being the lunch break from one-thirty to two-thirty. Promptly at twelve-thirty, they began on the appetizers. A general cry of admiration greeted the appearance of bottles and tasty-looking dishes, which were artfully arranged on two tables in the back room.

They started sampling bits of panettone and savoring tiny forkfuls of salad, sausage, and jellied meat. Then, a knock at the door. Intrigued by this unexpected disturbance, Viorica tore herself away from the delicious opening course and went to see who the killjoy was.

She was gone for an unexpectedly long time, returning slightly agitated and agreeably surprised.

"Girls, he wished me a happy birthday! He even brought me flowers. Unbelievable! He apologized for not being able to stay. He'd like to speak to Carmen. He's waiting for you in the other room, Comrade Petroianu. He has something particular to tell you."

It wasn't until a nervous Carmen had disappeared, without having understood from Viorica's hermetic summons who this intruder was, that the secret was revealed.

"Girls, it's Scarlat! He seemed rather depressed. He asked me to get Carmen for him."

Then they hesitated a long time, unable to decide whether they should invite him to join them or not. Since Carmen still hadn't returned, they finally gave up the whole idea. Even Viorica figured that there was no point, and she restrained Geta, who was insisting that each of them should take turns frowning through the half-open door to make the unwanted guest take the hint and leave.

So the first part of their festivities was spoiled, insipid, spent waiting for the team to return to full strength. They kept checking their watches; Carmen still hadn't reappeared. And when she did, it was just to pop her head into the room.

"Let's go, girls, I've opened up again, back to work! We'll continue the party later."

It was past two-thirty, in fact, time for the employees to return to their desks. One by one, they headed reluctantly into the office. Scarlat was gone. Carmen replied to everyone's curiosity with an explanation considered much too laconic: "Still got the same bee in his bonnet."

Which clearly served only to arouse further interest and suspicion.

Later, however, after they'd closed the office and gathered once more—with a little less energy, of course—in the hidden back room, the subject hadn't come up again. They spent the evening gabbing about the quality of the wine, how it wasn't right to make people ill by selling them this vinegary slop, how the peas were musty, and as for the salad, the mayonnaise smells bad because they make it with rancid oil, and have you seen the sick chickens they expect you to buy, what are we coming to, girls. And so on. Basically, all they did was complain, because they were drinking and "their mouths had run away with them," which is how the office manager of branch 46 put it as they arrived at the bus stop, rather late at night and frozen stiff.

III.4.

THE COMRADE PROPOSES THAT THE WINNERS OF THE NA-tional Savings Bank Lottery, as well as the winners of the State Lottery, Sports Lotto, and the State Insurance Lottery, should no longer be selected by lot. Instead, they should be chosen from deserving citizens. In this way, we would avoid the injustices caused by chance, which could result in choosing those who are not in financial need or those who may be truly needy but do not deserve to win. Many times, unexpected winnings enrich certain outcast elements, for example, drug dealers and criminals whose pockets are already full of dirty money. Or else this windfall ends up under the mattress of some stingy old woman who has one foot in the grave. The money or prizes offered at these drawings should reward the most honest and conscientious workers, farm laborers, and intellectuals. Therefore, State and Party would provide a new means of stimulating effort in industrial production, agriculture, and technological and scientific research, to raise the qualitative level in the present phase of the multilateral revolution. This proposal is also ideologically consistent with the concepts of dialectical materialism regarding the world, life, and the active role of man, who is not subject to fate, but is the master and creator of events.

III.5.

THE COMRADE BELIEVES THAT THE DRAWING OF WINNING numbers, for the Savings Bank or other institutional lotteries, should remain to all appearances unchanged in terms of frequency, operation, and monies awarded. Winners will have to be secretly selected in advance, but not too long before the drawing, by a highly secret committee of qualified experts. There should be a preliminary study to determine ways of keeping the names of the designated winners from becoming known to the public, so that no one could have the slightest suspicion about this new strategy. The comrade proposes that a careful analysis be undertaken so that the rewarded persons might be led to feel, in one way or another, that their success is due to their exemplary behavior. Only comrades of irreproachable moral character, whose devotion to the cause shall have been amply displayed over a long period of time, would be able to understand the justification of such a measure and keep this state secret in strictest confidence, for it is a secret that could be entrusted only to the best and the brightest.

II.4.

THE INSOMNIA HAD LASTED FOR SEVERAL WEEKS NOW, torturing him night after night. When dawn sputtered into action, it found him huddled in his bedroom, prostrate with fatigue.

The pills weren't working; they barely enabled him to drowse for an hour or so. He would lie there, staring at the whitish mark that throbbed on the ceiling and at times spread out to cover its entire surface and all four corners. He'd close his eyes, open them again, toss and turn from one side to the other, then lie on his stomach, and nothing made any difference. When the first light of dawn appeared, a faint violet bruise trembling at the window, he'd curl up into a ball at the edge of the bed, chilled to the bone, unable to move a muscle, and wait for day to wash over him in limpid silence.

It wasn't just the solitude of age, increased by his wife's trip abroad to be with their daughter, who was expecting a child. On the contrary, he'd quickly become accustomed to living alone; indeed, he felt closer to reality, having been alienated before by domestic routine. He went into stores, wandered through parks, got on streetcars to go see some stupid whodunit in a crummy movie theater on the outskirts of the city. Every day he discovered new things that were literally suffocating him. He couldn't make sense of these impressions, assemble them into a whole, but he felt something heavy, viscous, and diffuse coming from all directions. Like an invasion of invisible poisonous crickets weighing on the minds and shoulders of everyone he saw. They were already panting with exhaustion on their way to work, they glared at each other in bitter irritation, wanting nothing but to be left alone. What was happening? What was going on? The only words he found had somehow lost their strength . . . It wasn't like that . . . in our time . . . So it was old age, because that kind of whining is the leavening that puffs old folks up with helpless, windy nostalgia. Impossible to say when and how it had happened, that's how time goes by, that's how the perfidious, venomous dust accumulates, imperceptibly, clogging your lungs and the sky. Because the sky itself seemed darker, and it wasn't just his own lungs, his own vitality that had suffered some irrational and inevitable loss, but everyone else's, too. The energy and intelligence of the rabble had grown; those hooligans were livelier, indispensable, full of fun and enterprise, they'd multiplied, covering wider and wider areas, they were circulating at high speed underground, in passageways, on the roofs. But he thought once more about others like him; it made him want to puke to hear his former friends rant about how they'd believed in this or that and the questions they'd asked themselves, come on! Big deal, yes, big nothing . . . Just like him, they'd been ordinary young people, swept along by the tide, a little learning, a little foolishness, a little enthusiasm, a little ambition, that's all it was and nothing more. Average people, but they'd tried, yes, they'd tried, there hadn't been this pathetic, desperate lethargy he found everywhere he went, in the whispering and the prematurely bowed shoulders, this fed-up syndrome, as somebody said.

As though nothing depended on them anymore! As though they could no longer make anything that belonged to them—it was someone else who decided things for them or twisted their intentions, preventing them from wanting and from undertaking anything, someone who neutralized them, denied them, relieved them of their responsibilities and their personalities. A syndrome, yes, a generalized tiredness, a sickness, yes. All they did was inhabit predetermined, presliced slabs of life. It didn't matter how these lives were parceled out, it wouldn't make any difference . . . it was a generalized syndrome, yes.

They'd need a fanatical faith or the fear of punishment; they'd go nuts! They just don't care about anything, all they do is store up disgust, spitefulness, apathy . . .

It wasn't the aging of a single body or mind, in fact, but the disastrous process ripening in everyone. Not so much a specific age as a general state, a surrender, a slow shriveling . . . A diabolical encroachment, the incarnation of evil with myriad invisible mouths and arms, spying on our idiotic daily lives, robbing us of courage and hope.

It was a bright rosy afternoon, but all these thoughts, tangled in his skull, left him no peace. Barely two weeks had passed since his wife's departure abroad. Now it was dusk, a pale, sweetish, trembling light, and he was alone. He'd turned on the TV without thinking about it, program followed program, he'd remained motionless before the familiar face of the hated clown,* in silence, for he hadn't turned up the sound. Laziness, mimicry, jokes, tears, pervasive lethargy, lies, the house and the bed . . . He woke up mumbling things and punched the TV power button so hard to turn it off that it popped out onto the carpet.

---

* When *Composite Biography* was first published in Romania in 1981, Ceaușescu could be identified only by allusions, and even that was risky.

As the image of the ugly, retarded fellow vanished, darkness engulfed the room. The perspiring man unbuttoned his shirt collar. He went down on his hands and knees to find the telephone, no, the light switch, no, he changed his mind, wound up in front of the bathroom. He shoved his bristly head under the sink tap.

He didn't feel able to remain alone in the house, he had to get out at any price, forget this stupid afternoon.

He no longer remembered if it was that very evening he'd been to visit his former comrade, who'd been pressing him with invitations for a while now. He didn't have the slightest desire, actually, to be warmly greeted, with that gleam of joy in the eyes of a man whom—he had to admit it—he'd once wronged, or whom he hadn't protected, rather, from this wrong, even though, if one really thought about it, there hadn't been much he could have done . . . Never the tiniest sign of reproach, from this generous comrade, not even an understandable uneasiness, nor the slightest stiffness in his attitude—nothing at all! Only affection and friendly chatter . . . Senility, really! Injustice doesn't always make someone more combative. After all, he'd been intelligent and steadfast and worthy before he was rehabilitated. That's what did him in, lobotomized him—being restored to his rights, getting back his Party palace and his seniority and his pension. How else could one interpret the fact that Comrade Whosis, formerly a great orator and dialectician, was working as a puppet these days? As an extra! That's right, as an extra in a historical movie, along with a whole bunch of hags, oldsters, whores, and bums . . .

"What do you want? It's a way of killing time," the wretch had explained, relating how he'd rounded up one of his ex-subordinates for the film, and going on about how this would have made an interesting (ha!) study of progressive change in relationships.

"Of course everything changes—Aurel plays a general, while me, I'm just a major. You should see him on the breaks, when we go off for a smoke or a beer, he hardly talks to me, I can barely get him to spit out two or three words in a tight-assed, dried-up voice, because that's what happens with a uniform, it changes a man." And the old combatant had blathered out more such nonsense.

II.5.

ON A BITTER, NASTY EVENING, PERHAPS THE SAME DAY HE'D almost broken the TV, he wound up ringing the doorbell of a comfortable house in the northern section of town. Immediately seated in an armchair by his host, he stiffened beneath the onslaught of sticky logorrhea, like a fly in a bucket of glue. Then he gave up, allowing himself to be carried along by the rumbling wave. Which is to say that he held his own, which is to say that no, he was simply overwhelmed, exasperated. He had to think of something he could talk about, something else, something different that would put a stop to his host's affected drivel, his plaintive lowing. At that point Sonny Boy made his entrance—the offspring-manager, the young boss before whom one had to bow and scrape and smile timidly, in a harmless, elderly way, like an employee afraid of losing his job. As though he hadn't known him when he was still in diapers, pissing himself in his baby carriage, spotty with measles, sent home from school after being caught in the girls' bathroom, hospitalized for an entire semester after a fight with hockey sticks . . . Ugh! Now here he was, clapping you grandly on the shoulder, how are you, how're you feeling, Uncle Sile, so what's new, it seems you're a whiz with the account books, hey, Mr. Victor, that's what your charming colleagues say. Interesting, very interesting, that business I heard about, you'd have been better off coming to me about it rather than Papa, I'm really interested in it, seriously, you've got something there, a great idea, you've really got something . . . Sometimes Sile, sometimes Vasile, sometimes Mr. Victor, just to show he'd known him before he'd legally changed his name to his former pseudonym.

He really had something there, true enough! Whatever had gotten into him on the fatal night when he'd come up with that wild idea? So he ran through it again, that strange inspiration he'd had, giving it lots of conviction, cutting no corners. A bombshell, sure! Control over chance, yes! A bombshell! He'd put it into writing. In writing, come on . . . just so this young twit and others like him could take a squint at it and curl their fat lips, well, well, quite a genius, this Mr. Victor, who would've believed it, this Sile, Vasile, he's really something, the geezer racks his brains and look what happens! Still in there swinging, these old guys, I tell you . . .

A bizarre, twisted, distorted evening, a nest of vipers in

an infirm and damaged heart, a demented impulse born of anger . . . As though the thought had always been quietly holed up in there, waiting to emerge, slender, sinuous, an incandescent red thread.

A toxic moment, a dizzying rebellion, shunting the flood of anger so that it burst out elsewhere. To astound the audience and leave them openmouthed, as before an apparition of the Virgin in a hamlet of hayseeds. Myohmyohmyohmy, well I never, imagine that, what an idea, yes, worthy of interest, yes, yes, serious interest!

Worthy, absolutely, and of tons of interest, even if it was only an unforeseeable transference, a gloomy mood becoming a provocative idea . . . Go figure how long it had been lying around there, that stagnant, putrid dynamite, which could still fuel whole years of rancor and guerrilla warfare, so that no one would ever have enough time to grow bored, ever again! Actually, it wasn't even all that gratuitous and scandalous, this brouhaha, this little farce . . . No, actually, not at all! Because they deserved a bigger one, all those crooks and fakes! Should've gone at them with heavy artillery, not like that, with just a gentle adjustment, a simple regulating valve on a measly secondary tube, far from the main pipeline of juicy swindles and royal payoffs! After all, it was only a small contrivance, much too localized, a simple filter, a mini-attempt at rationalization, something like "why don't we tidy up just a smidgen of this chaos, by rewarding merit, by applying the principles we used to believe in and which we still trot out for parades, these principles we still spout from rusty balconies" . . .

And so tonight's guest is raring to go, and will now

129

show off his idea at top speed. This idea he'd sniffed out by accident, when he was pissed off or hung over, or that he'd unwittingly cherished through years of waiting, of disgust and smoldering rage . . . Now he was whipping it up into a real froth! A rainbow of bubbles, so that the manager was practically in a trance, he'd even forgotten to wear his jolly smile, he was so overcome by the bottomless pit of possibilities opening up endlessly before him.

It wasn't exactly a sudden impulse, since the employee had agreed to set out his proposal in writing. How could he have known that Sonny Boy, the comrade manager, was hoping to get the comrade general manager embroiled in this business, and get him to sign his own death warrant and get the minister embroiled, and so on, up to the very top? So the author of the proposal had agreed to present his ideas in person again, if desired! Yet Mr. Victor hadn't pressed anything beyond providing additional details and clarifications when asked to do so. He had no idea how unprincipled these new young wolves were nowadays, the type that would sell their own mothers—the first crook works himself into a good position edges out the second crook sucks up to the third crook slips lands on his ass, that sort of thing, constantly, you can go crazy. Poor bastard, with his ideas and his lofty ideological concerns! . . . No, not even a whim, just something twisted and inexplicable, from out of nowhere, the depths of the unknown, the way it is for everything that seems strange to you, until you notice that the stranger is you, having discovered yourself going around and around in your drunken rat's cage one winter evening, a mess, a disaster area, and that TV, and the ugly National Instructor, and the boredom . . . You needed something else, anything at all, and so you showed them how to get revenge . . . By stirring the dog packs to even greater frenzy . . . By letting them struggle and foam pink at the mouth, while you watched over their rations . . . There you are, order and discipline! That's all they deserve, let's keep on the alert, there'll be no more jokers left to slip through the net, no more slipups, no more breathing space, no more muddle, no more wild, spontaneous joy! We're going to screen everything, we're going to drive them bananas, we're going to howl, lashed at from all directions, the way they laughed and sneered at me that night when I'd left the house in the north side of town to go home, in a grinding rush of energy and cruelty. I was coming back to life, excited, vigorous, inspired, inventing more and more systems of filters and gears and shut-off valves, while the snow crunched underfoot, white and icy. The streets were cold, rough, I fell asleep quickly, the way I hadn't done for a long time, I closed my eyes so I wouldn't see that face of the stammering National Speaker anymore, the one on the TV screen and in the window and on the ceiling and everywhere. I opened my eyes again, and the ghost face was still there. I closed them once more and fell asleep like a baby being rewarded after a long day of games and tantrums.

And night went on spinning out sleep, compact, gray sleep, skein after skein, thick and rancid. Nothing else in the world existed anymore but dense, black sleep; thought was dead, had vanished along with anxiety and the earth itself, which stirred up sticky waves of sleep and oblivion, shaken by rumblings, a red foam, incomprehensible words, the growling and wheezing of a sick wild animal, dragged over the coals, through the slough of despond: What if cars ran on blood? If we could find another fuel for automobiles, dear Comrade Sile, Vasile, what about this? When will they replace gas with blood, Victor old boy? Gas with blood! Blood, the new fuel of our century, whispered and belched the exhausted night, a seething soup of lumpy tar. A nightmare of nattered words, at long-drawn-out intervals . . . Heart attack, oil crisis, blood crisis. A brand-new fuel, brand-new. His chest heaved, crushed beneath the weight, cynical rhythms, punishment, *just imagine, blood—a brand-new fuel*, think about it, motors running and the slaughter begins, the inevitable torment, the tower would start to tremble, blood, blood, tarantula thunder tavern, blood, blood, *chickens, cats, sparrows and horses and pigs and people*, yes, yes, my dear fellow, dis-memberment, no question about it, this business of chance and winning numbers and manipulating prizes, a human being's merit quantified by another human being, one win-ter night, fucking mess fucking disaster fucking TV fuck-ing boredom, something was missing, the real thing, *the blood of chickens, whales, then human blood*, obviously the mirror's our next stop. *First criminals, madmen, cripples, the incurably ill, then the elderly, adversaries, repeat offenders, then the uncle, the lady next door*, then then then, oh yes, my dear fellow, controlling luck, manipulating chance, selecting rewards, surprises . . . Big nothing, waste of time, a retiree's pipe dream! The deal of the century, energy, the

Middle East, petrodollars, Islam, the sacred precincts, the most terrible of all discoveries! The fuel of the future! And the control of chance! You'll see just how far we can go with discipline and fear, humiliation, submission, the schizophrenia lurking within the most highly developed computer-mammal . . . And we all contribute to it with our fuel and we'll eventually wind up with this collective portrait, the composite that will enable us to recall the time, the place, the individual.

And so it will be a black, freezing night. Frail Chickadee, bruised by the blows of the child-monster swelling her belly, will writhe in her sweat-soaked sheets, terrified, flinging out her arms in search of rescue; alone in a mountain chalet, startled awake by a bad dream, the traveler with the face and speech of an ageless adolescent will rush to the window and fling it open, blinded by the chilly torch of the moon, motionless and mute; somewhere the political police archive containing the biography files will screech, grating on the walls of a shabby office; at the streetcar stop over by the Abattoirs, the poor distraught and shivering employee will hang his head in horror, frightened by the huge scope of the Project, a project that tortured and terrorized him, a virile and impotent exaltation that illuminated him, as though he'd instantaneously recovered the madness of his crazed childhood. To control chance, to become real masters now as long as we still have time, until the slaughter starts, the massacre of chickens and horses and cats and fools and aunts and kids and bureaucrats, the new fuel, the brand-new fuel!

And only the rippling violet light, just before the dawn

---

of a modest day, will connect us once more to the maniacal spirit of fellowship, our share of hope, constantly deferred, forever postponed, our poor forgotten personal contribution to the happy future. The confusion of the incessant, robotized, and out-of-sync pulsation that sums up our punctual rout, fluttering impulse of an instant, shattering din of silence.

IV.

Rejuvenated by a brief convalescence in the mountains, the stranger will go back down into the big, flat patchwork of the city, groping his way for a while through the dawn darkness, in the shadowy streets riddled with potholes. He'll walk from the station to the outskirts of the city, stepping over puddles of waste water, looking among the new concrete boxes for the house where, it seems, he once lived.

The morning will be mild and sunny by the time he stops, at a noisy intersection crowded with buses and streetcars, before what used to be a slum-street stall and is now a branch of the National Savings Bank. He'll shrug off his worn backpack and loop the strap around his arm. He'll grasp the doorknob and gently push open the door, alerted in an instant by the ringing of the little bell overhead signaling that his strange wanderings are over. These ladies in the savings bank must have been amused at first by this noise, but they probably haven't noticed it for a long time now.

An ordinary ageless gentleman, polite, somewhat head-in-the-clouds, watching the people around him with a pleasantly curious expression: that's what he looked like, this stranger with the face of a teenager. The high-school kid, the college student, the scholar of indeterminate age, the recluse, the mountain climber—God knows who he was—sat down in a chair and put his backpack on the one next to him. He contemplated, overheard, memorized . . . the dance, the words of the foursome gathered around a pale, elegant young woman whom the others called Chick-adee and who was speaking in a soft, composed voice.

"I really didn't feel well last night, I was all alone in the house. I was scared when the phone rang, it was right before dawn. He was very upset, he told me that the idea had been his, but he didn't think it was going to work out. The idea came to him just like that, and he'd thought it was something worth looking into, something new. He wouldn't have taken it any further if the boss hadn't shown any interest, but then he'd gotten stubborn about it when he'd seen that the boss wanted to take over the idea for himself. And he'd known him for a long time, ever since the boss was little. But he got scared when he realized that he was being asked to defend his proposal one more time. He didn't want to give up without a fight, but there wasn't anything they could do to him anymore. There's nothing more they can do to him . . . But he couldn't stand the fact that the boss seemed to be making fun of him, once he'd realized he wouldn't let him use his idea for his own schemes. At first the boss had been enthusiastic, making him come up with further details to prove his points and fancy quotations from the classics of Marxism–Leninism, but he wasn't sure this wasn't some kind of ploy to discourage him for a while so that the boss could appropriate the idea later, at a more favorable time, but me, there I was, nauseated and everything, sick all night long, and I didn't understand any of what he was telling me. He was all alone at home, he seemed a bit unwell. I felt sorry for him and let him talk until he was finished. He'd spent hours in a streetcar stop, somewhere over by the Abattoirs. He'd just gotten home. But I was feeling so awful, I could hardly hear him."

Her colleagues seemed more astonished at the sick young woman's talkativeness than at what she had to say, so they soon drifted back to their seats when she'd finished. There weren't many people in the office. The place seemed very familiar to the stranger. The bell over the door reminded him of something, of some old story . . . The employees didn't bother him, letting him rest a bit, slumped on the seat near the door. He had all the time in the world to reflect on the fact that a survivor fresh from the still smoking ovens of the war, without any other piece of identification except his membership card in the Association of Former Prisoners, had to locate a distant uncle or some vague cousin or other of the occupant of the house next door to the one where they'd come for him so long ago, it seemed like an eternity . . . Then he might have been able to understand *what had happened all these years since to the minds and bowed shoulders of the average citizen*, the journey the paths the very narrow paths rising falling, how did this bizarre Idea take root, what connections were there between a hypothetical neighbor or uncle and the child-man who was supposed to give a speech this afternoon at the Institute of Futurology on "The Conditional Reflected in the Biography," a rather pompous title for a longtime member like himself, an ordinary child-witness, himself inflammable, fuel of the blood-century, which the little futurologist director wanted to see expressed in "octane numbers." That telegenic star, that charming, sly informer, polyglot, constantly cooking up paradoxes and hooey: the *ultimate composite picture!* Publicity for a secret establishment, a trap for derelicts and rebels.

Lolling on that chair near the front door of the bank, I realized that I would have to include—on the personal data sheet that's supposed to accompany the description of the symptoms of being fed-up that have plagued me these last hundred years—the barbed remarks of the gossiping employees, and the policemen, police files, police speeches, and the fight that broke out at the store across the way, where the waiting line for cheese had poured out into the street in a general melee, and the crematoria and the astronauts, and the streetcars immobilized at the intersection by a power failure due to the energy shortage, everything. Everything. Finally, *the new fuel capable of modifying mobilizing massacring everything, absolutely everything . . .* Please take note and work out the obvious correspondences! Stratified, diversified, hundreds of pages of autobiographies and reports, and I was going to go into all that in detail in my lecture, mentioning the sources that lay the foundations of such a scholarly descriptive undertaking, such a delicate analytical experiment . . . The ambiguity of any "solution of continuity," as the experts say. A gap, a break . . . ?

There is no other solution of continuity besides the clear and ordinary morning, and so I will display the absentminded expression and dithering gestures of a brilliant student in some obscure field. I will stand up, confidently, to collect my prize forgotten long ago, before the war, before the crisis. I don't even know what a savings-bank book looks like anymore.

But there won't be any surprise, or resentment, perhaps just a misunderstanding, a small oversight, because the thin blond employee didn't speak Romanian very well. She noticed the mistake, though. She had to admit that my address was out-of-date, my old, forgotten address, the card absolutely had to be renewed, my new permanent address had to be on it, plus the required stamps.

She had a sense of humor, however, and was very gracious, just like the soft, pleasant winter morning. She didn't see any reason why it couldn't be taken care of right away, we could simply make out an affidavit for the record. A record, of course, a recording, recited by the two of us, each in turn, whispering each word before writing it down again . . . A preliminary exercise that we were going to carry out, consecrate, perfect, together, in writing, in the present. *It was the only possible way to possess some kind of proof, to preserve, to prolong the present* . . . As a result, we were going to tackle the retranscription with a cautious hand, stopping after each word, trying to make sure we'd chosen the right one, every stratum of the morning had to be in there, the history of the event, the person, the day, if you like, something that would become day, week, or century, *still present, because recorded in writing*: "We certify that today, so-and-so, on such-and-such a date, presented a claim at this agency, in support of which claim the aforementioned, to whom by rights . . ." Which could amount to this: on a chilly, mediocre, and conciliating morning, we press forward, with our bag and baggage, calendar, certificates, cartograms, risks, chitchat, prattling, the cold childish expectation of dawn, our punishment, and joy and pain, all the troubles each one of us packs up in that old kit bag.

A WINDOW ON THE WORKING CLASS

Sunday keeps stretching out its arms . . . a grasping, famished octopus. A net with threads as slender as a hair. Eiderdown and clouds, a treacherous nest sailing on the endless, swollen ocean of night.

Blessed, cursed peace . . . To make it last forever and ever, to erase all sound, thought, the poison of fatigue, the nightmare of our times, places near and far, the past held frozen in a lowering sky, the future tossed into the clock grinder. The rusty toad devours pell-mell seconds, cells, flesh and dreams, tick-tock, no exit.

Light darts its first shaft, its first oblique ray, straight into the huddled body, which lazily divides in two: one

-----

being flops softly to the left, the other to the right. Shaken by gloomy storms, the placenta of sleep splits open in an instant, destroyed with a single movement: cruel day calls back her orphans.

The woman settles lightly on the right, the man rolls heavily to the left, while behind its bars the morning grows brighter.

And then a whisper: "You see, it's that light again . . . I've asked you so many times to . . ." A mist of childish breath, rocking the words. "That . . . light . . . asked . . . you knew . . . again and again . . . This torture, this same torture."

And sure enough, Sunday recaptures its prisoners one more time. Really, that damned blind should have been repaired by now!

"That window again . . . even though I asked you. I reminded you about it every day. You know it's driving me out of my mind. I asked you to find someone to fix it. I mean, it's just a blind—it can't be all that complicated. There must be someone around who can fix it."

They grope, haggardly, in terror of a new day. Shower, black coffee. Wide awake, sluggish, alert, groggy, sitting in front of their cups. Already belonging to this new day, no way out, none.

The rumble of streetcars somewhere, in the distance, close by, below, above, trolley bus motor bus blunderbuss, impossible to detect the teasing tick-tock of the stocky toad squatting in the bedroom. They keep an eye on the clock, without hearing it. But they know the pendulum is conscientiously nibbling away at the calendar's poison.

Face to face, slumped in the two armchairs of worn velvet, they contemplate the black circles of the cups placed symmetrically on the small shiny black table. The slim white hand runs a long pale finger around the black rim. The transparent blouse slides across the shoulders with a brief rustle, as though coaxing.

"I didn't sleep as much as I'd have liked . . . There's still this endless morning to get through. I'm going to visit the cemetery. But I won't stay long. I'll be back in an hour."

She stops talking. She watches him remain silent . . . Symmetrically, they take a sip of coffee, looking at each other. The morning authorizes such preliminaries. Silence as well—for a moment—from the motor bus trolley bus blunderbuss streetcars. They can hear the measured pulse of the toad chronometer rhythmically swallowing every last flicker of hope.

"Why don't you sort through his notebooks? And they ought to be hidden somewhere else, you know. They're too easy to find, here with us . . . That's probably what they wanted from him, that night: the notebooks. Maybe that's why he died . . ."

He keeps quiet, closes his eyes, waits for the rest. He opens his eyes, still waiting.

"We have to take care of the notebooks right away. They have to be sorted and put in a safe place. They're all we have left of him. And you know perfectly well there's more than just poetry in them, too . . ."

Nothing more is said, or happens. The barbarity of the street breaks in on all sides, surrounding the nest.

———

Suddenly they're both startled, on the alert. The door-bell. A long ring, then a long pause. Another ring, short, timid.

"Who could that be? On a Sunday morning, no less? No rest for the weary! Who could it be, at this hour?"

In front of their door, no, a certain distance from the door, practically up against the wall across the landing, there's a kind of grayish raincoat that hangs almost to the floor. Above the tight collar, a face with pale, sunken cheeks. Large eyes, glittering uneasily.

"Excuse me if . . . perhaps I'm disturbing you."

The hollow voice adds to the impression of shyness and humility.

"Your shade is broken, you know. Your Venetian blind. In the window, I mean. If you want, I can fix it."

Bull's eye, bang on, a one-in-a-million shot. A sure-fire surprise.

"Uh, yes . . . yes, but . . . how did you know?"

"You can see it from outside. The cord's broken . . . You know, the lift cord, the one you pull. It's jammed inside, I can tell. That's why your blind's drooping at one end. Not up, not down. The slats going every which way, you know what I mean?"

"It's true! You're right. But how did you figure out . . . How did you find our apartment?"

"I counted, from out front. Fourth floor, door to the left . . . It was easy."

"Mm yes, well, what can I say? Please, come in, come on in."

The door opens wide. The little man comes forward,

then takes a step back. He's left a heavy, battered toolbox sitting on the landing.

"Do come in, please. Oh, no, you don't have to take your shoes off, really . . ."

The man does so anyway and in no time stands there in his stocking feet. His raincoat is hanging on the coat tree in a trice; his toolbox, sitting on the floor next to his shoes, is already open, displaying screws, screwdrivers, pliers, wing nuts, keys, nails, bits of string, his stock-in-trade.

He moves at a slower pace through the living room, enters the bedroom. Short, bony, stooped, master of the situation. He examines the window from one side, then the other. His movements are relaxed and decisive. No trace remains of his initial hesitancy.

"It'll cost you one hundred lei. If you want, I'll get started. A hundred lei."

He shrugs his shoulders. Frail shoulders, large hands, long arms for such a small, gaunt body. He turns around, runs his fingers through his hair, which he wears in a brush cut. Hands on hips, expectant, keyed up.

"It'll take me an hour. For a hundred lei, as I said."

"That's expensive. Why a hundred?"

"That's my price. A hundred lei. When I mend something, it stays mended. A good cord'll last you forever. I've got some old ones that don't fall apart."

"Well, all right, but a hundred's a lot . . . Why don't you get to work and we'll talk about it later—I'm sure we'll reach an agreement. So don't worry about it."

"No, no, I have to settle this first. A hundred lei, I told you."

"Don't worry, we'll work it out. Please excuse us, we haven't had time to make the bed yet."

"Would you have a stepladder? I'll need one. And newspapers, for the parquet, so it doesn't get dirty."

The stepladder is brought from the den. He opens it up and spreads around some old papers found in a closet.

At that point, the woman emerges from the bathroom, all perked up and ready to go out. She stops on the threshold of the bedroom. She glances distrustfully at the little workman perched on the stepladder. She's delicate, blond, tense, a woman with a busy day ahead of her. She closes the bedroom door abruptly. Whispering is heard. Then a rustle of clothing. Then the door to the apartment.

"Well, how are you getting on?"

"So far, so good. The cord's broken on the inside, just like I said. I've got some old ones, sturdy material, it won't break again."

The man of the house, in jeans and a comfortable sweater, leaves him to it. Fifteen minutes later, the workman appears while he's reading his paper. The little guy stops in the doorway, looking around at the chairs, the desk, the bookshelves.

"You've sure got a lot of books! . . . Books, books, and more books, everywhere."

The other man looks up from his paper, nods in agreement.

"I've never seen so many books. I knew right away that this place was something else, really special, no doubt about it."

Smiling, he puts down his paper. Waiting. As tiny as a

splinter, the instant has already vanished into the maw of the chronometer, hop, croak, murmurs the old batrachian.

"I see you're busy, so I wouldn't like to . . ."

"I was reading the paper. Nothing important, you can come in."

"Well, since that's the sort of thing that interests you . . . books, I mean. You're a reader, I can tell. I bet you spend all your time reading."

"You can come in, you're not disturbing me."

"Your missus has gone out? In that case . . . I'd like to ask you . . . since we can talk now . . . otherwise, I wouldn't . . ."

"All right, tell me what you have to say. Come on, say it. Let's see what this is all about."

"I saw the books, so I got to thinking . . . Maybe you'd be willing to help me write something."

An angular face, knitted brows. Pants with the waist bunched up under a shabby belt, a child's short-sleeved shirt, very clean. Lively, penetrating eyes.

"You've got a problem? You want me to compose some sort of petition, is that it?"

"I've got a problem, yes. A lot of problems. But I'll come back another time, when it's more convenient. Some afternoon. Or some evening, when you've finished work . . ."

"Fine, come whenever you like. I'm home in the mornings, too."

"Oh? You mean you work at home? Then the morning would definitely be better. Perhaps I'll come by some morning, when you're alone."

Taking tiny steps, he withdraws, seeming to sway on his short legs and big feet in their socks.

He finishes his work in the allotted time, collects the screws, nails, pliers, the balls of string, puts everything back in his tool kit. The wife reappears at this juncture. He makes himself even smaller, hurries a little more. He asks for a broom, sweeps carefully, requests that the gentleman verify that the blind is once more in perfect working order, asks for permission to wash his hands. He wraps the hundred-lei bill in his handkerchief. Then he's gone.

A slow, rainy morning. The doorbell. One long ring. A long pause. Another ring, short, timid, then silence again. The man is drowsy, befuddled with insomnia. He has difficulty recognizing the visitor, who stands at a respectful distance from the door.

"Oh! It's you . . . Do come in, please."

The shadow detaches itself from the wall. Approaches, enters, takes off its shoes, boom, they're already in his left hand.

"You didn't need to, it's not necessary. So . . . Come in, come in. Leave your toolbox there, in the vestibule, and come in. No, no, you're not disturbing me. Please sit down. I'll be back, I'm just going to make some coffee. I'll make some for you, too. I'll be right back."

And he does return quickly, bringing the cups on a tray. His visitor sits stiffly, self-consciously, in the armchair. After about half an hour of laconic answers, he finally begins to feel more at ease.

"I was right . . . You're different. I feel I can trust you.

There's only two people in the whole country who can still help me. The big boss, but I could never get to him. Or else that fat guy you see all over, on TV and in the papers, that show-off who screws everybody left right and center."

"Drink your coffee, please, or it'll get cold."

"It used to be that you knew what you were dealing with. You could manage to get by in the old days. There were eight of us kids at home. A family of poor country people. It was hard, real hard. I got away from that village. Twelve years old when I left, off to the city. I knew where to go. To the comrades. I waited in front of the door for hours. But finally they let me in, they listened to me. They put me in a trade school. That's how I learned my profession. Back then, you could find doors to knock on, people would listen to you . . ."

"Drink your coffee, you haven't even touched it."

"Troubles, worries . . . They've sure put me through it . . . I went to the doctor. I don't drink coffee anymore, it's better not to. Everything's changed now. No one pays any attention now to a poor bastard. These days nothing's open and aboveboard. You have to have family connections or some other kind of connections in high places, where they divvy everything up. Ten or fifteen years ago, you could still get by. I was living with my wife and our two kids in a maid's room, nine square feet, like sardines. One day I went to the park. I found someone with a camera. You know, one of those strolling photographers. I told him what I wanted. He gave me a funny look. Won't do it, he told me. It's too risky, I know exactly what you're

---

up to, I don't do that kind of thing. I slipped him five hundred lei. Five hundred! Even that frightened the stuffing out of him, poor guy. He thought I was loony. He wouldn't take my money, scared shitless. He finally came and took the pictures, but I had to swear I'd never admit that he was the one . . .''

"Would you rather have some tea, or perhaps a snack?"

He doesn't hear. His voice is steady and his brow is furrowed in concentration, just as it was that Sunday morning when he spotted, from down in the street, the broken blind that he and he alone would fix, and for a price agreed on in advance. Now there's no trace of the hesitation or the embarrassed humility he showed when he first appeared, glued to the wall across the landing, standing as far as possible from the apartment door.

"One morning, I jumped in front of the official's car. Right outside his villa I mean, one of the big guys . . . I knew everything: the time, the itinerary, the precise moment. How? Well, it's a long story . . . I made it my business to do odd jobs for upper-class types. I found out how to get into their restricted neighborhood. Someone got me work in the home of a second fiddle, as he put it. I sweated for that guy for months, fixing this and that. Not much money, but I didn't quibble, I put everything right. I can mend anything: locks, stoves, plumbing, cabinets, whatever. Afterward, I said to him, okay, I've slaved for peanuts, fine, now it's your turn to help me out. Some advice, that's all. I'd turned up at his place after work at the factory, every day, stayed late every night, I'd fixed up everything in sight, practically for free. He couldn't refuse. He gave me a lead: one street over, there's Comrade Whosis who lives at this number . . . A big shot, a major heavyweight. Doesn't matter who, someone well known, now he's long gone, like the rest of them—the top dog keeps shuffling them around so that none of them gets a chance to grow too powerful. I kept watch for several days running . . . I dashed out in front of the car. Well, I can tell you, those guards were all over me in five seconds flat, from out of nowhere and from all sides. But the man motions to them to let me go. Come over here, what's going on, what happened? I give him the photos. An entire file, with the written statement, the pictures, the whole bit. Just like the other one suggested, the cross-eyed guy I did all that work for. This man, he takes a good look at me, he checks out the papers, then he goes through the papers once more, and looks me over again. So he says right, if what you're telling me is true . . . we'll look into it and we'll see . . . Two days later, we're moving. They'd assigned me an apartment. That was then . . . I'm not saying those were the good old days, no way. It was a sewer even then. But you could run around, complain, scream your head off. Now it's nothing but money and lies and pulling strings and making dirty deals."

He grabs the dossier rolled up in newspapers he's been holding between his knees, and brandishes it, a dangerous weapon.

"Today, getting all the way up to the guy on top, it's just not possible. And the rest of them, they can't do a thing anymore. Some people have managed to get what they want through that fatso who's on TV, plus he's got that magazine that comes out every week. I suppose you know him, you must know him."

"No more than anyone else in Romania. In other words, I don't know him, but I can write your letter for you, if you like. Perhaps you'll be lucky. If your problem intrigues him, he'll help you. But only if he can turn it to his advantage. Maybe you'll be lucky, maybe he'll help you out . . ."

The visitor undoes the rolled-up dossier and places on the table between them a bundle of papers covered with large, childish handwriting, slanted to the left.

"It's all written down here. But let me tell you about it first. My rating's A-1. I've been at the boiler factory longer than almost anyone else. Before the foreman retired, things were all right, I didn't have any problems. Two years ago they brought in this new guy from the provinces. A real operator. They gave him a place to live and everything. He had first-class connections that worked like a charm. He spent more time in meetings than on the shop floor. As long as you didn't try to cross him, he wasn't a bad man. A wise guy, on good terms with the director and all the others, he knew how to handle them. Me, I didn't ask him for anything, and he left me alone. Except that I didn't go out drinking. He's the one who started that. On payday, everyone getting blind drunk. Together, the whole crew. Everyone has to go, no exceptions. You know, me, I don't drink . . . and besides, I do odd jobs after work, off the books. It's not easy when you've got four kids. My wife, she doesn't work, it wasn't possible, not with four of them. I wanted her to stay home with the children."

The other man leans across the small glass table and picks up the papers. He glances through them, nodding, as though seeing exactly what he'd expected to find.

"So I wouldn't go out drinking, but one day I did go along with them. I couldn't help it, I didn't want him thinking I'd got anything against him . . . They had this place they went to, they called it the President. The real name was something else. I forget what. A crummy little bar, smoky and crowded, but with red velvet banquettes and prices that were way out of line. They'd start out slowly and just keep going until they were all blotto. That was the rule, you weren't allowed to slip away quietly. Hour after hour, all night long. At the end, when it came time to settle the bill . . . Well, the boss didn't dig into his pocket! The others paid for him. I kept my mouth shut and forked over. But I never went along again. Afterward, the others asked me . . . to contribute my share for the boss, as they put it. I didn't want to, so I didn't pay. Yeah, well, that's how it got started . . ."

The other man listens, nods in understanding; he puts aside the pile of papers, considering the person before him with great attention.

The silence lengthens; the papers will lie there quietly for several hours. Dusk would be the proper time to leaf through them . . . The tired man's hand reaches out for them again, in a hurry, pulls a few from the pile, separates them, holds on to them. He walks up and down the room, alone. Violet, ash-gray curtains veil the windows, and the murmuring night drowns out the chronometer.

"Has it been pointed out that on the only day this worker

was ever late, in twenty-five years of service in the same factory, transportation was at a standstill throughout the entire city?" The sentence has an impressive cadence and tonality . . . "Why was he reassigned from the boilerworks to the janitorial department, which cost him a quarter of his salary?"

"The questions in these pages are all framed as though prepared for a court of law," the man explains that evening to his wife. He holds the bundle in his hand, which trembles in his excitement.

"It's all laid out simply and intelligently. You can understand perfectly what happened . . . Why did the comrade foreman put him on the night shift, when it had previously been decided to exempt heads of large families with seniority in the factory? Why did they give him the most difficult and urgent work assignments without adjusting his pay accordingly? Why was he transferred from the boilerworks? . . . Why, when he fell ill, was he told that there was no place for sick people at the factory? . . . Why was he docked an entire work day for being one half hour late? . . . Why, when he asked to see someone in authority at either the trade union or the ministry, was he warned that if he didn't keep quiet, he might get into much more serious trouble?"

"Did he fix the stove, during all this? Or did you spend so much time talking that he never got around to it?" asks the wife with a smile.

"He fixed it. He fixed it while I was writing his letter to the newspaper. He thinks that fat pig will help him solve his problem. A kind of second head of state, that's what people think he is. They know he looks out for himself above all, but as they've got no one else to complain to, they turn to him as though he were a magician. So that he can put them in his articles, so they can become human beings once more, have their troubles taken under consideration by someone. That's basically what they hope for: some consideration. To have their confidence restored, that's what they want. Burdened with anxieties, surrounded by pitfalls, they don't know which way to turn . . . I composed his letter carefully, to arouse the interest of that bastard of a finagler . . . I tried hard to persuade our worker to accept a compromise with the people at his factory, but it was a complete waste. I explained to him that you can't take on such a system all alone, that he'd get himself crushed. He didn't even hear me. There's a ferocious stubbornness in that little man. Well, you've seen him, he's knee-high to nothing. Industrious, honest, proud. Clever at everything, assailed on all sides."

"How much did he get from you? The same, a hundred lei? An even hundred?"

"No, not this time, no. He fixed the stove, the bathroom door, the lock on the suitcase. When I tried to pay him, he said no. I insisted, he refused. He said, while I was working, you spent the same amount of time on my letter, so you don't owe me a thing."

When the really hot weather arrives, something goes wrong with the shower. They telephone the workman, who turns up the following morning.

A hesitant trill at the doorbell, barely a flutter. He stands, as usual, away from the door. Already he's used to the appearance of this childlike, sleepy gentleman wearing a cowboy-style shirt he hasn't bothered to tuck into his too-tight jeans.

"Am I disturbing you? But I thought that . . . My wife told me you'd telephoned."

"Come in, please come in. I'll make coffee for us. Ah! I forgot, you don't drink it. I'll fix you some tea, all right? It won't take a minute . . . You don't need to take your shoes off . . . No, really, there's no need."

The visitor's shoes are already in his hand, his toolbox is already sitting open beneath the coat tree, he's rummaging around in it, poking about among the screws, faucets, wing nuts, tubes of cement, coils of wire, bits of string, and other assorted junk.

The gentleman goes off to drink his coffee. He returns with a tray bearing a cup of tea and a slice of brioche, which the workman leaves untouched. The master of the house returns a few moments later, stands in the doorway, tries to think of something to say.

"So, what's new? How's your claim going?"

"Oh, that . . . I won. I won, but they wouldn't go along with the fourteen thousand I put in for, they only awarded me six thousand."

"You won? I wouldn't have believed it. That's great! That's the first time I've ever heard of anyone winning a case against a company, which means winning against the state. I take my hat off—you're incredible! And without a lawyer, that's what gets me . . . You did tell me that you weren't going to hire a lawyer, that you were perfectly capable of explaining the truth on your own, right?"

"I've filed an appeal. I don't take small change tossed at me like that, out of charity. I demand my rights. They've got no choice. They have to give me what's mine. Fourteen thousand, I counted it all up. The salary they docked me and the layoffs and the work bonuses."

"Let it go. You're going to wear yourself out in the courts. Now that you've won the judgment against them and they have to pay you damages, put an end to this business. You'll finally have some peace, instead of having to run around all over creation day after day."

"That's not the problem. I can earn my own living. But I want my rights. My place in the sun. Because otherwise—listen to what I'm saying here—the world has gone all to hell. Nobody believes in anything anymore. Honesty and faith and keeping one's word—out the window. What's the point of living like that, not giving a damn for God or man? I refuse to play that game . . . Can I wash my hands?"

"Of course. You may use that towel over there."

He washes his grease-blackened hands for a long time. He hesitates before using the towel. He holds his hands suspended over the sink for a moment before clumsily grabbing the towel. He puts away the screws, faucets, wing nuts, asks for a broom, tidies up carefully, gets ready to leave.

"How much do I owe you?"

"Well, a hundred lei."

It's hard not to smile.

"So, you always charge the same fee?"

"A hundred lei doesn't mean anything anymore. I replaced the shower pipe. At the plumbing-supply store, it costs thirty-two lei and it's a piece of garbage, rusts right out. I put in a good one, it'll last. I replaced the washers in the faucets so they won't drip anymore. I cleaned out the crud in the drain; it shouldn't get stopped up now. Give me a hundred lei and you'll have a bit of credit for the next time. I keep track of my accounts, don't worry."

"Which means we'll be seeing you again . . ."

A little more and the smile would break into laughter.

"You bet. So, goodbye and stay well. Above all, stay well."

In other words, let the warm weather last a long time . . .

No other news from the lone warrior until a chilly December evening, when a bulletin arrives in the form of a retrospective summary.

A great mass of people, all jammed together, waiting at the bus stop. It's not the first time that public transportation has been the target of curses and insults, bitter grumbles distilled from the hatred and despair of would-be passengers. They mill about, bump into one another, lean out once in a while to gaze into the distance, hoping to see this monster that's supposed to take them home finally heave into sight. Numb with cold and fatigue, they bitch unmercifully. Anyone overhearing their choppy burst of resentment might think they're working themselves into a rage and will shortly explode in revolt. But whoever has heard them too many times, pouring out over and over the same hopeless torrents of abuse as they wait on line for meat, soap, matches, toilet paper, milk, cigarettes, shoes, or the bus, whoever has heard this daily chorus of humiliation and anger from these endless lines has already learned not to expect anything beyond such periodic sullen grousing.

A huge crowd at the bus stop on this dark, frigid evening in December. Shivering children, women lugging bags and shopping baskets, but quite a few men as well, stamping their feet to keep warm and contributing their fair share of profanity.

He's easy to spot among them. Short, glum, three bulging plastic bags in each hand. Unlike the others, he stands quietly, stock-still. He doesn't make a move, or a sound. Bareheaded, wearing a thin, frayed lumber jacket, he doesn't seem to feel the cold. His brush cut is immaculate; he's close-shaven, slender but broad-shouldered, with arms that seem too long for his frail body. He stares indifferently at the black winter sky. He looks like some lost adolescent bound for boarding school, where other young people just as poor and proud as he is confide their problems and ambitions to one another.

The gentleman who approaches him hesitates for a good long moment before addressing him. First he examines the man closely, from a few steps away, as though to make sure that he hasn't been mistaken. He walks around the other man a few times before tapping him lightly on the shoulder, to rouse him from his reverie. They recognize each other, would like to shake hands, but those plastic bags are in the way. They lean their heads together, though, and begin to talk.

The city lies prostrate, overwhelmed by the night. The streets running into the public square by the bus stop seem like tunnels in a cavern deep underground. Darkness settles more and more thickly along the great arteries of the metropolis, as though it were a village lost out in nowhere. Only the headlights of an occasional passing car illuminate for brief moments the compact mass of black ants, a clump shaped like a dragon that occasionally opens its huge, gaping jaws to moan. A poisonous volley of invective. A chilling, somber rumbling.

The two men are oblivious to their surroundings, however, completely absorbed in each other.

The worker Valentin Nanu appears before the Supreme Court of Bucharest on June 8, 1982. He submits to the presiding judge a voluminous dossier containing statements, affidavits, and copies of medical records. These last concern not only his own state of health, which for the past year has been considered psychologically precarious, due to the plaintiff's stressful situation at work, but also the health of his children: Maria, nineteen years old (anemia and hypocalcemia); Angela, sixteen (asthma and kyphoscoliosis); Mihaela, thirteen (acute rheumatoid arthritis and a defective mitral valve), and Marian, ten years old (rheumatoid arthritis and dysfunctional thyroid). About two months after this hearing, Valentin Nanu receives in the mail the decision of the Supreme Court in favor of his appeal. On September 26, 1982, a court order is issued requiring the reinstatement of the worker Valentin

Nanu at his place of employment with no loss of seniority, and payment by the Republica Factory of Bucharest of damages to said worker in compensation for his arbitrary transfer from the boilerworks as well as the full salary due for periods of paid leave that were improperly denied him. This sum amounts in total to 8,750 lei. The plaintiff declares himself dissatisfied with this judgment, on the grounds both that it does not require punitive action to be taken against those responsible for the administrative abuses in question and that the said monetary award does not reflect the full extent of the damages to which he is entitled.

On September 27, 1982, Valentin Nanu reports to the personnel department of the Republica Factory to sign a contract of reinstatement with the firm and to collect the money awarded him by the court decision. Although the political authorities at the company try to convince him to return to work immediately, explaining that the official court order might not be delivered to them until almost a month after the actual decision in the case, the plaintiff refuses. He maintains that he will not come crawling back to the factory where he has been an exemplary worker for twenty-five years and that he will wait until all the relevant documents are in order and in his possession. In addition, he makes it clear that he is not completely in agreement with the judgment rendered and that he will continue to press, within the framework of the law, for the satisfaction of all his rightful demands. He is finally persuaded, after much urging, to go on leave without pay until such time as the new work contract is duly signed, which it is on October 22, 1982. On Monday, October 25, 1982, Valentin Nanu returns to his job in the boilerworks; he is absent on Friday the 29th, having been advised by his doctor to go on sick leave. He returns to work again on November 8.

On the eleventh, the firm's cashier pays him 8,750 lei in accordance with court order #4444 dated September 26, 1982. On October 28, the plaintiff Valentin Nanu sends a petition to the Attorney General to request a review of his case and the decision handed down upon appeal. On December 18, 1982, he is notified by letter (docket #567,132) that the Attorney General of the Socialist Republic of Romania has declared the judgment of the Supreme Court in his case to be final and without appeal.

The man tries to tell his wife what the worker Valentin Nanu has related to him. With a brusque gesture, she cuts him off. She's preoccupied by something else. Some painful reflection from which she cannot bear to be distracted.

"You went there again," he says. "Were you at the cemetery? I can feel it. Each time, you seem to fall into a trance."

"Not at all. When I've had a good day, suddenly I remember . . . But it can happen when I'm depressed, too. So I go back. To remind myself that things might be even worse. As though it gives me strength, somehow."

"I hope you don't go there . . . to remind yourself that I'm vulnerable."

"No, but what I remember . . . involves you. I come home terrified at the idea that something might have happened to you."

"That's absurd, it's impossible to live like that."

"No more absurd than the absurdity of all these misfortunes. They're real, concrete, even though they're absurd. Not even absurd. Mysterious. Incomprehensible. For the moment. Because we don't know what's behind all this. Perhaps one day we'll find out, one day. And then everything will seem logical, only too logical . . ."

"I live a fairly quiet life. I don't see what else I could do to protect myself."

"Your friend, he led a quiet life, too."

"Not entirely. He wasn't married, so that implies connections, affairs . . . But what can we do? No longer allow ourselves the most simple, the most natural actions? We might as well accept or even scoff at danger . . . In any case, you only die once. It's easier than dying a thousand times a day . . ."

"You see, that's it . . . You—you can live in despair. It even goads you on. Me, I just can't. I need stability. And a bare minimum of hope . . ."

She lights a cigarette, only to extinguish it almost immediately. She unbuttons her silk blouse. Her long, beautiful fingers gleam against the indigo silk, which casts a metallic reflection across her neck. She looks down; the tired blue grows dull, fades away.

"I admit, I'm nervous these days. But that guy, 'the worker Valentin Nanu,' as you call him, he irritates me. He's bad luck, if you want my opinion."

"Bad luck! But he fixed our blind . . . and by sheer good luck. Otherwise, it would've stayed broken for I don't know how long. That would have aggravated you a lot more than his turning up like that . . . which was bizarre, I admit."

"I've nothing against him. I just told you how I feel . . . He's got too many troubles. It's as though he were a magnet for disaster."

"So we distrust everyone? Fear everything? Everything that smacks of the unknown? We need to take risks as well. To reopen the wound every once in a while. To come into contact with unhealthy things. With dust, brutality, raw simplicity. We need antibodies acquired through contamination, believe me. From microbes and filth. We have to regenerate ourselves! Despite everything. Or else . . ."

"Perhaps, but some of us aren't up to it. Me, he gives me the creeps. And that's putting it mildly."

A long silence. They're too close to the dangerous terrain of truth, within an inch of turning aggressive. He's disturbed once again by her. The noble enigma of an unshakable pride? A strict and honorable code? But their neuroses are incompatible; his demands the stimulation of a break in routine, the speedy relief that comes from upsetting an equilibrium.

"He intrigues me more and more each time I see him, in spite of all his worries and pigheadedness. I don't have much contact with people like him. But there's still something lukewarm in me, something purulent, petty, resigned, something painful and rebellious that feels solidarity with guys like him. Even if only for a moment . . ."

"You're not going to start in on me again about my inability to relate to other people! Reproaching me for loathing confessions, hating to humiliate myself, brooding over suffering instead of rushing to offer sympathy! I refuse to indulge in compassion as long as I'm unable to make myself useful. Which is simply beyond me, because I can barely manage to keep going myself. Frightened by my own vulnerability . . .''

The husband goes off to his books; much later, around midnight, he goes out on the balcony. He gazes up at the night sky. He goes back inside. Distractedly, he studies the ceiling, the walls, the darkness. His thoughts become disjointed, chaotic. Blurred images on a phosphorescent screen of fuzzy cotton.

The second hand, tick-tock, swallows up sleep, digests insomnia. Insatiable, implacable toad. Tick-tock, tick-croak, croak-croak . . . and now it's climbing the wall. Fragile green feet. Huge, moist pop eyes, blinking rapidly, with only croak-what, croak-what for their viaticum. Jaws clamped shut, a steady rhythm, tick-hush, tock-shush. There are so many of them, they've multiplied, the wall is disappearing beneath their viscous, teeming mass. A wall of luminescent cotton wool, dozens of nosy periscopes beating out the same marshy, hellish cadence.

Little heads, all lined up next to one another. Identical faces, jeering, leering. He's sticking out his tongue—whoa! That's too much . . . What do you think you're doing, how did you get in among . . . ? Just a second, tick-tock, then he was gone. A frowning, ashen face. Sticking his tongue out, talk about gall! The deceitful toads couldn't have cared less, they'd disappeared, what did you expect . . . They didn't give a damn.

The screen is murky, greenish. Random flashes of lightning, white bubbles, red, bulbous shapes. The clock faces have vanished. So has the unexpected visitor. A seething, swampy wasteland from which rises a thick, glaucous fog.

Just a single second, tick, it's becoming an obsession, he's back again. Suddenly face to face once more with the strange visitor . . .

All dressed up. A navy-blue suit, good material, Chinese style, the Mao collar buttoned right up to the chin. A clean shave, hair *en brosse*. Getting ready, one would have thought, to attend some fancy ceremony . . . except that his hands—and they're large ones—are streaked with the stinking slime he's busy dredging from the sewer.

He bends low, plunging his arms deep into what looks like a dark pit. Each time he straightens up, he hauls out a fresh batch of excrement, which he carefully drops into the gutter, without staining his impeccable suit. He seems unperturbed by the astonished gaze of the passerby who's just appeared out of nowhere at his side. A gesture of bored resignation . . . which means that he still has a bit more to do, and he can't take care of anything else at the moment.

So he goes on leaning down, practically burying himself in his pit. Then he sits up and holds another double handful out for inspection—by no one—before tossing it neatly into the gutter. Another time, ten times, so many times. To the same rhythm. A robot, with great, dark, tranquil eyes.

Precise, perfectly executed movements that leave not a single wrinkle on the elegant party clothes or the fresh-shaven face, as ready as could be for the festivities. Again and once again and yet again, until the spectator feels dizzy, feels faint and nauseated out in the middle of this bog of a nightmare. Concentration is fading away, sapping his strength . . . A loss of contact, a slippery descent into cottony fog, collapse.

Then the voice of the worker Valentin Nanu: "Speak, say what you have to say. Get it all out, I'm listening."

A timid order, an expectant pause; now a kind of ironic indulgence, a staccato delivery: "Speak up, come on, say what you have to say, get it all out, I'm listening."

Despite this urging, he can't make the slightest sound. Not a syllable, zero, although the words are banging around somewhere, deep down, struggling to rise up and make themselves heard. Sounds strangled at birth . . . and yet they'd made a beginning, it seems, of some kind, enough for Valentin Nanu to notice, and he was even repeating snatches of sentences left unspoken.

The face was no longer visible, only the voice could be heard, falling in with his thoughts, only the large hands could be seen, emptying the cesspool, only the voice could be heard, translating the words of the man whose voice remained stilled.

"And so this poet, this gentleman, your friend, was found dead in his room. Stretched out on the couch, naked. Yes, yes, completely naked, I got that. I understood, you don't have to keep repeating it. Naked and dead, on the couch. Two glasses and a bottle of red wine on the table. All right, I heard you, it's not that hard to understand. Keep going, we'll see, come on, say what you have to say, I'm listening, I want to hear everything . . . Go on, I'm listening."

One couldn't see the face, only the large hands, and the toad he'd dredged up from the foul muck, the big hands cradling the frightened, stinking toad.

"He was supposed to attend a conference a few days later? Okay, I didn't quite get that, it wasn't exactly a conference. Oh, all right, an international symposium of poets, fine. So he had his passport, his ticket, everything. I heard you, the door was bolted on the inside. The neighbors and his mother, yes, yes . . . They broke down the door, I understand. His mother had come up from the country, poor woman, to see her son off on his trip abroad, yes, I understand. He hadn't been waiting for her at the station as usual. She was astonished, of course, absolutely astonished when she rang his doorbell and he didn't let her in. The neighbors, yes, then the neighbors, the forensic pathologist, the inquest, naturally. They didn't order an autopsy? His mother asked for one but they refused, I see. Did she insist on having one or just let it drop? You've got to be more specific, you know, so let's have it: did she insist or not? It's an important detail, after all, I should hear everything you've got to tell me . . ."

So he was instantaneously intercepting the thoughts of a person unable to utter a single word. He was instantaneously voicing the thoughts of the terrified person over there next to him and at the same time over here—and where's that? Somewhere . . . somewhere . . . in front of that cottony screen on which the nightmare is unfolding. To be here, who knows where, but also over there, which is where? Next to the drain opening . . . To say not a word, but to hear one's thoughts on a simultaneous sound

track . . . He knew everything, every single last thing . . .
The marks on the body, the burns from cigarettes stubbed
out on the skin, the lipstick on the rim of the glass, all the
grotesque details . . . Certainly, I understand, a very private
person, taciturn, yes, yes, too reserved, yes, someone
staid, very serious, a loner, of course, a solitary man. In
good health, no doubt about that, perfect health . . . Pardon
your son who has died without confession, without the
last sacraments, receive him into the Kingdom of Heaven
. . . Pardon your son who has left us unshriven, without
extreme unction, chanted the priest before the coffin, yes,
yes, so few people at that strange funeral, useless, those
visits to the cemetery, your lady's too emotional, she
shouldn't keep going back there. No one has ever figured
out that sort of mystery, your wife's torturing herself for
nothing . . . Without confession, without extreme unction,
that's right. Naturally, hearsay, vicious rumors, people are
like that, cowards and scandalmongers. And then that bottle, very suspicious, definitely, it's all a muddle, what's the
use . . .

He tried to stem this flood surging out of his control.
Cold sweat, a slow descent, drawn by thin threads, so
thin, helplessness and befuddlement. Time stopped, cut to
ribbons, the body fraying, surrendering . . . until where
when how, the tinkling bell . . . a twittering, a chiming,
a mountain spring, the booming monastery gong, bells in
the sheepfold, jingle bells on a horse's harness, a school
bell, a church bell, cow bells, a child's rattle . . . the doorbell. The doorbell's ringing.

Silence. And . . . the doorbell rings again. A timid buzz,

---

a faint lapping, a rattling toy. He clutches the bedposts, he must feel the bedposts. Something solid to lean on, proof of purchase, a guarantee one won't be torn away and swept into the void. He feels around at the foot of the bed, pulls on his jeans, his shirt, his slippers. He staggers, still half asleep, toward the door. Yes, it's morning, it's light out, tick-tock, the alarm clock on the bedside table, tick-tock. Daylight, another day, off we go.

The man stands, shyly, far from the door. How, how did . . . when just a few moments ago . . . back there, what were you doing in that other place . . . and now, so quickly . . . Who knows if . . . The man stands, silently, far from the door. He leans down to collect his toolbox. A few steps and that's all it takes, he's inside. A slight nod in greeting, that's it, he's inside.

"How did you . . . Listen, there's no need to . . . Don't take off your shoes . . . Put it down right there . . . The bottle . . . the bottle of red wine, yes, it was half, only half full, that's what's suspicious. It had been left uncorked, and that is just something he never would have done. Ab-so-lute-ly nev-er, you hear me? Anyone who knew him knows that . . . No, there's no need . . . Yes, I got out, but only just . . . The swamp, sleep, sliding, yes, yes . . . So, come in, I'll make some coffee. A cup of coffee, yes, that'll help . . ."

One drinks coffee; the other, tea. They exchange furtive glances, ill at ease. The handyman replies without enthusiasm to inquiries concerning his health, his lawsuit, the latest presidential decree ordering that apartments may not be heated to more than 54°F. He sets the same bundle of papers down on the table. He repairs a switch on the desk lamp, reglues some tiles in the bathroom.

"I'll dismantle the glazing on the balcony, what do you say?"

"No, it'll wait . . . I've filed an appeal. There are tens of thousands of people in Bucharest in the same position, who've enclosed their balconies to gain a bit of space. They had permission from the municipal authorities. Now they're being forced to tear everything down. Because someone, and we know who, took a walk around the city one day when he was in a bad mood, waved his hand, and said, 'Get rid of all that glass on those balconies!' In our case, the previous tenants had enclosed the balcony by the time we moved here eight years ago. The work had already been done. We have the papers to prove it. The people down at city hall can just come and tear everything out themselves! It seems that's what they're doing, after first raking in outrageous fines."

The little man doesn't seem to be paying attention. He washes his hands. He shakes them vigorously over the sink to dry them. When he's handed a hundred-lei bill, he appears not to notice. But he pockets it in a twinkling, without a word.

"I'm in a hurry, the attorney's waiting for me."

"Which attorney?"

"Well, yours, the one who lives in your building. Right above you, except that he's got two apartments he's made into one. As big as yours and the teacher's put together."

"Oh yes, I know who you mean. He's the president of the tenants' association. Very polite, well-mannered."

"But stingy, take it from me. I've been doing odd jobs in his place for years. An attorney . . . I told myself, you never know when you might need one. With that guy, I have to haggle each time until I'm exhausted. It wears him out, too, but he never gives in . . ."

He disappears, the worker Valentin Nanu, just as he had appeared, here one moment, gone the next. You can't even find him again at night, back in that stinking fog of darkness he was trying to muck out.

It's winter again, in the afternoon, when a ring at the doorbell is a sure sign. Someone rang, no one rang, it's as though someone rang . . . as though one hadn't dared to ring. And then there he is, standing away from the door, backed up against the opposite wall. The distorted image glimpsed through the spy-hole shows him perfectly: a gray jacket, too tight, with worn lapels, a clean white shirt, pants twisted and gathered at his waist, arms hanging down, too long for his short, bony frame. Gaunt, with deep-set eyes. His hair *en brosse* . . . and those huge, those ancient shoes, so patiently polished over the years. And no overcoat.

He knows he's being studied through the Judas. He approaches, he murmurs, "It's me."

The door opens a crack. The woman, that lovely woman, stares out at him with frightened eyes. "Oh, it's you . . . I'm sorry, my husband isn't home just now."

The apparition doesn't budge an inch.

"And it's so cold out, too . . . You should have telephoned, I'd have told you to come by later in the day. My husband won't be home until this evening, but he'll call you. Or you can call him tomorrow morning."

"But . . . it's just that . . . It's you I wanted to talk to . . ."

"Me?" She hesitates. "Well, come in, then, if you like."

The words lack spirit, as though she regrets saying them even as she speaks. As for him, he's in no hurry. He lingers an instant in the doorway, picks up his heavy toolbox, another step and there, he's inside, shoes already off and in his hand.

"Come in, come in. Sit down here, I'll be right back."

She does return quickly, in fact, wearing a large, bright red housecoat. It's cold in the apartment; the blanket she had wrapped around herself before the doorbell rang is lying on the couch.

"I thought of you . . . because you've got a job. Perhaps you could find me something, where you work, or you might hear about an opening from someone you know . . ."

"What kind of . . . I mean, since you're already employed, I don't see how . . ."

"But it's not for me."

It's his daughter he's talking about. Soon she'll be finished with school, either trade or business school, it's not clear which he means. If the lady could find her a quiet job, in an office, among nice people . . .

"They're not hiring, where I work . . . They keep laying people off . . . They're running out of excuses for letting them go. First it was your sociopolitical background, then it was your material situation, those who didn't have any

---

175

children, and now . . . I just don't know. But your daughter will be assigned to a position, all the young people who graduate from a school are given a job."

"Sure, they're going to send her the hell out into the sticks somewhere. She'll be posted to a lousy factory, she'll live in a dorm for female workers, I know how it goes. It won't be long before someone takes advantage of her. Off among strangers, with that kind of job, these days . . . She's a child, she has no idea what's in store for her. And besides, her health isn't good at all."

Silence. The woman shivers, crosses her arms over her chest.

"If necessary, I'll . . . I mean, I'm ready to pay these guys what it takes, if I have to. That's how it is everywhere you look today, I know that. I'm prepared. I put a little money aside, on purpose. I need to find somebody in charge somewhere who'll fix things up . . ."

"To tell you the truth," says the woman, now speaking in a direct and friendly manner, "to tell you the truth, I'm not too close to the higher-ups at my job. You're right, that's how these things work, as you say, but I don't really know those people in my office. I'll try to look around for you, I promise, yes. I promise you I'll ask around, I might come up with something. Call me in a little while. Or rather, no, my husband will give you a call if we have any news."

One Wednesday in March, the worker Valentin Nanu is busy taking down the glass enclosure around the apartment balcony, which has a view of the greenery in the

Botanical Garden. Thick glass, a very heavy metal frame, deeply anchored in the wall. Frail but stubborn, he sweats for hours, wielding his hammer, screwdrivers, pincers, blowtorch. Even after the sections are dismantled, after so much effort, they still seem too heavy for him. He keeps going, though, straining under the weight of the panels, which leave streaks of rust on his overalls.

"Good steel and thick glass. You should have saved this marvel. They don't make anything as solid as this nowadays."

"There was nothing I could do, I told you. The order came from the very top. The courts have cold feet, they don't want to hear a single word about arguments or appeals."

"The courts weren't the place to handle it . . . since they're useless anyhow. You should have found someone who would've lost track of the paperwork. You would've slipped him a nice little piece of change under the table and the paper would've gotten lost. Lots of balconies have been rescued like that."

"I know, but they're on the garden side, they don't look out on the street. The First Lady doesn't see them."

"Courts, they make you sick. Nothing but lies and dirty money."

"But you went through all that, too. I advised you to give up, and you wouldn't. I didn't think you'd be able to get anywhere. You won, though. And you still weren't satisfied. You went back again."

"Well, as long as you can hand out money right and left, you can manage like that, with underlings. In my

case, that wasn't working anymore . . . I told you the story
. . . I was used to taking on the small fry first and then
working my way up to the big shots. You didn't need to
pay anymore . . . In the old days, you just needed a fucking
big mouth, excuse the expression. Now it's bribes everywhere, only money talks. You take this as far as it will
go, until the point where . . . the point where money
doesn't mean anything anymore. Then you need something else. It's hard to find a way out. You realize you've
come to a staircase different from all the others you've
climbed. The old step-by-step routine no longer works,
that's all."

Tired, crouching down on the cement strewn with bits
of glass and metal, he speaks quickly, without looking up.
"So that's where I am now. After a whole . . . a whole
lifetime of troubles. I see that this is what I've come to. I
need a hand, I need a hand from someone big. But I can't
see who, I just can't. Luckily, above all these staircases,
and all these devils, there's still someone . . ."

A long silence. But he's not sure he's made himself clear,
he feels the need to be more precise. "There has to be some
hope left somewhere, or else . . . Who's still looking out
for us? Everything's going to hell, everything . . ."

"Are you a believer, perhaps? That's a question I hadn't
asked myself. I mean, I hadn't wondered if . . ."

"Well, what do I know . . . otherwise . . . what've we
got left? We've lost everything, you know. It's all gone.
That's the problem."

He accepts a cup of coffee! He drinks the steaming liquid
in quick little swallows.

"Did you get a job lined up for that girl of yours? For your daughter, I mean."

The workman stiffens, his cup held motionless in the air, no reply.

"Have you found something? You were worried, weren't you? You seemed quite upset about it."

Valentin Nanu emerges from his few seconds of torpor, sets down his cup. He gets to his feet, goes to pack up his tools, quickly, then he changes his mind, wipes his hands on his overalls.

"She got married, what can I say? I wanted to spare her that, help her find her way. An idiot, that's all. And now . . . the idiot's teamed up with another idiot. They had to rush to prove they were idiots through and through. Too bad. So, now . . . in poverty up to their necks. She'll figure it out real quick . . . Tied to the grindstone with a man but no money. Too bad, that's not what I wanted, it's a pity."

Now he's in a hurry. He finishes putting away his tools, sweeps up, deftly pockets the two hundred lei. His coat's on, he nods, that's it. He was there, now he's gone. No time! Times are hard, no time to lose.

. . . He returns, but at night. More and more often, at night. He approaches slowly, through a sticky, steamy tunnel. His figure grows larger, comes closer, becomes familiar: short, frail, with long arms, a youthful brush cut, and a hard look in his eyes.

These absurd nocturnal encounters happen suddenly but are preceded by a murky incubation period: sleep, insomnia, tick-tock. Staring vacantly at the wall opposite the bed. More and more cotton wool on the phosphorescent screen. A blurry image slowly takes shape, grows larger, becomes clear.

. . . In white overalls, like a parachutist. A white helmet in his right hand. Approaching . . . Unbelievable—he's approaching the speaker's platform. The huge deserted public square stretches out endlessly in all directions.

The silhouette of the diminutive orator stands out crisply on the black rostrum. He doesn't move a muscle. You can see his pale, angular face, his dry lips. Standing stiffly, he delivers packets of words, in equal portions. In a weak, monotonous voice.

"We've had enough of your flattery! Liars, from all around the world! Leave us in peace, liars! Stop tricking us out in gold braid and angels' wings!"

The screen quivers frenetically, matching the rhythm of his sentences, but his voice remains low and even. The screen undulates . . . oily, green mud . . . black foam.

"Into the flames with our gold braid, our angels' wings! The proletariat doesn't want to unite anymore! We've had it up to here with these masquerades, leave us alone. We want bread and sleep, that's all. We don't want any more of your promises or your persecution! Tell the truth about yourself and about us! Our own little everyday truth! We're poor, weak, lost creatures, no better than anyone else! We snuffle about in our pigsty, like you, we clutter up the earth. Leave us to hell, leave us to swarm all over the planet! Naked, without your uniforms. Leave us alone . . ."

His pathetic appeals are broadcast by hundreds of loudspeakers. A timid, monotonous voice, on hundreds of loudspeakers. There is no one in the square, only loudspeakers. He lowers his head slightly, brings his hand to his mouth, coughs. Once, twice . . . The loudspeakers repeat, once, twice. One time, another time, hundreds of times, in hundreds of metal funnels, on hundreds of poles.

Silence, for a moment. There—the words are coming back, little by little, an even murmur.

"Leave us alone, liars! We don't want to rule the world, we don't want to be its salvation . . . Tear off these heavenly wings, toss our gold braid into the fire! Stop insinuating yourselves among us, stop speaking in our name. We've had enough of your promises and your terror. Get us out of these uniforms . . . Our truth is so much smaller . . ."

The cough drags on, amplified. A tumultuous, jabbering cannonade from all the loudspeakers. The screen has gone dark, too dark to see a thing. But then he's back, sitting on a stool this time, in the middle of the square.

"The window blind is fixed, sir. Don't worry, I did a good job . . ." A sugary voice, a humble procession of sly, sarcastic words. "Was I an interesting case? You tried to listen to me as a philosopher, to understand me . . . An experiment, this voice from the underground? A mole who amused you for a moment? How annoying, sir. You started avoiding me? You can't help me, man, we can't help each other. They've taught us fear and selfishness, and so we're all off, each in his own corner."

He rubs his hands nervously. His white Adidas keep kicking the white helmet sitting at his feet. In his hands is a round toad, as big as his paratrooper's helmet, and . . .

he's already tossed it into that white pot-shaped thing
. . . He takes aim, gives a quick kick, and the missile is
out of sight. Apparently reassured, from then on he stares,
I mean really stares, at his audience, he takes up the entire
screen of the nightmare. He runs his hands over his brush
cut, wipes them on the front of his overalls.

"You're not strong enough for my tomb. You've already given up visiting the poet's, and he was a friend of
yours. Perhaps I'll make up my mind to do it, to blow it
all sky high. The hell with everything! Everything, everything, in our cemetery . . ."

The screen goes dark, lights up again. It'll light up again
tomorrow night, of course . . . The worker Valentin Nanu
no longer has any spare time except at night. His days are
too full—one fucking nuisance after another, his damn job,
dealing with all this shit. It's only at night that he still visits
his friends, pops in on them with his astonishing routine.

In fact, these nocturnal visits are becoming more and
more frequent. And there's no way to prevent them. Sleep-
ing pills, tranquilizers, late-night reading, booze—all useless.

Day, on the other hand, brings some measure of peace
and forgetfulness. Even his name isn't mentioned very
often anymore. One hears questions like these much more
rarely now: "So, whatever happened to him, that worker
of yours? He's forgotten all about us?" The husband
doesn't answer. He doesn't want to talk about his secret
meetings at night, he knows his wife is too fragile for this
sort of thing. He avoids answering, just as he avoids ar-
ranging to have the handyman come around, in spite of

all the stuff that's falling apart in their home. He claims he can't get hold of him. And so the worker Valentin Nanu no longer shows up during the day at the apartment near the Botanical Garden, and his name no longer comes up except during those inevitable nocturnal tempests he brews with such cruel indifference. And yet . . . Suddenly, just like the first time, when no one was expecting it: the doorbell.

A timid ring. The lightest touch, barely brushing across the skin of the morning, almost imperceptible, as before. After a long pause, the sound is repeated. Finally, something or somebody moves, in the quiet apartment. Dragging steps scuff over to the door.

A long gray raincoat, glued to the wall, across the landing. Above the tight collar, a pale, wasted face. A stubble of black beard. Raw suffering still glittering in the angry, brooding eyes.

They look at each other a long time, and then some more, carefully, each one waiting for release.

"They killed my wife," mutters the little gray man.

The ensuing silence grows almost palpably heavy.

"They killed my wife. I had to . . . I wanted to tell you."

"Come in, come in, please," stammers the other man.

The raincoat on the hook, the shoes on the floor, by the door. His hands are shaking. That rough beard . . . His gaunt cheeks have been invaded by a wild growth of black beard . . . He sits down immediately without waiting to be invited. He tells his story quickly, in choppy, hesitant phrases. A changed voice, hoarse; whenever he stops talking, the silence is painful.

It was Tuesday morning, March 16, 1985. His wife had died the week before, at the hospital. In accordance with the latest presidential decrees, she'd had the right to request an abortion, since she was over forty years old and already had four children. She'd had to obtain official permission from the authorities, however, and the proceedings had been complicated by new provisions, still somewhat confusing, designed to raise the age beyond which abortions would be permissible. Finally, all the papers were signed on a Friday. In the opinion of her doctors, the patient's case was neither serious nor pressing, and the operation was scheduled for the following Monday. By noon on Monday, she was dead.

"I'd promised the surgeon money, of course. I know how these things work. But seeing how poorly dressed I was, he probably thought I was broke. Those bastards in their white coats! Supposed to help people, them? Not on your life . . . All they think about is stashing away as much money as they can get their hands on . . . An infection, can you believe it! An unexpected complication, that's what they're claiming, those sons of bitches! They're all covering for one another. The nurse on duty left early on Saturday; on Sunday the doctor only looked in on the most serious cases . . . as usual, what do you expect. I spoke to the two women who were in the beds next to hers, they know the truth. I wrote everything down. They won't get away with it like that, they won't get away with it!"

He'd brought a whole file. Medical certificate, death

---

certificate. Statements from the doctors and nurses. Memo of his interviews with the other pregnant women. Report sent to the city's health department. Report sent to the Ministry of Health. Report sent to the Supreme Court. Report sent to the World Health Organization. Report sent to the Patriarch of the Romanian Orthodox Church. To the Secretary General of the United Nations.

He apologizes at length for this visit. He'd had no intention of ever bothering them again . . . Just a prayer . . . if he might be allowed to ask . . . from the lady . . . If your missus . . . if she still goes to the cemetery, for your friend the poet, she might perhaps also stop at the tomb of Valeria Nanu. It would please her so much, the poor woman. He'd often told her about that lovely lady and her kind husband.

The husband can't stand the cemetery. One Sunday, however, he goes there with his wife. They stroll around a long time on the side paths, to the right, to the left, before heading for the two graves. At the modest tomb of their friend the poet, bare of offerings, they leave a bouquet of flowers. They find the other grave at the far end of the cemetery, near the fountain. A massive slab of imposing black marble, covered with flowers and candles. They add their sprigs of lily-of-the-valley to the tributes and hurry away.

The visitor reappears that night. In the small hours, at the uncertain approach of dawn. In suit and tie. His face stern, clean-shaven. He explains in great detail, but with few gestures, how he intends to reorganize the running of the establishment. Cleanliness, order, supervision! New schedule: limited hours, but greater convenience. Support services, competent personnel. A well-thought-out, meticulously planned project . . .

He returns the following evening with additional information. And again the next, with ever more elaborate explanations.

Husband and wife are growing increasingly irritable, ill at ease. An unhealthy situation. They almost avoid looking at each other, and speak only when necessary. Sometimes they huddle together at night, but after a few moments they withdraw tensely, each to his own side of the bed, one on the left, the other on the right.

One day, the husband takes the initiative. Simple good manners: to return all those visits, see his guest again, at his new place of work.

At night, the cemetery is well lighted. Everything is spotless. The plots are nicely cared for, pedestrian traffic has been efficiently organized, the tombs are clearly numbered and easily located on maps of each section. Flower shop, refreshment concession, a checkroom for one's belongings—nothing has been forgotten. Capable management for the public good. Open only at night, so that people won't be cutting into their workday, neglecting their family and other obligations. The entrance fee is stiff: a hundred lei. But worth it, considering the quality of the services provided. And then, there's only one price, general admission, no exceptions, no discounts pegged to age, sex, class. Here, instead of proliferating, injustices, machinations, and influence-peddling are completely unknown. No effort has been spared to guarantee profitability and self-sufficiency, in the interest of the general welfare. Otherwise, it would be chaos all over again, bankruptcy, a shambles.

In fact, the improvement has been outstanding, and remarkably rapid. Provision has even been made for friendly conversations, like the one taking place at this moment . . . Any subject at all may be discussed, for here there is no room for fear. But idle chatter should be kept to a minimum, there's no time to waste on empty words. There are constant, varied, and pressing matters to be attended to, explains the manager, shyly running his big hand across his close-cropped hair. It's important not only to maintain the plots but also to show the proper solicitude for their tenants. You can't have one without the other. Absolute peace and quiet must be assured. Silence, regeneration. Regeneration, future, new order. A period of recovery, as I suppose you've already gathered. Reconstitution and preparation. Preparation for a new time. We speak to them regularly about this, we prepare them for the crucial moment. Here they're at rest, able both to understand why they were defeated and to find a way to recover everything they've lost. Here, no more fear, no more terror, no more lies. They've got the time, a lot more time than we have. They're calm, untroubled. Our efforts on their behalf will be rewarded, I'm sure. We speak to each one, we assist every one of them. You'll see how well prepared they are when they get going again, you'll see for yourself . . . The tranquillity they so longed for guarantees complete recovery, believe me. Really new people for a new time. Honesty, order, order and cleansing. New times.

His face truly glows with tranquillity. No longer rigid with tension, his features have somehow acquired more clarity and resolution. His countenance, radiant with faith in the future, fills the entire screen.

Yes, a deep tranquillity indeed. Tranquillity is boiling away, its red vapor clouding the screen, which quivers under the intense light of the fire. Impossible to see anything anymore.

But here's a whole new morning coming up, ignorant of what may happen, peeping through the huge windows of the calendar. Tick-tock, singsongs the toad on the bedside table.

"That light again, a different window. Another blind must be broken . . ."

The blind . . . the blind . . . the word whispered over and over, the voice drowsy, slurred with sleep.

A childish murmur. The click that starts the great wheel of day rolling once again.

THE TRENCHCOAT

"FROM NOW ON, YOU DON'T GIVE YOUR REPORT IN AN office. They've got a new system, they've found something more original," Alexandru I. Stoian was to explain a few weeks later to his friend, the Guileless One.

"In people's apartments? Private conversations with informers? What's that supposed to mean? The interview's more relaxed?" A guileless question from the Guileless One's wife.

Confusion . . . The confused voice of a confused time, a jumble of voices, the murmur of time. The panting, the choking, the sputtering called time.

"With the permission of the tenants, obviously. Confidential agents, or forced to act as such. Two sets of keys and meetings set up in advance." Further details, in the concise style of the code, would come from Al. I. Stoian, known as Ali.

Voices of the times, the modern chorus, the cacophony of the present to which the Narrator listens, attentive to the timbre of this muffled rumble.

"Well, it's possible that they use these apartments even without the permission of the tenants, when nobody's home. It's possible, but I don't think so," Ali would add doubtfully, evasively, cautiously, in the style of the times.

But all this was still in the realm of the future. The future: conjugation of uncertainty?

The future: small and immediate. Already present, already past, already small, shrunken . . . enormous.

For the moment, the present means this rainy Sunday evening. A dark, dense deluge. The city has collapsed underground, dozens, hundreds of meters underground. A spectral subterranean site buried beneath the watery night.

The Stoians' car moves slowly and painfully through the flooded, shadowy streets.

"We wound up having no choice. You kept inventing excuses, but here you are, finally," complains Ioana provokingly.

The couple in the back seat are quiet; Ioana keeps at it.

"Sorry, but personally, I'm glad. Other people's troubles make me glad? Well, at least we won't be alone. We'll all have to suffer together through the boring conversation and Madame Beldeanu's snootiness."

"Yes, but there are compensations," remarks the husband from behind the wheel. "The dinner, the music. Don't skip over the positive side. Don't forget the positive side, comrade teacher; it's important for educators, dear comrade."

"Have you noticed how dinner parties have been disappearing over the last few years?" Ioana starts to blabber, like her husband. "A Latin people like ours, so addicted to conversation and celebrations? Exhaustion, depression . . . not even enough energy left to improvise a potluck supper. Then there are the long distances, and the buses that never run on time . . . But it's the desire, above all, it's the desire to get together that has disappeared. Everyone stuck at home, no one going anywhere. So we ought to be grateful to our precious hosts. A rare chance to get out and see people. An adventure, that's what it is."

"Me . . . well, I would've accepted their invitation a long time ago," the soft voice of Felicia observes, floating up from the back seat. "After all, they've been trying for years. A courtesy visit, basically, and *basta*. So they don't think we've got anything against them. The problem was that . . ."

"The problem was that the Kid didn't want to. The Kid can't stand Lady Di, I know, he's told us all often enough. He can't stand her, and he avoids that husband of hers. A purely preventive measure, I know. A sanitary precaution, yes, I've heard the whole rigmarole. We also feel no undying love for the Beldeanus. But Ali couldn't very well refuse Bazil. Not when he's a colleague on the editorial staff, it's just not done."

The gears grind, the headlights poke their stubby beams out into the drenched black streets. Advancing cautiously across town, a long and difficult journey. A deep-sea dive, one might think, with colonies of organisms bursting into view for a brief instant, sinister monstrosities outlined against an unpredictable fluid vastness. But here, inside the diving bell, it's really cozy. Ioana wears her hair boyishly short, in what's called a typhus cut, which looks rather good on her, while Felicia is in her new black mohair vest, so perfectly chic, Italian, isn't it nice to be cruising along lazily underwater while, all around, nature is putting on a show of vitality and grandeur.

"Bazil's a great guy, I'm telling you," announces Ali enthusiastically from the driver's seat. "Two weeks ago, I went with him to a teaching farm outside Bucharest. The guy in charge was a former buddy of his at the Political Institute. He keeps him in chickens, and that's not all. Every once in a while he needs Bazil to do him a little favor in return, obviously. A journalist, in the capital— you never know . . . He supplies him with chickens, but also with the latest jokes about . . . ah . . . you know who. He telephoned Bazil to let him know that he was sending the car from the farm to pick him up, but Bazil didn't want that. Forget it, he tells his pal, we'll manage on our own, thanks anyway."

"Uh, a journalist, in the capital, who knows," comes an echoing purr from Felicia, just to show she's keeping track.

"Of course, Bazil invites me along on this chicken chase, and I can hardly refuse, naturally. These days we'd be happy with sparrows, as long as we didn't have to spend the best years of our lives waiting on line for them. So we set out Tuesday morning in Bazil's car. Now, I was wondering what he was up to. There are people today who're ready to kill for a drop of gas. Thirty liters a month! That's not even enough to get to the office, I mean, really . . ."

Embarrassed silence. Could that be an allusion to this evening's gas consumption? Ioana rummages nervously in her purse as though she hadn't heard that last remark. A gaffe, Ali felt it immediately, but there's nothing he can do about it. So he goes on in the same vein.

"We stop in front of the first gas station. Comrade Beldeanu gets out his press card, of course. He starts explaining that he's on an assignment, he needs gas. The attendants couldn't care less. They've heard it all. The only argument they listen to is a big fat tip, and even that doesn't always do the trick. Nothing impresses them anymore, not the press, not the Party, nothing. Talk about blasé, they are blasé to the core, you have to come up with a real stunner to jolt them out of their apathy. Bazil doesn't admit defeat, obviously. He insists and finally asks permission to telephone Comrade Colonel Adam, the chief economic watchdog in that area, everyone knows who he is. Well, you can imagine, they don't wait around for that phone call, naturally—they give him a full tank. Now, that's Bazil all over! Unbeatable! You know how he introduces himself? He's not Comrade Vasile Beldeanu, like before. Bazil. That's all, the American way. The name's been Hispanicized . . . but the style's cutting edge, very U.S.A. Simple and direct. Bazil, journalist. On the way back, what do you think? He pulls the same thing again. Goes home with a full tank, naturally. Unbeatable! To look at him, you'd think he was nobody in particular. But a real go-getter, I'm telling you. Even that house he has. Right in the middle of Embassy Row! And as for what we'll be eating and drinking tonight . . . Just wait. You're going to forget what kind of a world we live in, you'll see."

"Stop blabbing and pay attention to the road! It's pitch-dark, and with this rain, we'll end up wrapped around a tree," warns Ioana sharply. "It's like wartime, like a black-out. In the streets, the apartments, everywhere you look, darkness . . . The elevators all suddenly go on the fritz, then the running water comes back when everyone has given up on it. The children refuse to ride in elevators, did you know that? No food, no electricity, nothing. Dorin, our son, recited the new children's patriotic oath: 'I'll be tall, healthy, clean and neat, without ever needing a bite to eat . . .' "

Laughter at this seemingly recent joke. Laughter, jokes, signs of the times. All around them, the urgent and festive forces of nature, and here, in the torpedo, a sudden clear-ing. Ioana's new suit, her long, white gloves, her waspish sting form a contrast with the driver's moderating role, with Felicia's proletarian Mona Lisa smile and her limpid radio announcer's voice.

"That's what they'd really like. Not to be asked for food, money, heating, nothing—nothing," continues the wasp.

They, meaning *them*, meaning *Him*, the audience knows it.

"Speaking of children, what's happened to the Child, hmm? He hasn't said one word, he must be bored stiff by our chatter."

"Not at all, no, really," stammers a baritone voice in the back seat.

"Not at all, not at all . . . So why don't you say something? Well, poor Bazil isn't a gorilla, just your basic pig. But Dina Eisberg . . . that is her name, isn't it?" asks the wasp, swiveling around toward the man in the back seat, who continues to stare with indifference out the black window, rippling with rain. "Eisberg, I'm sure of it. Icicle, that's what Ali calls her, and he's an expert on refrigerators. She freezes everything she touches. Unless it's the other way around? You never know . . . It might very well turn out to be the other way around. Well, what have you got to say about it? You're from the same background, after all, you've known Miss Goldberg for a long time. Or is it Salzberg, Süssberg? Now that I think about it, it must be Süssberg . . ."

Felicia tries to stem the attack.

"Dina thinks very highly of him, if you want to know. When I run into her, which isn't often, the first thing she says, every time, is . . . how smart he was in school. The local genius, more or less."

You'd never guess she was talking about someone right there, yet it would seem that this absent mind is the unique receiver, the only one listening.

"Yeah, sure," mumbles Ioana, without turning around this time, studiously contemplating the dripping windshield. "And why, may I ask, doesn't the Boy want to see his former friend and classmate again? Watch out, Felicia, there might be something behind all this."

"No, not this time." Felicia laughs childishly. "No, that's not it. We just try to stay away from the new class, that's all."

More embarrassed silence . . . Could that insinuation . . . A blunder, perhaps, who knows . . . But Ioana wastes no time in returning to the attack.

"An after-effect of puberty, why not? Those are the most dangerous love affairs. If they crop up again, later in life. Nuclear explosion, catastrophe, end of the world. You never know . . . What does the Kid think about all this? We'd like the Kid's opinion."

The Kid, the Guileless One, the Learned One . . . prolongs the silence. Finally, the baritone voice announces, "No danger, no problem—I've sampled all life's little temptations in my time. Well, almost all . . ."

"Will you stop squabbling!" Opportune interruption once again from the quiet one's wife. "Don't forget you promised me we wouldn't stay late. I'm taking an early train tomorrow and I have to get up at dawn, I told you. Otherwise, I'd never get back by Tuesday. Monday is all I have off, the boss only gave me Monday. Ioana, you know what it's like having to deal with Comrade Chibrit. I don't want us to hang around forever tonight."

Next come questions about Felicia's mother, who's ill, off in some tiny Danubian village. Comments are made about the plight of the elderly, who are being refused aid by hospitals and ambulances . . . The mingling voices of the evening, the confused muttering, evasions, humor and indulgence and pretense . . . Ioana's poisonous barbs and Ali's strategy of mollification and Felicia's contemplative distance . . . For you, the observer, the Guileless One . . . The miracle of the instant already past, the deep, inaudible breath of the instant to come, chance and void and question: the uncertainty.

The Stoians' car proceeds quietly, with infinite caution. As it approaches a wealthy neighborhood, some lights can now be seen, imagine that, the avenue grows wider, the streets are more and more elegant, the landscape becomes gracious, what's this now, sentry boxes, before which stand militiamen, chilled to the bone. The roads, lanes, discreet little alleys interweave freely, leading at last to homes and gardens.

The car has barely enough time to brake in front of the armed guard who suddenly heaves into view. Ali lowers the window, the sentry leans down, checks the identity card, listens to the explanations: the Beldeanu family behind the embassy, in the courtyard, all the way in the back, friends, invited for the evening. Yes, he knows the Beldeanus, he knows the lady and gentleman, or rather, Comrade Beldeanu, of course. A snappy salute, yes, they may proceed.

"It's not next to the American embassy or the French embassy, only the Ghanaian embassy. But, all the same, it's not bad, you'll see," says Ali, as though trying to boost his passengers' spirits.

The car turns to the left, past the sentry box, into the courtyard, near the clump of trees, turns to the right, here we are.

"This is it, we're here. This is the house."

A last moment of hesitation. The passengers don't dare leave the vehicle. They're still staring doubtfully at the lustrous black night welling out of the deep sky, the deep and troubled waters of an ocean without moon or stars.

"Okay, everyone out now," orders Ioana. "Tuck your head under your umbrella, huddle in your raincoat, let's go. Quickly, come on, just a few steps and we'll be on dry land."

And yes, in fact, only two, three, four, five strides bring them right to the door. Ali leans firmly, insistently, one, two, three, four, five times on the doorbell.

The heavy door of solid wood springs open. There on the threshold, with open arms, stands Don Bazil.

"I'm so happy you've come! Too bad about the weather . . . Make yourselves at home, put your things there, on the coat tree. It's quite comfy in here, we've got everything we need to help us forget about the rest. Rainy outside, cozy inside. Come in, why don't you, come on in."

Very pleasant, it's true, toasty warm, with big electric radiators everywhere you look. And the house, so spacious, so bright, and the furniture, yes, yes, white furniture and pink furniture, amazing, who would have expected that, these days . . . So much elegance and bad taste and prosperity and such a warm atmosphere, isn't it . . . And here's Dina, emerging from the bedroom, coming down the stairs in an evening gown and matching turban of yellow velvet. Hugs all around, I'm telling you. Only the Kid manages to complicate this joyful reunion. Dina goes to greet him, smiling, opening her arms, but her guest simply holds out his hand. He's never been able to stand her, has he, that painted scarecrow, whose slightest gesture betrays a certain conventional theatricality—no, he's never been able to bear her. But Lady Di is unflappable, and slowly, ceremoniously, she extends her hand to him. The Kid bows quite low, kisses her hand, then keeps her slender fingers in the hollow of his own small paw, as though to study her manicured nails, before consenting at last to a brief formal embrace.

"Since this is the first time you've come here," says Di, turning to Felicia, "we must show you the house."

And so a tour of the premises gets under way. Vasile's office. Madame's boudoir. ("Just a former pantry, that's all," explains their hostess modestly, opening the door to the pretty little room with its sofa and mirror.) The kitchen, the huge storage cupboard with its gleaming shelves, the gigantic refrigerator. ("These days, when you can't just go to the corner store to buy what you need, you're lost without a fridge and ample storage space, so we're reduced to stashing away food like barbarians in caves.") The living room, the bedrooms, the sumptuous bathroom, pink and white tiles, look at that. Everything clean, shining, spotless, charming.

"What'll you have, whisky or vodka?" asks Bazil, returning to his role of the attentive host. "The two super-powers! So, which will it be? The capitalist imperialists? You bet. We've had a bellyful of Big Brother, we prefer the imperialists. For the moment, just for the moment. Bastards, same as the others, but that's human nature, to crave illusion, novelty. So, whisky?"

The gentlemen acquiesce; their wives hesitate.

"For the ladies we have a liqueur, if they'd rather. Imported from Cuba, marvelously delicious, you bet. Unless you'd prefer some other aperitif?"

Felicia smiles, yes, she'd prefer some vermouth. Ioana declines with a sharp little wave. No, Ioana wants vodka.

"Then I'll allow myself to join you, old militant that I am," announces Comrade Bazil gallantly.

Lady Di makes another entrance, from the kitchen this time, rolling a tea cart in front of her. Tiny hors d'oeuvres, as big as thimbles, on a large silver tray. Minuscule canapés, with sardines, tarama, cheese, ham. She passes in front of everyone, in front of Ioana, in front of Felicia, in front of Ali, in front of Bazil, in front of the Guileless One. Each of them chooses one, no, on second thought, two morsels. They taste, they smile, they're amazed, they're thrilled, they're in ecstasy, the Child nods away along with the others, yum, excellent, mute approval from the Guileless One, who can't take his eyes off the hostess's hands. A mouthful, that's how long the miracle lasts, a mouthful. Short, savory, sinful, a brief but exquisite pleasure. Have another, why don't you, do have another, no one can resist, yum, the cries of delight are convincing, yes indeed, they flow as freely as everyone's mouth is watering, full of appetizers and saliva. All help themselves again, again and again.

Dina returns from the kitchen. Another tea cart, another silver tray. Cunning little pastry shells, fresh from the oven, marvelously warm and tender, filled with cheese, with meat, with spinach, spiced with pepper, cumin, sunflower seeds, dill and paprika, yum, warm and tender, they melt in the mouth they've teased and inflamed and tainted with pleasure, no one can resist. Ioana and Felicia and Ali, they all help themselves, again and again, swiftly swallowing these appetizers. Ioana and Ali and Felicia and the Learned One and Bazil, even Dina finally has a cheese tartlet, and one more, so scrumptious. They all have more, Felicia, Ali, Bazil, Ioana, and the Guileless One, who keeps nodding as a sign of approval, yum, marvelous, all these dainties are just marvelous, aren't they, the Kid would like to say, his eyes riveted on his hostess's hands.

Another round of drinks, of course, and even Dina has a vermouth, what a surprise, a convivial atmosphere, isn't it, really relaxed, the usual topics are trotted out for discussion, the dinner-party repertoire. The waiting lines for bread plus milk plus toilet paper plus rubber bands plus plus plus. The loused-up public transportation and the poorly lighted streets and the badly heated apartments and the armed patrols, and the neuroses and the illegal abortions and nationalism and the demolition of the lovely old residential neighborhoods, but also the latest scandal in the papers—that superb, that subversive poem, how did it slip past the censor? "We are a vegetable people," superb, super, surprise, however did it come to be written by that actress, a privileged person, and such a fragile woman, how come it was published, they got permission somehow, you bet, permission and collusion, you bet, collusion all up and down the line, obviously, that's how things work with us, you never know who, what, how, why, everything's on the take and on the sly, a thousand-year-old tradition, tradition and innovation, hand in hand. And dictatorship and poverty and suspicion and fear and widespread complicity and the cynicism of children, yes, yes, the cynicism of children no taller than your knee. Divided souls, their souls are already split in two in their mothers' wombs, you bet, they learn the code, the lies, the deceit, right there in the womb, obviously. And the West, that West so addicted to consumerism and entertainment, the savage, civilized, naïve, selfish West, not a chance, not a hope in hell, kaput, *das Ende*, they couldn't care less, naturally, they're not going to give up their petty little jobs and their little treacheries, you bet, we're all-alone-all-alone-all-alone, of course, they've got the money and we've got the lies, right, alone with our misfortune, that's how it works, you bet.

And another round of whisky-vodka-vermouth, shall we go in to dinner, the fish course awaits.

A long, plump fish, and a short, plump fish, so there'll be enough for everybody. Delicately browned, just out of the oven, pink-and-white flesh, drizzled in lemon juice, sprinkled with salt and pepper. The glasses clink gaily, a crystalline sound, the real thing, from Bohemia, and crystal-clear wine, the real thing, as golden as honey. And the roast veal, done to a turn, meltingly tender in its thick, spicy, appetizing sauce. The succulent meat, and the hearty, dry red wine, and the salad, so crisp, with fresh, delicate colors, and the heavy silverware, and the even heavier silence. Stomachs as round as cannonballs, stuffed solid, somnolent, and vague, erratic, drowsy thoughts, and increasingly labored and tired congratulations addressed to the hostess, even though everyone knows that Lady Di employs an elderly German cook on such occasions. Tired congratulations, so tired, aren't they, and the stomach is tired and the mind is dulled, sleepy.

"A break, a break!" shouts Ali. "My kingdom for a break . . ."

And sure enough, the guests move to another room for coffee and cognac and dessert and chatter.

"Shall I put on some music?" suggests the indefatigable Bazil, Marathon Host. "What would you like? Tina Turner, or Michael Jackson? You bet! Or maybe one of those little French girls who sing those old-fashioned chansonettes, real sophisticated and racy. Unless you want some Yoko Ono, the Japanese muse, or Homo Lennon, that old druggie lemon. Or some classical, how about classical? Anne Sophie Mutter, old Kara's last find. Karajan, Kara-adolf, Karanazi, with Fräulein Mutter, yeah, yeah, a special couple, hoo-hoo, ha-ha, you bet. Or maybe you'd like some Israelis, grade A, Zuckerman, Perlman, Barenboim . . . or else those others, hmm, closer to home, from the barbarian East? You know what Oistrakh replied when the Yanks asked him who were the better violinists, the Soviets or the Americans? Know what he said?" inquires the tireless Comrade Vasile Bazil Beldeanu, studying his groggy audience. "Get this, here's what he told them," continues their host, drawing out the suspense, rolling up the sleeves of his spotless white shirt and pouring some port into the Learned One's glass. "Who's better?

Well, he says, doesn't matter which side you pick, they're all our good old Odessa Jews. That's right, ha-ha, he knew the score, you bet."

The whisky, the vodka, the hors d'oeuvres, the fish, the roast, the salads, the white wine and the red wine and the cheeses and the dessert and the cognac and the coffee, yes, yes, there's even coffee, real coffee, not ersatz, and excellent imported cigarettes and baroque music, oh yes, when one's this tired, baroque is the only way to go. Everything's perfect, isn't it, yes, yes, and the perfect bowl of fruit, and the décor and the cuisine and the fancy conversation, everything, everything's perfect, of course. The perfect hosts, you bet, indefatigable, flawless, constantly trying to make the evening seem informal, to create a less sophisticated, more friendly atmosphere. Hard, very hard to do . . . Prosperity doesn't draw people together, it's an irritant. Comfortable house, Pantagruelian meal, relaxed atmosphere, a chance to have a good time, forget one's troubles, fears, regrets, that's all, and yet, there you are, it doesn't work, that's what happens, nothing you can do about it.

Conversation has lapsed, despite the energetic efforts of the hosts—who are experienced at this, well trained, in tiptop shape, wired up.

"And you, Felicia, do you still visit churches and synagogues?" asks Dina, taking the initiative once more. "Do you still think those are the only places where one can find interesting faces? You've stopped painting? Ioana told me that you were still at it, that you hadn't given up. I can imagine what it's like being a drawing teacher in a technical school. But you haven't stopped painting, I'm sure of it.

I'm not asking about the religious aspect of this—it's a question, if I understand correctly, of a purely aesthetic interest."

Poor Dina, unbearable Dina! She does her best to act natural and friendly, but she can't overcome that fatal barrier, that's all, she simply can't, whatever she does always comes out stiff and conventional. That's how she fell into the trap named Vasile, the lure of the rudimentary, wouldn't you say, that sudden relief when someone else takes over all social interaction, everyday contacts, favor for favor, social chitchat, comfort, the whole bit.

Felicia's laconic reply has startled her, since any refusal to go along with that artificial spontaneity she affects throws her rudely off her stride. But nothing in the world would make her show it, and she has already turned toward another guest.

"I've always admired the way you behave so naturally, Ioana. Your soul is an open book, to use the popular expression. Ali is really to be envied. Wives these days have no time to do anything anymore, whereas you, you still manage your teaching and your embroidery, and your canning for the winter. What energy, what patience it must take to instruct these farm boys, these future technicians, in the fine points of English pronunciation! I can imagine what that means, school on top of housework and the child. You're a champion, that's what you are. A heroine, one of our truly impressive modern women."

Little gem-like phrases, intended to be simple, appealing, which, once spoken, sound arch and precious, all because of her inability to communicate, you see, that's why he succeeded, Vasile, that's why she has stayed resigned, content, who knows, she'll have gotten used to the trap named Vasile, she'll have understood it was a trap, she must have understood, in the end, don't you think, but she got used to it, yes, yes, it's rather comfortable, all this, rather comfortable. She tries to make little jokes with Ali or her husband, and they always misfire laboriously, poor, poor Dina, the unbearable, the useless, the poseur. Only the Learned One escapes her inept attentions, she leaves him to his own devices, asking nothing of him, neither participation nor approbation, nothing at all, she leaves him alone.

The Kid hasn't said a word all evening, although he's seemed extremely attentive, tolerant, approving, he keeps nodding yes and keeps his eyes glued to Dina's thumb. The club-like thumb of the left hand. As though he wanted to convince himself that this thumb is the same one he knew quite a long time ago. Delicate, slender hands, so very slender, with a pale purplish-blue tinge, a faint reddish flush, her circulation, isn't it, she's got poor circulation. Delicate hands, certainly, but the left thumb mars the picture: clubbed, inflamed, it looks as though the tip has been sliced right off. Delicate hands and a delicate profile to the oblong face, with its bluish, Oriental shadows, and a delicate figure, with a slender waist—and that horrible thumb on the left hand. There have been many changes, of course, but this unnerving thumb has remained just as he remembered it. The passage of time hasn't softened this distressing detail one whit.

It's late, very, very late, Felicia's sending desperate signals to Ioana. The train at dawn, the trip, her mother, the hospital, her boss Chibrit, Ioana had promised they wouldn't stay a long time.

Bazil senses the discomfiture. He knows, you bet, that his guests can say all the nasty things they want on the way home, but still, they'll have to admit that this so long delayed get-together has been a success. A pleasant, luxurious evening with perfect hosts, charming people, unpretentious, attentive, convivial, the guests will agree, these are good, honest folks, they're bound to agree on that.

He takes a last mouthful of cognac, savoring it at length before swallowing, and closes his performance on a melancholy note, with an important announcement.

"What do you want, I'm an apparatchik, a self-serving little apparatchik. No, don't contradict me, I know what I'm saying. After all, I'm not stupid. Perhaps a bit of an ass, now and then, but not stupid, no way. An apparatchik, that's what I am, you bet. On that point, can't do a thing, to each his own. *Jedem das Seine*, as *the others* used to say . . . Oh yes, I even know a smidgen of German, you bet, it's not so surprising, I've done a lot of traveling. I'm just saying that all this isn't that simple anymore, the way some people seem to think. No, it's not at all simple anymore, believe me. They're mistaken, those who think that this new social category is a simple, homogeneous one. No, not even those guys in the Securitate . . . No, not even them, they're not all in the same bag. And let me say that there are lots of people who get us mixed up with them. Especially these last few years, people figure everyone's a snitch, on the payroll of the secret police. Well, that's more an expression of widespread exasperation than the truth. A shortcut like a lot of others, you bet. But what . . . what was I saying? . . . Oh, yes: the newspapers say that the Party official is the true hero of postwar life. Or else the true hero of postwar literature, hey? What do you think?"

Proud of himself, he looks around at his audience. And his audience is attentive, his audience hangs, breathlessly, on his every word, and follows as well, and just as attentively, his faithful observer, which is to say the innocence and astonishment and childish participant enthusiasm and torment of the bookish man suddenly fallen among down-to-earthlings, but also the joy of the researcher, the pure joy of the scientist.

"So, which one? The true hero of life or of literature? *And*, not or . . . The hero of postwar life *and* its literature! The same old line. Pure demagoguery, everyone's fed up with that blah-blah-blah. And yet! And yet . . . if you think about it . . . the paradox is that . . . yes, yes, it's even true! Days and nights and years wasted in Party meetings and campaigns for a goal that's . . . unattainable. The authorities have no desire to admit this, you bet. If they admit the truth, which is becoming clearer and clearer to them, well then, it would be obvious that the heroes of these gigantic and useless efforts, dedicated to an absurd and never-ending mission, yes, yes, you've got it—they themselves are the heroes. It took me a while to realize this, little by little . . . We've all realized it, the dreamers and careerists and hangers-on. I won't mention which category I belong in, oh no, forget that. I'm simply saying that all I am is a poor *parvenu*. An apparatchik, a postwar hero . . ."

The hero has finished his number, but the Learned One continues to gaze at him in fascination. He'd like to add a comment or two, but his lips are moving too rapidly, silently. He'd really like to say something, though, and he makes an effort, but still can't get the words out, and, turning back to Dina, gives his full attention once more to the club thumb of Madame Beldeanu. Yes, the same thick, stumpy, truncated thumb of their adolescence. For here is a flaw to which time has brought no stunning remedy, has it, no remedy, how about that! And yet the fine wine and the delectable meal and Felicia more beautiful than ever in her noble serenity and discretion, and Ioana so vivacious, so scintillating, and Ali so generous, so at ease, even Dina, hitting just the right note of gracious warmth, don't you think, yes, yes, even Vasile with his imposing, majestic belly, a classic paunch, isn't it, and his bristling pepper-and-salt mustache, and his thick, unruly iron-gray hair, very distinguished, isn't he, a patrician *bon vivant*, affable, courteous, yes, even Vasile, and everything, everyone is perfect, a really perfect evening, isn't it, such blissful relaxation, away from the bitterness and depression and fear, yes, far from the fear that permeates our daily lives, yes, yes, a moment of respite, a moment stolen, wrenched from the system, as it were, an escape, a stubborn, rebellious, and passionate disregard for our present predicament.

The evening ends in a flurry of handshaking and cheek-kissing. A real but agreeable feeling of fatigue. Even the

---

Stoians, initially reserved and anxious not to seem too thrilled about the whole thing (because you never know), so that they wouldn't seem like close friends of the Beldeanus—even the Stoians have loosened up, they're having a grand old time, bubbling with enthusiasm and pleased with the success of this little get-together, so it looks as though an evening at the Beldeanus' isn't the last word in utter boredom, you can have quite an enjoyable time there as long as you accept the kind of relationship involved, obviously, obviously.

The gratified hosts accompany their rowdy guests to the door with affectionate zeal, Don Bazil's hoarse voice booming out paternally, "Make sure you haven't forgotten anything! Drive carefully, that wet asphalt is slippery. Watch out you don't skid, be careful, careful, don't forget!"

In the courtyard, near the car, the Guileless One manages, belatedly, to utter the word he'd tried in vain to produce after their host's speech. "Ma-magisterial! Magi-magisterial," stammers the Kid. "Ex-periment, ex-quisite, ex, wasn't it? Magi-magis . . ." mumbles the Learned One, dead-drunk, clinging to the arm of that beanpole Ali, who's just as drunk, soused, pickled, bombed.

"Perfect, perfect, obviously, ob-vi-ous-ly," agrees Ali, while the Kid agrees with him, "Mar-mar-marvelous, I sw-swear." And they stagger around like that, in each other's arms, slowly, so slowly, teetering around the cosmic, yellow, aerodynamic craft that awaits them.

Ioana's the one who takes the wheel, ticked off but sober,

full of contempt for masculine weakness, but sober, in control of the situation.

The rain stopped quite a while ago. The air is cool, the night clear, the city lost in darkness, in sleep, and galaxies. Overhead, an ocean of stars, and the moon, here's the moon, glacial, somnambulistic, cadaverous, the ancient moon, lyrical, demoniac, the vigilant moon, perfidious, all-seeing, surrounded by the ocean of harmless stars. The ocean above and confusion within us, beyond us, before us, chance and the law, stars and the moon in the sky up above and the gamble of daily life here below, for us, *Terra incognita, confusa*, chance and the law, the enigma of tomorrow, and tomorrow, and after tomorrow.

Monday was the proper day to make the thank-you call. The Stoians were probably dragging listlessly around their apartment. Wiped out, with an extra dose of the blahs because it was raining again.

"We should phone Bazil and Dina, to thank them," suggested Ioana.

Ali looked up from his typewriter. "Thank them? We're colleagues, after all, Don Bazil and I, we don't stand on ceremony. He should be the one to thank me instead, for going over today to pick up his stupid article and drop it off at the office. Mister High-and-Mighty didn't have time to do it himself. He got up late and had to go off and do something else."

"Fine, but what about Lady Di and her grand airs? Come on, you couldn't have missed how hard she was trying last night to seem relaxed and informal, poor thing. Playing at being just us folks, with her fancy dishes and furniture! Then she's amazed when her guests never come back . . ."

"You know times have gotten hard even for people like them. Bazil has to perform incredible contortions to get hold of the slightest trifle. Before, it was a piece of cake to get that stuff, and now he has to go through all sorts of crap. For the little things, obviously, for every little thing."

"Perhaps, but I'm not going to waste time shedding tears over their fate. I mean, there are others who deserve compassion a lot more than they do."

"So you're going to give them a call?"

"Me? Why me? Why don't you call her, she'd appreciate it more coming from you."

"I think you're the one she's expecting to hear from. Or else she'll think something went wrong. You know how women are."

"And how would I know? I'm a woman? Me? All right, fine, I'll call later, after I've had my bath."

But Ioana Stoian doubtless forgot to call the Beldeanus Monday evening.

The other couple didn't manage to rise to the occasion as promptly as they should have either, it seems.

Returning home late that Monday night from her sad trip to the countryside, Felicia had barely strength enough to relate the exasperating details to her husband (the filthy, overcrowded train, the arrogance and indifference of the doctor, her mother's terrified weeping over her approaching end) before collapsing in bed, exhausted.

Since she taught only three hours on Tuesday, Felicia was able to come home early the next day and get some rest. That evening, presumably, they finally got around to the appropriate discussion.

Felicia's clear, even voice wafted in from the kitchen. "If we call now, we're still within the bounds of good manners."

"And if we don't? It would only mean the end of something that never really existed" was the probable baritone reply, launched from the depths of a comfortable reading chair.

"It took you five whole years to accept that invitation. Dina has always been nice to me. She's helped me get paper supplies and frames and paints. While I, I've always been standoffish with her. For no reason. Except that you absolutely didn't want to get involved in any way with the Beldeanus. Now the visit's over and done with, so we ought to wind the whole thing up properly."

"Fine, call her, if you like," agreed the husband, joining her in the cramped kitchen.

"I have no desire to get Comrade Vasile on the other end of the line," objected Felicia, tossing back her heavy curls with an irritated shake of her head.

"Comrade Beldeanu left Monday morning on a business trip. Ali told me so. Worn out, I understand, from doing the dishes the previous evening. Did you know that Vasile was the dishwasher? A model husband, that's what I've learned. He bends over backward to make things easier for his wife. He's the one who does the errands, the food shopping, the housework. A veritable paragon, no question. He's definitely out of town. Yesterday morning Ali went to pick up some article for him, something Comrade Beldeanu didn't have time to drop off at the office himself."

"Apart from his biography . . . I think Vasile is rather pleasant. Well, not necessarily his political biography, I mean his social standing. You understand what I mean."

"I understand, but it doesn't interest me. Anyhow, he isn't home. You can telephone without any problem."

"It would be nice if you called. A nice surprise. A warm gesture, something to take the chill off this whole thing."

"You're asking too much, believe me. I'm already too exotic for La Beldeanu, have been ever since we were kids: the minor provincial celebrity with great expectations. Then the young scientist with so many prospects, a brilliant career ahead of him. Then, inexplicably, he jumps the track. Just when he's hitting his stride, what does this loser do but give up his career, suddenly, just like that, the way losers always do. Why do you think they wanted to invite me in the first place? To see this rare bird! The sideshow freak, the lunatic. Something to shake them out of their boredom, spice up that tasteless soup of their dull-as-dishwater daily routine."

"Tasteless or not, you can't possibly know a thing about it. Vasile can't be having an easy time of it either, these days. His political file isn't spotless anymore, after all. Married to a woman from a minority group that . . . the most . . . well, you know what I'm getting at. Ethnic purity, today's principal criterion of selection. And she's got her own problems, I mean you couldn't exactly say the past was a paradise for her, or the present either, for that matter. The camp, then coming back, and a difficult adolescence, then she has that love affair and gets thrown out of the house by old Berg, that bigot, and everything that happened next. Living with Vasile can't be all that exciting. It's true she's walled herself up in that sort of frozen ritual she goes through, the Great Lady, but . . . Besides, I'd be surprised if she were interested in you just for your novelty value. You've known each other since childhood, after all. It would be natural for her to feel a certain nostalgic kinship."

"You mean those games up in the attic? No, really, I don't feel up to calling. Each word would be checked out under a microscope, I'd wind up sounding like a Martian. Bingo, I'd find myself flirting with her out of sheer nervousness, some kind of ridiculous hysterical fit. You know what Ali said? He sure knows how to put things. She needs a good thrashing to loosen her up; otherwise, forget it. No, it would be better if we just forgot all about this polite thank-you business, believe me."

Two days after the dinner party, it seems, Ioana Stoian did get around to calling after all, to thank the Beldeanus, especially Dina, for the wonderful evening they'd spent together. On the dot of nine, as it happened, Dina recognized Felicia's lovely voice. Conventional expressions of gratitude, true, but spoken in such limpid, glowing tones that it was a joy to listen to her, all the more so in that Felicia seemed genuinely moved, yes, touched, pausing here and there, while the words that should have followed seemed snapped up by a silent void . . . A habit of Felicia's that Dina was familiar with.

"A most enjoyable evening for us. The gracious atmosphere . . . such a delightful dinner . . . sincerely . . . such a pleasure."

"Ah, but we wouldn't have done it for simply anyone. We did it just for you. I hadn't spoken to your husband for thirty years, can you imagine! I ran into him every now and then in the street, but we never stopped to chat. He'd say hello, that's all."

"Oh, you know how he is . . . not very sociable . . . never says a word . . . even at your house. But he had a lovely time, I promise you . . . He even got drunk, that's unusual . . . it was good for him, good . . . to get out and see people . . . a hermit otherwise, just a hermit."

Felicia let herself get carried away by this flood of banality, and quite without meaning to, went overboard. "Now, since Vasile isn't there, you're all alone, you could stop by and see us."

Her husband gave a start in his armchair when he heard this invitation, and flung his hands up in despair. Startled in turn by his antics, Felicia temporarily lost her voice, but Lady Di seemed to have sensed this element of hesitation in time.

"I don't know, I don't think so. I've got too much work at the moment. It's been getting harder and harder these last years. I'm in court every day, there's an endless stream of lawsuits. The laws are constantly changing, always new restrictions, more and more hopeless situations. It's not only the people who are fighting among themselves, institutions are at war with one another as well. You can feel how fed up people are in the courtroom, too, not just on the milk line. The judges are overwhelmed. Oh, I wanted to ask you . . . Did you perhaps forget a raincoat when you were here?"

Taken aback, Felicia has trouble finding something to say. She answers with some difficulty. "What? Excuse me? No, no, I don't believe so, maybe Ioana, try Ioana, I wouldn't know. What? Oh, no, Ali, I see, yes, perhaps Ali, I don't know."

"Someone left a raincoat behind the evening you came. I mean, I didn't see it until the next afternoon, when I got home. That morning, when I left, I was in a hurry, and too tired to notice a thing. Perhaps Ali, yes, or maybe Ioana. I forgot to ask. She just called me, too, a little while ago, but I didn't remember to ask her about it. No, it's not important. Nothing, really, I'll just call her now and find out."

In fact, it seems that Dina Beldeanu did call the Stoians right away, but no one answered.

It was only two days later that Ali had a long, friendly conversation with the wife of his absent colleague, at the end of which he was asked the same question and gave the same reply.

"A raincoat? What raincoat? No, it's not ours . . . Absolutely certain, it's not ours. No, me, I don't wear them. Besides, when I stopped by your place on Monday, around noon, yes, it must have been around noon, I didn't see any raincoat on the coat tree. Well, I didn't look very carefully, obviously—so I don't know, haven't a clue."

Two days later, however, Dina called back. "Ioana? You know, I spoke to Ali the other day. I don't know if he mentioned it to you . . ."

Silence. A long pause. Each waits for the other to speak.

"Well, it's not important. I asked him about a raincoat. I don't know if he spoke to you about it."

Another pause, even longer. But the dialogue finally gets going again.

"You asked him about . . . about what? A raincoat? What raincoat?"

"I don't know, a raincoat, that's all. It's silly, excuse me, I must be overreacting. The next morning, after you were here for dinner, I noticed a raincoat in the hall. I mean, no, not that morning, that afternoon, when I got home. I asked Ali if it belonged to you by any chance. He . . ."

"He told you he doesn't wear a raincoat. I suppose that's what he answered, right? He said no, and that's true. As for my raincoat, it's hanging right here. No, I'm positive, it's not ours."

"I'm sorry, it's irritating, I don't know why this silly business is bothering me so much. It's just a stupid little thing. But it's . . . how can I put this, it's unpleasant, simply unpleasant, I'm very sorry."

"I understand, I quite understand. You never know, a strange object that turns up in your home, I understand, it's aggravating, naturally. There's an explanation, don't worry, these days nobody's simply going to abandon his belongings. Someone will claim it, you can count on that, especially since . . . you're not dealing with careless people who can't remember where they've been or what they were wearing. I suppose you've asked . . ."

"Yes, yes, I spoke to Felicia, too. I bothered them as well with this mystery."

But Dina—big surprise—couldn't resist calling the other couple again.

The telephone rang a long time, a long time . . . Finally someone picked up the receiver, although no one actually spoke. There was no voice, even though someone had answered the phone at last. And yet, yes, yes, it seemed someone was there, hesitating to speak.

"Hello, yes, who . . ."

"Oh, it's me, Di . . ." Then she fell helplessly silent. She hadn't expected him to answer, she couldn't manage to go on talking, she was completely lost . . . Now, what use was it to bring up . . . that idiotic business of the raincoat . . . No, it didn't make sense anymore . . . She didn't know where to start, had forgotten what she'd intended to say.

"You wanted to speak to Felicia, right? Hmm, yes, I'm not usually the one who answers the phone. Well, what can I tell you, you've got no choice, you'll have to chat with me, that's just the way it goes."

Dina tries to protest, what a nice surprise, for a long time now she's been wanting to . . . but it's too late, his monologue is off and running. All attempts to interrupt, to object, or to qualify the suppositions and reminiscences that pour forth in a torrent, in a frenetic hodgepodge—all attempts would prove useless.

"I'm not an easy person to talk to, am I, we haven't had a conversation for a long, long time, since childhood . . . a lifetime. And even then we didn't really talk, just those weird games, in the courtyard of the Berg house, with your cousin and my classmate . . . what was his name, whatever was his name, Snookie, Mookie, I can't remember, but him I remember perfectly, with those big teeth, buck teeth that stuck out beyond his lips, a sweet boy, really kindhearted, I heard he'd become a soldier, it surprised me, maybe he never even had a choice, everyone in that country's gotten tougher, too big a clash between ancient ways and new ones, yes, yes, the climate, the Arabs, the waves of new arrivals, wars, neurosis, yes, I remember Hymie perfectly, oh yes, Hymie, that was the name, yes, yes, your cousin, the big courtyard, with all those trees, and that sort of 'penthouse' we had . . . up in the attic, you had to climb a ladder to get there, remember, too precocious, the two of us, weren't we, yes, yes, a lifetime ago . . . Thirty years, a lifetime, we haven't spoken to each other since those days, that's how it goes, growing more and more set in our ways, losing that spark, that lively curiosity, yes, yes, curiosity and playfulness just fade away, don't they, experience wears them down, the spark dies out, we turn into lumps, trapped inside our own images, stiff, uncomfortable, inside our legends, our coffins . . . An arrogant woman, why not say so, arrogant, elegant, privileged, yes, that stupid word is the most appro-

priate one, isn't it . . . I'm taking advantage of this unexpected phone call, who knows if we'll ever . . . I mean,
I'm not very talkative, practically a recluse, yes, yes, I'm
not very sociable, not much for conversations, something
different for me . . . I hope I'm not offending you, my
naïve sincerity, isn't it, another experiment, isn't it, yes,
yes, cruel, I mean, and there's no reason for it, no reason,
but still, it's a sign of sympathy, with me sincerity is a
sign of sympathy, and it's only with people close to me
that I try this experiment, yes, I'm constantly ex . . . ex
. . . An arrogant, vain, stupid woman, that's what I wanted
to say, that's what you seemed to be . . . then there was
that legend, wasn't there, when you ran away or were
kicked out of, you know, during your last year of high
school, the great love affair with your classmate Vasile
Beldeanu, of all people, why him, was it, I ask you, inexplicable, inex . . . ex . . . inex . . . Young girl at a difficult
age, that must have been it . . . Completely unforeseeable,
I mean, who could have imagined that this poor clod, how
shall I put it, just impossible to foretell the future, not an
option, ruled out, excluded, ex . . . And even if we'd
known, yes, known what was coming, it wouldn't have
made any fundamental, essential difference, would it,
well, that's not the question, no, no . . . Not even
your father, poor old Berg, I'm sorry, that terrible episode . . . No, he couldn't have known what would
happen, not even your own father, but it wouldn't have
changed a thing in any case, would it, hardly likely that
we'd ever be able to talk to each other, I know, a con-

ventional woman who in the past, however, did defy con-
vention . . . I mean, when, you know . . . when the father
curses his daughter, I mean the malediction, the expulsion
and ritual burial, as though his only child were dead, you
know, as though the old man, without knowing it, without suspecting that, without, no, it's not possible, he had
no idea that within a week he would be, he of all people,
I mean, he was the one who, well, barely a week later, his
own funeral, he was actually dead and buried, poor old
Berg, the old bigot, poor man . . . And yet social conventions are back in favor, except that now these standards
are perfectly stupid, frivolous, superficial, whereas that
dramatic faith, as irrational as it may have been, was still,
yes . . . Well, that's not the point, the old man couldn't
stomach his daughter's relationship with, well, with those
who, yes, yes, the age-old psychosis of the ghetto, right
. . . No one knew what the future would bring, and anyway it wasn't important, I know, the years at the university, years of poverty, estranged from your family and
friends, then suddenly the career, it's been an outstanding
one, hasn't it . . . Although his wife's background hasn't
exactly helped him along, I know, that's the least one can
say, otherwise he'd have been ensconced in a choicer position a long time ago, right at the top, just look at the big
shots we've got now, lousy employees with their pathetic
privileges, yes, yes, Vasile could have gone much further,
a remarkable career . . . What I meant to say was, we're
all prisoners of our images, our past, it was hard for us to
communicate . . . And the stories about me, the legend of

course, the non-violent protests, giving up my scientific career, a sort of Gandhi, one would have thought, who knows, I was some kind of hero, not at all, far from it, a tired man, worn out, yes, all the reading, yes, a joy, I won't deny it, and the book, well, I won't deny it, a success, yes, yes, one shouldn't exaggerate the success of a book, crisis, no more, no less, the expression of a sense of impasse, absolutely true, but mine wasn't the only dilemma, we've all been there, it's the story of our generation, the children of the war, not only the war, there's something else, we haven't found the right label yet . . . I'm rarely off in a trance like this, very rarely . . . It's the morphine of boredom, that's what it is, another experiment, isn't it, 'developed multilaterally,' that's what all those newspapers say, stuffed with lies, no, it's not society that's developed multilaterally but boredom and poverty and terror . . . We're used to it, of course, we've been used to it from childhood . . . Yes, yes, let's keep things in proportion, sure, I was talking about boredom, I mean, that deadly monotony and the multilateral boredom of language, of submission, conventions, don't forget those murderous conventions, incurable, real killers, unless we can find something else, a new experiment, an explosion, an ex, yes, we know exactly which one, but before then there will be other ones, ex, extra-, lots of others, soon, extra-, always more, plenty more . . ."

And so on, for almost an hour.

That very evening, the guilty party will probably report this fit of uncontrollable logorrhea to his wife.

"I was vulgar and aggressive. The thrill of saying mean things. An impulsive, crazy, sadistic thing to do. The neurosis of boredom. I mentioned that to her, by the way, I must have babbled some stuff about boredom, perhaps she saw the connection, an incriminating excuse. In any case, we've definitely gotten rid of Lady Di—it'll be a long time before she turns up again! I don't think she'll even say hello to me now. Stuck-up and bitchy the way she is, I couldn't have offended her more if I'd tried. Especially since I'm not even a drunk, I haven't even got that excuse, I'm not Vasile, that's another excuse down the drain. Well, that's how it goes . . . So much for the Beldeanus. We're all of us better off like this, aren't we, since there wasn't any point to the relationship anyway."

And yet, only two days later, Dina called and spoke briefly to Felicia, referring curtly to the impulsive invitation made during their previous conversation. "Perhaps it was simply idle talk, but as it happens, I would like to stop by one of these days. In the afternoon. For a half hour, if I may. Nothing fancy, just to see you . . ."

"Yes, of course, please do," said Felicia with a sigh, giving in without a fight. "I'll speak to . . . Yes, yes, I'll call you tomorrow."

"No, don't bother. If we put this off, we'll lose interest, especially since we probably don't have much in the first place. There's no need to change your plans for me, no need for the both of you to be there, or even for anyone to be home at all, if you're busy elsewhere. I'll simply stop by, and if you're there, fine. If not, there's no problem,

I'll come by some other time. Half an hour, no more.
That's all, really. Tomorrow, after court. I've two cases
tomorrow. Let's say around six o'clock. Tomorrow, then,
if you can. For a half hour. So, six o'clock, six-fifteen.
Don't go to any trouble, please. No preparations, nothing
fancy . . ."

And *basta*, goodbye. Click, finished, end of conversation.

Felicia paralyzed, still holding the receiver. The guilty
husband—livid. Now what do they do? How do they get
ready for this confrontation? Dina, with her grand manner,
think of it, Dina: I'll drop by to see you, just like that. I'll
stop by, a simple visit. What a thought, Dina. Dina suddenly being friendly, familiar, informal! Tomorrow, or
some other time, no problem. What an idea! A long, vast,
swelling, infinite silence filled the room.

Dina appears the next day, at the appointed time. Elegant, as always, especially since she was coming from work
at the courthouse. A very simple hairdo, a chignon, with
a clip to match her dark hair. Relaxed, rather tired, cordial.
No sophisticated airs, quite natural, period.

She takes part in the usual review of current topics, the
same old ones, of course. Multilateral ennui, the lack of
heat, the press and its lies, the black market, the long lines,
the long ideological meetings, the long-lived Boss, the
censored letters, the tapping of phones, but also the
crappy paper used to print fewer and fewer books, the
abolishment of subsidies to theaters, which get by thanks
to their scenery departments, where they make and sell

coffins, a rare commodity, almost impossible to find . . .

The moment the judge arrived, the brains of the household had tossed out these hot topics for discussion in an effort to keep certain others from being mentioned.

Lady Di chats without enthusiasm, but also without her usual affectation. She drinks her tea quietly, smiles at a few of her former playmate's sarcastic remarks. She behaves absolutely . . . normally, excessively so, even with undue moderation and good sense. She brings the visit to an abrupt end shortly after a half hour, as promised.

That very evening, the Stoians will be given a full report of the occasion by phone.

The men will comment jokingly and at length, in rather vulgar terms, on the effects of Bazil's absence, but their main topic will be the humanizing impact—that effort to seem natural and down-to-earth—so noticeable in the privileged class during periods of crisis. One man will fidget constantly with his glasses, while his friend on the other end of the line scratches his kinky black African hair.

The bomb will explode only at the end of the conversation. So Dina has invited herself over to the Stoians' as well! A short visit, the following day. She just wanted to stop by and see them. A half hour, that's all. No particular reason, nothing special. Just half an hour, to say hello. Not really a visit, simply dropping by for thirty minutes or so on the way home from court.

It seems that her visit to the Stoians' is just like the other one. Dina stays only half an hour. She behaves extremely naturally . . . abnormally so, Ali will remark. The humorous commentary had already taken on a slightly artificial tone, a routine that had lost its punch line.

There were no further visits. Only long-short-long phone conversations, Morse-code communications, sometimes with Ioana, blinking behind her eyeglasses, sometimes with Felicia, cooing in her soothing, velvety voice, both of them growing more and more indifferent to these repeated phone calls. The men's jokes begin to grow stale, sheepish, almost intimidated as well by the constancy of that strange natural behavior flaunted by Dina Beldeanu. A friendly, agreeable simplicity. Extremely, extra-agreeable . . . Imagine that! All four of them gradually realize that it's true—and it's just too much! The Guileless One keeps exclaiming excitedly over this marvel. It's the last thing anyone would have expected, isn't it, never ever ever, what an experience, an ex, I swear!

When Vasile gets back, we'll see what comes of it . . . Comes of what, I'd like to know . . . We'll have to see how we'll get out of this . . . We might end up buddy-buddy with Comrade Beldeanu . . . As though the ambiguous position we're already in weren't enough, oh no. If you think about it, we don't really know anything about the Stoians, either, except that they're nice people and that they're the ones who urged us to visit, at long last, our distinguished friends from way back when, no, we can't forget that detail, can we, mustn't allow ourselves to forget that.

Luckily, Felicia wouldn't hear of such suspicions and preached love for one's fellow man: This is ridiculous, no one has the right to think like that, nobody's forcing you to get involved with other people, you can stay all alone for as long as you like, but if you accept, then . . . As for Ioana, you've worked together for so many years, over at your research institute, you know her, you know her even too well, I'm sure of it, there was something going on between you two, I'd bet on it, I can feel it, I'm not wrong, I can sense it, I'm convinced of it, she did more than just translate your work into English, I'm certain there was more to it than that, and I wonder . . . how can you talk that way, you suspect everyone, you're afraid of every-body, even though, even though . . . you know for a fact that those you fear the most can spy on us how and when they like, they don't need intermediaries, and what's more they don't even need to spy on us, they own us, in any case, they can do whatever they want whenever they want.

Everyone knew that little Felicia was capable, if neces-sary, of phenomenal bursts of energy.

Which was about to be proved once again, naturally, be sure of it, sure of it.

"What can you possibly imagine they might need from us? It would more likely be the other way around, believe me. Vasile's told you a million times to come to him if you have the slightest problem. Problem, that's the word they use, that's how they speak. The slightest problem, that's what he said to you. And God knows you've got some! Why do you think they might call us? What have we got to offer them? Empty pockets and long faces."

It's clear the Kid won't take this lying down, no way.

"Yes, but they haven't anyone else! Bigwigs bored shit-less with other bigwigs. They want something else, something more exotic. Milady Dina feels like a change of air; as for Vasile, Comrade Vasile . . . You never know what he's up to, so it's useless to try to reassure me!"

Surprise: after the return of Comrade Beldeanu to hearth and home, there were no more phone calls from Madame.

Not a peep, from either Lady Di or Comrade Vasile. A day goes by, then two, then three . . . Go figure! Felicia and the Kid waited, tense with anticipation. They'd cooked up all sorts of convincing pretexts for avoiding another visit. The Beldeanus' silence amazed them. They seemed to grow more and more anxious. It's not good to play around with *that kind of person, they* can be really vindictive . . . Arrogant, inhibited, and screwed up! shouted the Child, losing control in a burst of panic. Of course, anyone can become vindictive, sighed his long-suffering wife. Maybe she's upset, angry, they're only human, after all. The Learned One had decided, however, that he would absolutely not make the next move.

It seems that after about a week Felicia called Ioana to see if she had any news. No, Dina hadn't gotten in touch with the Stoians, either. Had anything happened? No, nothing. Ali would have heard about it, Ali saw Bazil every day, no, nothing in particular.

The subject must have come up again in the men's conversation. Felicia's husband asked Ioana's husband if he'd heard anything lately about the wife of Vasile Bazil Beldeanu. What's going on, what's happened? She'd vanished as suddenly as she'd appeared. A comet, come and gone, joked the Brat. His friend calmly ignored this display of teasing adolescent humor. The question was repeated. A grunt was the only answer. Intrigued by this mystery, the Guileless One wouldn't give up. Ali replied as though reciting a lesson in school: nothing in particular. The phrase had a decisive ring to it, clear and definite. Clear and false. As though, somehow, there was still something . . . something unusual, perhaps.

And so the men took a walk together in town.

"Well, what happened? Come on, spit it out. I could tell, you couldn't say anything on the phone. Now let's have it."

"Things aren't going too well . . ."

"What do you mean? The trip didn't work out? He wasn't able to stuff the car with chickens or booze? Or was it that he couldn't cadge enough gas?"

"No, he's not the problem. I'm not talking about him."

"Ah, Lady Di. She finally caught him with a secretary or a Party groupie?"

"No, that's not it. You'll laugh, but Bazil's scared to death of Dina. He doesn't try any funny business within three hundred kilometers of home."

"So, what then? Three hundred kilometers wasn't enough? You told me he traveled all over the country. Romania's pretty big, isn't it, and it isn't the Holy Land either, if you get my drift."

"It's her, she's the one who's not doing well. Poor Bazil, he's deeply worried. Really worried, believe me, I'm not joking. These problems, you know; it's not easy to find answers for them."

"It was inevitable! An organic reaction. No, not organic, a reaction of the entire being, body and soul and spirit, to alienation. Self-alienation. Marriage produces breaks like that, you know. Or the tyranny of the state, of parental authority, a routine job, lots of other things. A void, nothing, unavoidable emptiness . . ."

"Drop all this philosophizing, it's serious."

"And philosophy isn't, right? But why don't you tell me exactly what's wrong? With all this secrecy, you'd think Dina had joined a dissident movement."

"No, that's not the problem, obviously. It's very confused. She's a bit . . . shaken. She can't get back on track."

Ali flicked away his cigarette and crushed it out beneath the sole of his huge shoe. He studied at length his short friend's glasses. He studied his friend, with a look of boredom and irritation on his face.

"Since that business. With the trenchcoat."

"Which trenchcoat?"

"What? What which? *The raincoat*, I'm telling you . . . *that one*. The phone calls. After we went there for dinner. You don't remember?"

"What?"

"Don't you remember? She asked us if we hadn't left a raincoat at their place that evening."

"No, not me. She never spoke to me about it, not to me. Felicia, perhaps. But no, I don't think so. She would've mentioned it to me. No, I don't believe so . . ."

"You don't believe so? Are you out of your mind? Of course she called you. Apparently she called everyone. She even called our house one morning when she knew we weren't there so she could speak to our son, and of course Dorin didn't know what she was talking about. She was clearly checking up on us, checking to see if we'd been telling the truth about the kind of raincoats we had. She went crazy from asking all over town about this thing. Now she's clammed up."

"What do you mean?"

"What do I mean, what do I mean! As if you didn't know! She called you too, obviously. And not just once, twice. I checked. The people she trusted, she called them twice."

"Well then, she didn't trust us, because she didn't call us. Felicia mentioned nothing to me about it."

"She said nothing to you because it was nothing important. It just seemed like some nonsense."

"So, wasn't it? Nothing important, I mean? What trenchcoat . . . what the hell is all this fuss about, what trenchcoat?"

Ali lighted another cigarette. Drawing the collar of his jacket closer around his neck, he looked up at the sky. The clear, lifeless, inscrutable sky. Brisk, seasonable weather. The street along which they were walking was deserted. Neither said a word. Ali considered his candid companion once more.

"Monday, the day after we had dinner there, Dina found—I mean, she noticed—a raincoat that didn't belong to them, hanging on the coat tree in the hall. That's what she says . . . She asked us first, of course, to see if it might belong to us. Then she asked you the same thing. Then she asked other people. Over and over again, it just didn't make sense. She got completely worked up over this, it seems. Then she stopped asking people about it."

"You mean she found the culprit? The owner?"

"The owner! The culprit! No! No, no, that's not the problem . . . What owner? The raincoat's still in the same spot, hanging on the coat tree. That's what I'm told . . . In the Beldeanus' hall. No one knows whether she understood or not. Suddenly she just stopped talking about it. It's not clear why. From fear, evidently. But no one knows. Fear because she understood, or fear because she didn't understand at all? Bazil can't figure out exactly what's gnawing at her, where things have gone wrong. She refuses to see a doctor. As though doctors . . . Anyway, the whole thing's a mess."

"Oh, fine," observed the Kid, looking innocently up at his friend Al. I. Stoian, known as Ali, hoping he realized at last that his companion hadn't any idea what he was talking about, not the faintest idea. He understood, didn't understand, understood too much, hard to tell, with all the questions he was asking.

"You said you stopped by their place Monday morning."

"Yes, I went by before noon, before going to the office."

"Oh, right, so you did stop by. Actually, you told me that, that you'd been there on Monday."

"Bazil called to tell me he was in a hurry, that he'd hardly had the time to write his article, he was worn out from the dinner party. He had to leave, so he asked me if I'd come pick up the article and take it to the paper."

"Aha! Fine. He asked you to stop by and then you went over."

"Why, what do you mean? What exactly are you insinuating? You keep questioning me, what is it you don't understand?"

"Nothing. Everything. I'm repeating what you tell me. You went there, you picked up the text, you took it to the paper."

"Yes, I stopped by for a few moments. But that's not the problem, dammit!"

"Then what is the problem?"

"That's not the problem. It's got nothing to do with it, nothing to do with anything, Kid, that's not the problem."

"And the trenchcoat?"

"What trenchcoat?"

"*The raincoat!* The raincoat in the hall, where was it?"

"How am I supposed to know?" Ali screamed. "I've never seen the damn thing! I haven't laid eyes on it, and that's not the problem, I've already told you!"

The Learned One's mild, skeptical gaze wavered beneath the furious glare of the tall, lanky man.

"When I went over to their house," continued Ali, trotting out the same alibi, "I didn't see any raincoat. I didn't even look to see if there was, yes or no, a raincoat. There wasn't one, evidently. I had no reason to stay and look around. Besides, I don't even remember if there was one or not, I haven't the slightest idea! But damn it all, that's not the problem!"

"But then what *is* the problem? The problem, that's what you keep repeating, the problem. That's what you

say. So there must be one, some problem, somewhere . . ."

Ali stared at him, flabbergasted. The Learned One gave
him a long, suspicious, guilty look before turning away,
and Ali gave him a long, suspicious, furious look before
turning away. Neither spoke for a while.

The Kid looked up at a confused mass of clouds in the
sky, then down at *Terra incognita, confusa,* and his step
slowed even more.

"The coat, the overcoat then . . ." sighed the Guileless
One.

Ali was a few paces ahead of him. His stride was long
and swift, his bearing imperious, angry, awkward.

"What overcoat?" Ali turned around, raising his arms
to heaven, becoming even taller, one might have said,
reaching his long arms up to grab hold of the sky, of
something, anything.

"Well, the trenchcoat. The coat, you know," repeated
the Guileless One. "The overcoat! You've read his stuff?
The madman? The one with the big nose . . ."

"What madman? What big nose?"

"Well, the inspector. The inspector! The inspector with
the big nose. The nose! The madman. The diary of a madman . . . The little devil with the big nose! Nikolai Vas-
ilievich, who wrapped us all up in his Overcoat."

Every now and then, the Guileless One mumbled, in
time with his dragging footsteps, "The overcoat, right,
naturally, the overcoat . . ."

Ali smiled indulgently. He'd slowed down, stopped taking those long, hurried strides that the shorter man at his

side could not, it seemed, match, since he refused to alter his own moderate, calm, composed tread. Ali ran a hand through his kinky black hair. He rubbed his forehead and temples impatiently.

"Well, Dina must have figured out things, all these years. Perhaps she knew quite a lot, or maybe she didn't want to know. Marriage is marriage. People who live together live together, after all. Bazil isn't a thug, but he isn't an angel, either. When you go up a ladder, you push a little bit here and there, you knock a few guys down some rungs, you do a few things in the darkness too, when nobody's watching . . . Maybe it took her this long to crack. The straw that breaks the camel's back. The drop that makes the whole glass overflow. A harmless drop, like so many others, but suddenly it turns red, blood-red, and it changes . . . What's that stuff called . . . Right, litmus paper. It changes the color of the litmus paper . . ."

He fell silent. He didn't think his explanations were sufficient, or clear enough, for the complex and childish mind of the Learned One, who still clung to his guileless expression and insistent, naïve questions, questions that were suspiciously insistent and naïve. As though he'd known for a long time all that anyone could tell him, and even a great deal more, and as though he asked questions like that to conform to a script, because he didn't trust friend Ali or anyone else. He felt friendly only toward the truth, you see, just the truth, or because he wanted to avoid arousing friend Ali's suspicions by continuing to play the same ethereal, guileless role, incognito, experimental, far removed

from all those mundane imbroglios he found it so fasci-
nating to toy with.

"The drop isn't special in any way, any way at all,"
continued Ali the pedagogue, on his second wind. "It's
not blood, if you want my opinion, it's not blood anymore.
Even those creeps who keep an eye on us all, even they've
become apathetic. That's right, apathetic! They plod
through their jobs with their eyes on their paychecks at
the end of the month. They write reports to look busy;
otherwise, there'd be layoffs in the ranks, and they'd lose
their perks. Careless, quick work, with no point to it. It's
not just the hammer and the sickle that swing away in a
vacuum! Even that institution . . . THE INSTITUTION, that
is, you know the one I mean, obviously. The Fundamental
Institution! Ineffective, just like all its subcontractors. All
sorts of resources at its command, of course, and yet it's
humming along in a vacuum, my dear Scholar! In a vacuum, believe me. Just think about it . . . They're constantly
filling files and cabinets. Reports, nuggets of information,
boxes and boxes of it. And then? Zip! Big zero, Kid . . .
It turns out they can't make use of all this stuff they endlessly compile and sift and hoard. Gone are the days of the
guy from Soviet Georgia with the walrus mustache . . .
When I listen to those characters on the other side, over
there in the consumer's paradise, nattering away about
Utopia and Terror! What utopia—that idea fell by the
wayside some time ago . . . As though they and their
pragmatism had come up with a solution! Go check them
out, Simpleton, if you want to see consumer paradise, what
the absence of utopia looks like. And take a little look

around right here to see the absence of everything, utopia included. But they don't arrest thousands of people in the middle of the night anymore . . . even though the means, the motivation are still in readiness, the machine is there, obviously whirring away. In a vacuum! Rooms full of stuff. Files, files, and more files, hardly ever used. It's the same thing with them, minimum results, believe me. Minimal performance. Minimum results, Kid.''

Ali seemed tired, lacking the patience required to spell out, for the umpteenth time, things that were self-evident, things that he'd understood in good time, quite a while ago, obviously.

"And so this drop that overflows a glass that's already been running over for a long time—this drop is not a drop of blood. A simple extra drop, like so many others. Poor Dina, she got scared over nothing. There's no reason to be scared or conscience-stricken. It's not unheard-of, nothing to get hysterical about, believe me. Routine and boredom, as you used to say. Our little devil, boredom. You can get rid of the devil just as well by boring him to death. Because he gets rid of himself, obviously. A sleepy society! Deprived of the epic elements. Unspeakable boredom, that's what you used to say. Our little devil, he swallows everything, screws up everything, falls apart and gets swallowed down himself. No, you mustn't hit him, confront him, provoke him, or he'll rev up and destroy us. But if you simply accept him, you destroy him bit by bit. No acts of heroism, please, that's the rule: nothing epic. Here's our epic poem: hot air. Boredom! How right you were, obviously. Boredom!''

He was definitely on a roll, friend Ali, forced as he was to spout his tiresome truths that even children can figure out these days, figure out and then file away, which is just about all you can do with them.

The park was nearby. Night had fallen. A clear, cool night. The park was silent and empty.

Ali returned with renewed vigor to his initiation course. He'd recovered his composure, and his little exposé was becoming more explicit, more didactic.

Al. I. Stoian even touched once again on that troublesome point, this time with a strange detachment. As though it weren't an event they'd just been discussing, involving people they knew. He spoke of it the way people talk about scandals in the tabloids. As though he were only too familiar with weird occurrences, and they didn't bother him in the least. As though he were utterly used to such things. He spoke as if he were describing to a child how the world works, when the child hasn't even noticed the phenomena in question.

An official tone, an orderly presentation, a logic geared to the education of the ignorant: the appointments to which various people are summoned periodically, the places where such conversations take place.

His listener appeared extremely, exaggeratedly attentive. He listened, didn't listen, seemed to be intercepting something else, another voice, or voices, imperceptible currents, the rustling of air, a subterranean gasp, staccato commands, a frightened moan, somewhere, close by or far away, all around, or just the reverie in which he drifted off, longing to return to his games, his den, a world of his own.

Not in official surroundings, of course . . . continued a voice, God knows where and when. Reports weren't made in offices anymore, they'd given up on that, even though the people who ordered and organized such meetings were officials, obviously, I mean as official as anyone could get . . . The voice gradually imposed itself, its timbre, acquired its own personality . . . Unofficial surroundings, but official agents, wow! Even if the official assignment wasn't legal, well, in this case, definitely illegal, couldn't be more illegal, on the contrary . . . The voice was getting better and better at putting on a nonchalant tone, yes, yes, it was growing more distinctive, a familiar voice, wasn't it, yes, yes.

The apartments? Copies of keys? With the permission of the tenant, obviously, even though, well, I mean, you never know, things can get too complicated for their own good, obviously. Obviously.

"How would they get the keys?" asked Felicia in astonishment. She was ready for bed, that time when her husband would tell her, very sweetly, the most outlandish stories. "You mean that Vasile would have given them permission to . . . You mean they had the keys and they knew when no one would be home or . . . but how . . . and why, how does that fit in, the coat, the overcoat, I mean the trenchcoat, the raincoat, not the overcoat—now you've got me saying things every which way. So it had nothing to do with our visit? Left there a long time ago and . . . she hadn't noticed? Or else it didn't turn up until the next day, after the dinner party? So she figured it out, or it's precisely that she can't figure it out? And *the others, them*, what kind of meetings—conversations, I mean—and why, why wouldn't they use real offices for their interrogations, I mean their meetings, their meetings with *them, those people*, the informers, call them whatever you like, their stooges. Aren't they, they're on the official payroll, so they can use the offices. Why not, what do you mean they're not stooges? What are you talking about, they're not exactly their people? Forced into it? How are they forced into it? What, poor bastards, what do you mean, poor miserable souls? You mean that *you, you'd* agree to . . . No, no, I'm not talking about Ali and his theories, or Vasile, no, or their wives, no . . . *You, you'd* agree to . . . Why other people's apartments, what does that mean? Family atmosphere, domestic environment, how, what, no, no, I don't follow you, family setting, what kind, what mood . . . Excuse me, just talk, what do you mean just talk, an intimate atmosphere—what do you mean, intimate, private, how . . . What is this, increased efficiency . . . How can you say such . . . What does that mean, privacy, what privacy?"

This really isn't the kind of story to tell at bedtime. Too upsetting, and it leads to no end of questions. After a while, the tension inevitably gets to both the narrator and the listener, and, in any case, ordinary daily life provides more than enough worries and fears. There's no need to add to them, so why chase around after terrifying mysteries?

And so the couple decided never, ever, to talk of such matters again. To forget the whole thing, as though it had never happened.

The other couple, the Stoians, hadn't even tried to fathom the enigma, it seems. Wiser, probably. And also, perhaps, indifferent to this kind of transparent mystery, or quite simply more cautious, unwilling to burden their days and nights—especially their nights—with unanswerable questions.

A few months later, however, the inevitable happened. The wife came home in a state of indescribable agitation, which couldn't have been caused by the line at the butcher's, where she'd wasted several hours in the cold and darkness, since she was used to that, after all.

Her mute distress and the way she kept rubbing and rubbing at her glasses seemed to suggest some extraordinary event.

The husband was busy proofreading the text of an article due to appear in the newspaper the following day, and doing so very carefully, because the piece had been more or less dictated to him on the phone by someone from the top floor of power. He raised his woolly black head and looked at his wife in annoyance. And waited, still watching her. The woman smoothed her short hair, glaring at him through her glasses. A sharp, green-eyed stare.

"Why didn't you tell me?"

"What?"

"You know exactly what I'm talking about . . . I could

feel there was something going on. I felt it, but I didn't want to start asking questions. You never know, I thought, I could be wrong. I felt there'd been . . . that there were still things going on all the time with that business. I was waiting for you to tell me about it. I mean, I wanted to get to the bottom of it, too."

"What? What are you talking about? What's happened now?"

"What's happened? You're asking me what's happened? No, I don't believe this . . . You'd think the poor dear had just been born yesterday! *You*, exactly, *you*, the one who always knows everything, and before everyone else, and knows a lot more than he needs to!"

"I know what? What's going on?"

"The romantic lady, remember her? The one who killed her father, the old man who died of a broken heart when the apple of his eye waltzed off with a bum, a faker, a creep who wound up becoming a great big zero, or maybe Zero the Great? Fancy-schmancy Madame, remember? With her priceless house, her priceless wardrobe, and her priceless way of talking! The statue, right? I saw her! I ran into her! Just now in the street. And I saw what's happened. Only now you have to explain it to me. It's too much of a shock, I can't get over it. I want a clear explanation. Clear, you hear me? Clear, clear, clear!"

She was shouting. Her husband must have known she'd end up bursting into tears and pulling out all the stops. He set down his pile of papers.

"You have to speak clearly first. Tell me exactly what

you're talking about. Because right now I haven't the foggiest idea. Calm down, explain what's upsetting you, tell me what happened."

"Come on, do you think I'm some kind of idiot? Or crazy? I saw her, I told you. I met her! I ran into her on the street, two hours ago. I stopped, if you want to know. We had a conversation. A normal conversation . . . an absolutely normal conversation, even. You know what she told me?"

The husband dropped his mask of indifference. Bored? Relaxed? No, far from it: he was impatient, disturbed, frightened. It would probably have been impossible to describe precisely how he felt.

"You know what Madame told me? The story that's going around all over Bucharest! Everyone's heard it—taxi drivers, soldiers, old people, even children. The tale of the disappearing corpse. The story about the dead woman. You must have heard it a good twenty times."

"I haven't heard any story about any dead woman. I guess that means I'm not so well informed after all," muttered the husband faintly, in a resigned tone.

"Poor sweetheart! As though anyone would believe you anymore! As though anyone would still believe the tiniest word from you, or even a lousy comma . . . And the latest edict, regarding the obligatory burial of deceased persons in the locality where they rendezvoused with the Grim Reaper? You've heard about that, have you?"

The husband remained silent; who could tell what he knew or didn't know?

"From now on, the dead must be buried where they

died, how about that! Sure, right, the poor dear is completely at sea, I'm the one who has to bring him up to date on all this, fine, fine . . . So you don't know the story of the dead woman? It's told hundreds of times a day in cottages, offices, schools, everywhere, but the poor boy hasn't heard even a whisper! An old peasant woman . . . Well, she met Death, scythe and all, here, in Bucharest— not in her village, the way she would have wanted, with her old man by her side, in her old house that she'd lived in since forever. She'd come to visit one of her sons, here, in Bucharest. And the son? He wanted to take her home to the village, where the rest of the family was. To their own village, so she could be buried there. Forbidden! Against the law! The body goes nowhere, neither as is nor in a coffin. For-bid-den, courtesy of take one guess. Not even that, you haven't even got that anymore, the right to die when you feel like it, wherever you feel like it, to rot in peace wherever you want, instead of where Comrade You-know-who says."

"Ioana, if you could . . . Wouldn't it be better if you calmed down, tried to get a grip on yourself, you're talking wild, not watching what you say . . ."

"Not watching what I say? What, you want to see me die of fear right here in my own home? So what, what difference does it make? What do I care if they hear everything I say, what do I care if the walls have ears, fuck it, how about that, I really don't give a frigging damn! The son wrapped his mother's body in a rug. One of those big rugs, made a big, fat roll. And he put it on the roof rack of his car. He wanted to drive the rug to his mother's

---

house, so the old woman could be buried properly, with her family. He took along a friend from the office where he worked, and they went up north, to the other end of the country. They stopped along the way to eat, or sleep, whatever. So they entered a restaurant, and in the meantime, someone stole their rug! Someone stole the rug tied to the car! A huge rug, really beautiful and everything. They stole the rug, with the body wrapped up in it. That's it . . . You never know what's going to happen . . . So there you have it, that's the latest hot rumor going all over town. And . . . and . . . Madame! A normal conversation . . . perfectly normal. Everything was quite normal, utterly normal. The same short, well-thought-out sentences, lapidary treasures. Superb diction, like in the theater. The same distance . . . that ultra-correct, conventional stiffness which humiliates you and drives you out of your mind. The same, the same, exactly the way I've always known her. Translating that story into stiff academic prose. That story, from her lips! A high-level lecture . . . from her prissy, aristocratic mouth."

The husband stared at the floor, directing a heavy black look at the red flower in the precise center of the rug.

Ioana was pacing up and down the room; she stopped, waited, returned to the fray.

"Everything looked perfect. Expertly made-up, as always. Ultra-soignée, aloof, polite, just as we've always known her. Not a thing had changed. Except that raincoat . . . that's all. Italian high heels, impeccable hairdo, freshly manicured nails. Freshly manicured, even that revolting thumb of hers. Hairdo, nails, silk scarf. Makeup . . .

lipstick, mascara, eyebrow pencil. The perfect mask, Cleopatra, Queen Nefertiti, absolutely. This posture, conversation, everything flawless, as before. Except for the raincoat . . . A long one, a man's raincoat. That trenchcoat!"

Ali studied the carpet; Ioana marched back and forth, extremely upset. She stopped, looked at her husband furiously, suspiciously—sometimes suspiciously, sometimes as though she were about to explode, ready to release all of her pent-up anger.

"The trenchcoat! You know what kind of raincoat they were wearing? Perhaps not . . . They were wearing the same kind. The same kind, both of them! The cheapest kind, you know, the one you see in all the stores, the one hardly anyone buys. Those big, man's, faded-looking raincoats. A sort of cotton duck that used to be real material and used to have who knows what real color. Now it's the color of wind, fog, our bleached-out boredom. Big, long, a raincoat from a long-dead army, no shape, no style, no color. The same, you understand? The same raincoat, both of them! You'd have thought they'd escaped together from a loony bin, from that camp years ago, or from the moon, or from the circus. The same trenchcoat, you hear, the same! I'm mistaken? I'm seeing things, I'm crazy? Nightmares, visions, sure, I'm exhausted, hysterical, right? Right? Right . . . So, tell me, tell me where, where does madness come from, like that, all of a sudden? From apathy, from cowardice, from fatigue and passive complicity and normality, that abnormal, vegetative, pathological, stifling normality that's strangling us all? Just like that, all at once, from that sort of tepid sludge we put up with? Just like that, in the middle of the jokes and the rumors and the gossip and the harangues?"

Then, a rustling in the air, perhaps, trailed by the shadow of a long, thin, invisible snake. But no one heard a thing. The woman took a deep breath and fell silent. Her voice had sunk gradually lower, finishing in a sort of suffocated helplessness.

"So now you understand. And now I would like to understand, too."

The man didn't speak. His gloomy face had probably grown even gloomier. The woman watched him, waiting. Those little green eyes behind the thick lenses . . . and the pale, ever paler face, and the short hair, quivering with each nervous toss of her head.

"You must also know, I'm sure, who was with her . . . Perhaps you could explain that to me as well, while you're at it."

Her husband, naturally, kept his eyes fixed on the red spot in the carpet.

"Aha, you know that, too. So there's an explanation for everything . . . You knew that as well, of course. And you never said a word to me. You should have seen me, I was thunderstruck, petrified. Petrified, I mean it. Just seeing her, first of all. You never know . . . was it her, or wasn't it? I couldn't tell anymore. And then our conversation, seemingly so natural, with her usual tics, her stilted phrasing. Aloof, imperial. Talking of this and that . . . the current gossip . . . the latest story, the body hidden in the stolen rug . . . as if everything were fine, as if her elaborate phrasing were perfectly suited to the story—as if she'd always been interested in such things and used to talk about them all the time! I tried not to see that raincoat of hers, way too big for her, she was swimming in it, so slender and elegant, the way she is. And just then, whom do I see coming out of the cigar store on the corner? The Learned One! The Researcher! I didn't understand yet, I was going to wave, call to him. For all I knew, he hadn't seen me . . . but the Learned One was heading, in fact, very calmly, straight for us. Here the Guileless One came up to me and asked—well, what do you think he asked me? How are you! That's what he asked me, how are you! . . . That's what that Simpleton asked me. Never said a word to her, the other one. I was openmouthed, rooted to the spot, I didn't know whether I was coming or going, I was completely at a loss."

Ioana Stoian couldn't control herself any longer. She fled to the kitchen, from which came confused noises, the sound of a chair being knocked over perhaps, and the clank of silverware, and then she took refuge in the bathroom. She stayed quite a while in the bathroom. Finally, she reappeared, rubbing her forehead with her right hand, holding a glass of water in her left. She drank it all in a single draught and went on holding the empty glass.

"Suddenly I realized that they were actually . . . together. He'd gone off to buy cigarettes, and she, when I first spotted her, she'd been waiting there alone, standing listlessly on the sidewalk. That strange apparition . . . out of nowhere, in front of me."

Alexandru I. Stoian remained silent. He was no longer

looking at the carpet. He was no longer looking at anything.

"So he asked me, politely, how I was, and then he gently took her arm. He said goodbye to me and . . . they left. It's just too much for one day! After hours and hours of pushing and shoving on line, in the noise and cold and dirt, I was feeling faint and I'd finally managed to leave triumphantly with that disgusting package of rancid sausage in my hand. I run into her, and a few moments later . . . the Martian lands, right in front of us. You would've sworn they were from the same family, or else husband and wife, or lovers, or missionaries, or cellmates, escaped from the same prison or asylum or freak show. The two of us, and then him . . . The Child! The Learned One! the Researcher! There was some kind of complicity, I don't know . . . something strange. I was stunned, confounded. And those raincoats! The same, the same . . . I was going mad. As though they'd arrived from another galaxy, or were on their way there . . . I don't know, who knows, I give up."

Alexandru I. Stoian remained silent. He neither looked at nor saw anything, but he heard everything, every word, even if he'd lost the power of speech, and he'd lost that a good while ago.

"A nightmare! Then I stood around for an hour at the bus stop. Hundreds of people with their string shopping bags, numb, frazzled, frustrated, ready to scratch one another's eyes out. I was thrust into the bus, there's no other way of putting it, swept along by the crowd. I couldn't see a thing anymore, squeezed in like that. So there I was, in the bus, squashed by all those sweaty bodies. A nightmare. Paralyzed, held there stiff as a stick, pitching from side to side whenever that whole heavy mass of tired bodies swung right or left each time we took a curve. But I couldn't feel a thing, I just couldn't feel a single thing anymore. I was still back there, in fact, on the sidewalk, in front of the butcher shop, between the two Martians. All I could see was the both of them. I couldn't get over it . . . A nightmare."

"Hmm, yes . . ." Alexandru I. Stoian seemed to mumble, after another long pause.

"And . . . that . . . raincoat? What, what the . . . what the hell is it with that raincoat?" burst out Ioana Stoian in renewed fury.

"Well . . . it was left at their house. You see . . . it would have . . . it would have disappeared. It would have disappeared, obviously, eventually, just the way it turned up. The same way, just like that, the way . . . it showed up. You see . . . the same person, or someone else, or . . . anyway, it would have gone, it would have been picked up."

"What? What, the same person or someone else, what is this? No, really, this is too much. Too much! No way! Why, since it would have disappeared in any case . . . why . . . no, who should have picked it up and why wasn't it picked up, and so then how . . . no, it's too much!"

"Hmm, yes . . . It would have disappeared, except that there was this problem. Her illness, I mean, the breakdown. The trenchcoat . . . Well, you saw. That's why it couldn't be picked up again. It turned into something else. Anthropomorphized, as they say."

"As who says? Who, why, what anthropo, what morpho, you've got me talking nonsense again, so, what does that mean, now we're theorizing here, is that what we're doing? Anthro, phormo, morpho, that's it, that's the problem? You're trying to make me think you're insane, and that I'm insane too, everyone, we're all insane? You mean, and . . . and, and . . . the husband, I mean? What's he doing, this Mr. Fixit? Unless he doesn't even know what's going on . . . Of course, the husbands are always the last to know."

"No, it's not what you think. The poor guy knows, he knows everything, he told me all about it. The other one—the Researcher, whatever you call him—has been very touched by what's happened . . ."

"Touched?" shouted the madwoman to the madman. "Touched, that's the word? He's been touched by Comrade Vasile's distress, that's what you're saying? Who's touched in the head here, who? Me, you, all of us, who? You mean, anyone, anything, is that what you mean?"

The lunatic turned sharply on her heel, speechless with anger, and stopped in precisely the right spot to glare with phosphorescent, venomous, suspicious green eyes at the lunatic husband gaping in astonishment.

"Anyone, anything, that's it, that's the explanation? Anyone can do anything, feel anything, any time, toward anyone, that's the idea? Who, the Child, or whatever you call him? The prize pupil, the distinguished student who considered his classmate Vasile a prize moron? . . . The Brat, who was reading Marx and Rimbaud at thirteen while the other one, the dunce, was kicking a ball around with the neighborhood kids? And the mathematics, the physics, the fancy degrees? The crisis, the downfall? And—and his book, and its brief, bizarre period of marginal success? He's marginal, that's what he is, the Simpleton, off on the sidelines, with himself, with others, far from the crap, the general masquerade—isolated, peripheral, on the fringe, while the class jerk rises higher and higher, piling up the privileges while he's got the chance, for a rainy day, then whoa, all of a sudden, the Learned One is touched by suffering, he's touched by sin and mystery and the mud little piggies have to wallow in? Touched by the snobbery of *parvenus* who're dying to have them— the losers, the fringe-dwellers, the outcasts—at their table, to protect them and show them that their hosts are human beings, you see, poor, polite, hospitable, educated little piggies, full of fun and good manners, even liberal piggy-wiggies, you'd never know they were perfectly capable of kissing the devil's ass any old time at all, ready for any shit and all possible lies and treachery and cruelty and, and, and . . . touched by that? You mean, anything, anyone, we're all alike, no exceptions, that's it, that's the theory you're hiding behind? In the slender hope of getting out of this, if everything and everyone's the same so that nothing matters?"

"I said he was touched by what's happened, not sympathetic to Bazil, I didn't say that. But you're really not listening anymore. You're busy having your tantrum."

"By what's happened, that's it, exactly! That's just what I said, the husband's the very last to know."

"It's not what you think," Al. I. Stoian repeated softly. "It seems she's not well. You never know, with these episodes . . . with this kind of illness. It's a complicated situation. Sometimes she looks sick, sometimes she seems normal . . . It's not as simple as all that. You never can tell, these illnesses are tricky. He was calling up day after day to see how she was doing, and then they started discussing the problem. On the phone first, and then they got together to talk about it. They meet regularly. They seem to help her, these meetings. What do you want, after all . . . Afterward, she comes home calm and relaxed, that's what Bazil told me. She comes home quite serene, as though nothing were wrong."

"And him, him . . . old flabby . . . the Kid . . . What am I getting into? Shit, he couldn't stomach her. He said the most disgusting things about her, he couldn't bear the sight of her. And suddenly, wham! There's something wrong here! What the hell has gotten into him?"

"Why are you getting so worked up? It's an act of great kindness, that's what it is! And great patience, obviously. It can't be much fun, as you can imagine. He has to spend a lot of time going on all those walks. He's being very understanding and attentive, if you want to know . . . It's an admirable thing for him to do."

"Hey! No, now, really, I'm going batty! Patient, attentive, admirable! You think I'm a half-wit or a nut case. That's it, you must think I'm either retarded or hysterical . . . That's why you never told me a thing about what happened and what's still going on. An admirable thing to do, right, listen to him . . . There's something else, something else, I'm sure of it. I just can't see the Little Mouse leaving his cage full of books to play lady-in-waiting out of pure charity. And the trenchcoat, I mean the raincoats . . . What is this farce, they're playing ghosts, or what? No, no, there's something going on, something!" screamed Ioana Stoian, pale and haggard. "There's something going on! There's always something under the surface, obviously. Obviously! Nothing is what it seems, nothing or no one, not even your own husband, no one! Anyone can become anything! Anyone, anytime, anything? . . . Come on, answer. Charity? Don't be ridiculous! Research, yes . . . that's the best-case scenario. A subject for study, yes, I can see that, obviously. A kind of experiment . . . scientific research, a project, if you like, choose your own term. An exercise in pure research, an extra experiment, an ex, okay? And that's the best possible interpretation! He can't stand her, I'm sure of it," shouted Ioana Stoian, holding her arms out in front of her as though to ward off any reply contemplated by her husband, Alexandru I. Stoian.

She no longer needed to pause to catch her breath, no, she couldn't bear any interruption now—the flood was unstoppable.

"He can't stand her, he never could stand her! Even now, he can't stand her, I'm certain of it, absolutely certain! What good does it do to wear a raincoat like that! Unless it was his idea to have her wear a raincoat just like the other one? Simulation, right? Setting up an experiment? Conditions

---

for study and research, that's what the Guileless One is after, that Simpleton, that ex, that hypocrite! Who's he trying to put one over on? Me? You, perhaps . . . all of us. Himself? . . . What's he trying to prove? Anytime, anyone, that's it? That's the point? Who knows . . . Wouldn't surprise me, no, no, not anymore, obviously. He wants to observe, right, to probe around under the surface, get past appearances! Appearances . . . and then what? Appearances, those trenchcoats of theirs, appearances, come on! Scientific cynicism, yes, and that's the nicest way of putting it. I'm telling you, the nicest way. There could be something behind it, who knows, something else entirely . . ."

There were, in fact, many hypotheses. The two also discussed them, the old friends from childhood, the war generation. Not just the war generation, a new term had to be found that applies more accurately to that which was and that which followed.

Yes, they also pondered the same possibilities during their long weekly walks. They had animated, passionate discussions beneath the stony, inscrutable sky. They reconsidered the question, each time from a new angle. And this was what brightened up the sick woman, it seems, and steadied her nerves. She'd take an intense interest in their talks. About her life, their lives, the lives of their friends, their acquaintances, the lives of all the Martians they passed on the street or remembered from the past.

She seemed finally free, liberated. An absolute, cosmic,

intangible assurance. A focused, steady voice, and a happy laugh, incognito.

Time was as though sharpened, glassy, feverish, glinting with sarcasm. A sarcastic, happy, broken laugh, with cutting black shards.

The time of absence suddenly heard as sound. Sharpened, shattered. A glassy, guileless, ancient laugh.